THE GIRLS NEXT DOOR

ANITA WALLER

Boldwood

First published in Great Britain in 2024 by Boldwood Books Ltd.

Cover Design by Head Design Ltd.

Cover Photography: Adobe Stock

A CIP catalogue record for this book is available from the British Library.

Paperback ISBN 978-1-83533-906-0

Large Print ISBN 978-1-83533-902-2

Hardback ISBN 978-1-83533-901-5

Ebook ISBN 978-1-83533-899-5

Kindle ISBN 978-1-83533-900-8

Audio CD ISBN 978-1-83533-907-7

MP3 CD ISBN 978-1-83533-904-6

Digital audio download ISBN 978-1-83533-898-8

Boldwood Books Ltd
23 Bowerdean Street
London SW6 3TN
www.boldwoodbooks.com

To my two writing buddies, Valerie Keogh and Judith (J A) Baker, who keep me almost sane!

'The best protection any woman can have... is courage.'

— ELIZABETH CADY STANTON

PROLOGUE
SEPTEMBER 1987

Jason Kinkaid, the *Sheffield Star* reporter, arrived at the house on Larkspur Close in Hackenthorpe village, one of the oldest suburbs of the steel city, together with his photographer, on that lovely sunny day in September of 1987. Jason's best friend had given him information about four families living on one small road with only thirteen properties on it, and the four families had all produced baby girls over the previous few months, so surely there was a story there?

The reporter decided that as there was nothing much else going on, he would indeed follow it up. After contacting Suzanne Chatterton, who was still brain-befuddled by only recently giving birth to the fourth baby of the group, she agreed it would be a good idea. She would contact the other three ladies and get them round to the Roberts house, she said. Yes, they were all good friends, she continued, brought together by pregnancy, when he queried if they would all be there.

And so it came to pass. Three of the ladies, along with their babies, were waiting for the fourth one, Suzanne, to arrive; she was breastfeeding her child and that couldn't wait.

They offered the two *Star* staff members tea and biscuits, but both declined. Jason was uncomfortable around tiny children who didn't play football, and merely wanted to get the information correct, take a few photographs and skedaddle.

Jason made a start on names.

'I'm the first mum, Laura Roberts,' a very pretty woman said in an Irish accent, and he smiled. He liked pretty women. He wrote quickly. 'And your baby?' The little girl was sitting upright on her mother's knee and staring at him, her eyes very wide, gloriously dark brown. She was a beautiful child.

'Chantelle. And my husband is...'

Jason held up a hand. 'No husbands. They didn't do the work, did they? This is an article about mums, about friendship, about a close community, not about men.'

The three women looked at each other, and one by one they nodded.

'Fine by me,' Laura said.

'And Chantelle was born when?'

'She's almost six months now, born on 4 March 1987. She was the first of our four babies, born in Nether Edge Hospital.'

He scribbled down her words and moved onto Tracy Marsden, sitting by the side of Laura.

Tracy spoke quietly, hoping she didn't wake her baby. 'Melissa was born in Jessop's Maternity Hospital, on 6 June, just three months after Chantelle.' Melissa was clearly disinterested in anything; she was fast asleep in her mother's arms. Tracy felt relieved that he didn't want husbands' names – she didn't have one. It was only the whiteness of her daughter's hair and the blueness of her eyes that led her to believe Daddy could be Tony Smith, but there had been a couple more on that long weekend in September 1986.

'Thank you,' Jason said, making sure all details were accurately recorded. He wanted to impress with this, maybe get it as a full-page spread on page five.

He heard the front door open, and turned to see a tall woman enter the room, her long dark hair piled into a ponytail on top of her head.

'Sorry I'm late,' she said. 'Mine's a coffee.' She held out a hand to Jason. 'Suzanne Chatterton, husband Jake.'

There was a general chorus from the others of, 'He doesn't want husbands,' and she grinned and sat down, cradling the tiny infant held in her arms. 'That's understandable,' she said.

'So who's next?' Jason asked, with a smile on his face. He liked bubbly Suzanne.

'That would be us,' an older lady said. Her blonde hair was now tinged with grey, and she also was holding a sleeping baby. 'This is Jessica, also born in Jessop's on 23 April. St George's Day, Shakespeare's birthday, and now Jessica's birthday as well. I'm her nan, Nora, and she lives with my husband Arthur and me, because her mother... well, let's just say it was too much for her, having a child.'

Jason's head lifted. Was this a secondary story? He drew a circle around Jessica's name, and knew he would be looking it up when he got back to the office. Could 1987 be his year to shine, all because he'd interviewed the mothers of four tiny babies? He felt a shiver of anticipation run through him.

Jason turned to Suzanne. 'And this little one is the tiniest one?'

'She is. This is Erin, born on 21 August 1987, just a month after we moved into the house next door to this one. I had a home birth because the ambulance didn't get to me in time. Luckily the midwife did. It's a proper little incubator/nursery, this road.'

'That's what the article is about,' Jason said with a laugh. 'As well as celebrating the births of these four beautiful little girls, it's a story of community, and maybe a little bit of "is there something in the water on this road?" to it. It will be a feel-good article, should be out in the Thursday edition, so make sure you get it.'

The photographer stood and began sorting out the photographs he wanted to take, managing to wake up two sleeping babies as he did so, but twenty minutes later the two men left the house, moving on to the next item on their list for the day.

The four women sat back and sighed. 'Thank God that's over,' Laura said. 'It'll be a nice thing to save for the girls for when they get older, but it is *The Star*, I don't expect it to be particularly accurate.'

Nora Wheeler stood. 'Thank you all for your support. I need to let you know that it's been finalised, as of yesterday, that we are to be the official guardians of Jessica pending the return of Anna, but we've still heard nothing from her. It's been over four months now, and not a word. Arthur is going mad with the worry, but you've all seen her letter. She didn't want the child, and we can do what we want with her. As if we'd let her go... I'll head home now, she's almost ready for a feed, but that was good. Something different in my life.'

They said goodbye, and Nora headed home, just three doors away from Laura's house.

'She's a star, that woman,' Laura said quietly. 'She's got my support whenever she needs it. Bloody Anna never said a word about not wanting the baby, did she? Just said she'd fallen out with the baby's dad, so he was no longer on the scene. These four little ones will grow up knowing they can pop in and out of any of our homes, that they will be cared for, and we will have their backs. Yes?'

'Yes!'

'And now can we have a coffee?' Suzanne said. 'I'm knackered and need caffeine.'

* * *

And so the clique of four had arrived, announced to the world in a newspaper article that spoke of fecund vibes around Larkspur Close, with the births of four girls within six months of each other. Chantelle, Jessica, Melissa and Erin were temporarily famous, albeit for one day only, and their parents saved several copies of Thursday's *Star*. They grew together, they schooled together, they became sisters without linking genes. And they loved each other, protected each other, celebrated life events, and acquired a small collection of bridesmaid dresses, used for Chantelle's and Jess's wedding days.

* * *

By 2022, one would have given birth to twins, one would be a paralegal for the largest law firm in the city, one would be a reluctant stay-at-home housewife, one would be a bookseller in her own shop – and at least one of the four would play a significant role in a murder. A necessary murder.

Larkspur Close was a community; secrets were hidden, sometimes shared, but ever present. Families linked by the births of the girls were linked by death also.

1

SUMMER 2022

The long blonde tresses of Jessica Armstrong appeared around the kitchen door at her grandparents' home before her body did. The rest of her was trying to persuade a six-month-old puppy called Mabel to follow her instead of trying to chase a cat down the back garden.

Jess's grandmother, Nora Wheeler, smiled at this most welcome of all visitors. She looked at the little puppy, and said, 'Mabel, sit,' in the stern voice meant to show authority. Mabel wagged her tail and moved across to lick Nora's hand.

'This dog does not recognise who's the boss,' Nora said firmly.

'Certainly doesn't,' Jess said with a laugh, leaning over to kiss her grandmother's cheek. 'Grandpops okay?'

'He's fine. Down in the greenhouse at the moment. I've just made a pot of tea because he texted me to say he fancied a cuppa. These mobile phones have turned me into a slave for this man.'

'You were a slave for both of us anyway, so don't blame the mobile phones,' Jess joked. 'So, do you need anything doing while I'm here?'

Jess had taken to calling in most days on some pretext or

another, aware of how old they were getting, and how there were now things that were proving difficult to do.

'Bless you, my love,' Nora responded. 'No, we're fine, thanks. Unless...'

'Unless what?'

'Well, I stripped the bed this morning, and haven't put the clean bedding on yet. It's that duvet cover that defeats me...'

Jess snorted. 'Duvet covers defeat everybody, Nan. Don't worry about it, I'll nip up and do it now.'

By the time Jess was back in the kitchen, her grandpops's cup of tea had been delivered, and a fresh pot had been made for her and Nora. 'All done, Nan. That's a pretty duvet cover.'

'It's new. I like poppies.'

'As if we didn't know.' Jess smiled and picked up her cup. 'So, talk to me about Grandpops. Is he okay?'

'He's just getting old, Jess. We're now officially in our late seventies, and we're slowing down, but I make sure he takes all his medication, and although he has an hour's nap during most days, he's fine. Stop worrying.'

Jess reached across and squeezed the wrinkled hand. 'You'd tell me if there was a problem?'

'Of course. We're managing pretty good, apart from putting duvet covers on.'

'It just takes a phone call, Nan.'

'I know. Change the subject, before we get all maudlin. How are the rest of you?'

Jess knew her nan meant the other three girls, and she smiled. Sisters by nature, even if not by genetics, that's what the four of them were.

'They're fine. Chantelle is a bit frazzled since having the twins, but she's a person who just copes, and copes very well. Mel and Erin are good. We still see each other as much as we can, but we're always texting and such like. We actually met up three times last week. Chantelle can't always make it because of the children, but three of us do. Strong friendships, Nan, strong friendships.'

'And Mike?'

There was the briefest of pauses, but Nora registered it.

'He's good. His job takes him away more now, but he's always home for weekends, so I shouldn't grumble.'

'But you're feeling a little grumbly right now, aren't you?'

She nodded, and her mouth turned down a little. 'Just a bit. It wouldn't seem such a long week if he would agree to me working, but for some reason he doesn't want me to. Says I don't need to work, and he's right, I don't, not financially. But mentally is another thing.'

Nora put down her cup with some force. 'Do what you want to do, Jess. He's your husband, not your owner.'

Jess grinned. 'I went into the charity shop to see what I could get in the way of really old books – they save them for me if they get any in. I had a cuppa with the manager, and she said if I had spare time they would be happy to have me join the team. I said I'd get back to them, but I think it would suit me down to the ground.'

'Go for it. Get out from under Mike's thumb, and while you're at it, find yourself another man that will give you the baby you so clearly want. I don't like to interfere in your marriage, Jess, but I can see how unhappy you are. It's in your hands to do something about it.'

'Nan!'

'Don't deny it, young lady. I've seen the way you are around those twinnies of Chantelle's.'

'But I can give them back without having any of the hard work.'

'Children aren't hard work, Jess. Impossible work at times, but look at you, an absolute blessing to us, and you kept us young. If you won't leave Mike, maybe it's time to just accidentally forget the pills, Jess. If you want a child, you should have one. Having your mum...' She paused. Anna was ever present, ever absent, and just speaking her name caused Nora's heart to stutter. She took a deep breath. 'Having your mum was the cement that tied me and your grandpops tightly together, and brought us so much joy.'

'But she left you.' Jess spoke quietly. This was a rare moment to treasure. Her mother was rarely spoken of.

'And she gave you to us. That was our bonus consolation prize that turned into a winner.'

The two women smiled at each other. 'Am I like her?' Jess asked.

'In looks, definitely. She had long blonde hair, although she usually wore hers in a ponytail. You tend to be a little more sophisticated. Mike's influence, I suspect. In body shape you're very much alike, not too tall, both of you very pretty. I would say you got your mother's genes, but as we didn't know who your father was, I can't say anything about him.'

Again Jess squeezed her nan's hand. 'I have the best parents ever in you two.'

Nora gave a small snort of disbelief. 'I won't say it's been easy, young lady. We were too old to be taking on a youngster in any role other than grandparents, but Anna left us with no choice. We already loved you from the minute of your birth. But you've changed. And if Mike isn't giving you what you so clearly want, a baby, then it's time to rethink your life, or you'll end up being a cranky old woman.'

There was a moment of hesitation before Nora continued. 'You know, Jess, it has always been my opinion that in this world there is someone for everyone, some special person who will love you unconditionally and will be loved by you unconditionally. You just have to find them. And when you do,' she glanced down at her hands resting in her lap, 'you don't give them up. Not for anything.'

Jess felt a shiver run through her. 'And Grandpops is your special one?' There was a sudden compulsion to ask the question.

Nora lifted her head slowly, as if deciding how much to say. 'No, and that's why I'm speaking to you like this. I'm giving away no details, so this conversation will never be spoken of again, but I was simply waiting for Anna to have the baby and become settled with you, then I was going to leave to be with my special one. But Anna walked away, leaving our most precious grandchild with us. I stayed.'

For a few moments, Jess felt speechless. Of all the conversations they could have had, this one shocked her the most. Her nan! With another man! She wasn't sure if she should laugh or cry.

'Should I say sorry? For keeping you from him, I mean?'

'Never. That's another thing, Jess. Never do anything you need to say sorry for, and let's face it, nobody but me and my love ever knew of our plans. Oh, his wife suspected, but she never knew the full truth of how close we became. So nobody has anything to be sorry about. It was simply that we had the right love at the wrong time. I accepted the choice I made on the day I became a mother again, instead of a grandmother. And I've never regretted it for a minute.'

'But I grew up,' Jess said. 'You could have left when I went to uni.'

Nora shook her head. 'Not possible. The moment had already passed with the man I loved, we'd accepted it wasn't to be. You'd already met Mike, and I somehow knew that one day we would be having this conversation. Well, maybe not me telling you about the love of my life, but certainly one where I would be encouraging you to rethink your life and decide what it is you really want.'

She reached across and held Jess's hand. 'If you need time to think about things, your room is always ready for you here.'

'With Mabel as part of the package?' she joked, trying to lighten the mood.

'Let me guess where Mabel is right now. With your grandpops down in the greenhouse. Mabel is most welcome here, as you very well know. I'm serious about this, Jess, you need a life instead of keeping that perfect house spotless. What do the others say?'

'All three say exactly the same as you. But lately they say it more often. Mel and Erin aren't quite as vocal about it, but Chantelle brought the twins round one Sunday and Mike was there. She heard him say something along the lines of "Does she have to bring those bloody kids here?" and she had a pretty raucous argument with him, while I tried to be a peacekeeper.'

She finished her drink and stood. 'I'll nip down and retrieve Mabel, then head off home. I will think everything through, Nan, I promise. You... erm... don't want to tell me who this other man is then? Your right love at the wrong time...'

Nora laughed. 'No, I do not. Now go and give Grandpops a kiss, and don't ever think about this again. Just consider your own situation, my darling girl, and get yourself into a happy position, instead of where you are right now.'

2

———

Lily and Daisy French stared at their mother, waiting for her to hand over the ice lollies she was holding, one in each hand.

'Who wants red, who wants orange?' Chantelle asked.

The twins both responded with red, then both said orange. Their mother slipped her hands behind her back and asked them to choose which hand. Daisy ended up with red, and Lily with orange. Peace descended as they began to suck on the ice.

'Okay, my little monsters, listen to me. Aunty Jess is coming over later to babysit while I go and do a big food shop. I need you to be good for her.'

Lily bit a chunk of the lollipop. 'Sweeties?'

'Maybe. But mainly bread, milk, butter, you know, the ordinary stuff that people buy when they do a food shop. What sort of sweeties?'

'Jelly babies,' Lily said.

'Buttons,' said Daisy.

Chantelle sighed. She had always assumed twins were alike in everything, but it seemed with the set she'd managed to acquire, it was only their looks that were identical.

'I'll see what I can do. But if Aunty Jess says you've been naughty in any way, you don't get any sweeties. Is that understood?'

They both nodded with a solemnity that made her want to laugh aloud, but she reckoned that might not be a good idea. Serious moments had to remain serious.

There was a brief knock at the door and it opened. Both girls shrieked, 'Aunty Jess!' and barrelled their way down the hallway. Chantelle smiled. The cavalry had arrived, and she could enjoy a couple of hours of freedom, culminating in a Starbucks coffee.

* * *

Chantelle finished loading up the car boot, wondering how on earth she'd managed to spend so much money in such a short space of time. Maybe it was time to revise her normal shopping habits of simply chucking everything she needed into a trolley irrespective of prices, and begin checking just how much the previously paid price had increased.

She slammed down the boot lid feeling somewhat frustrated, and slid into the driver's seat. Starbucks coffee. Her treat. She checked her phone for messages and realised she still had a full hour or so to feel like a woman and not like a mother, knowing her girls were safe with Jess. If there were any issues, Jess would have messaged.

Driving to the Drakehouse retail park took a mere two minutes; she parked in the shade and walked across to the coffee house, trying to decide between a simple latte and something a bit more exotic. If only all decisions in her life were this simple, was the thought that flashed through her mind.

Andrew. The decision that was causing her so much angst, yet she knew things had to alter. A change of sleeping habits hadn't helped in any way; he had slowly but surely moved all his clothes into the guest bedroom, the intention being clear to her that he was not returning to the marital bed at any point, never mind the six weeks they had initially agreed would be good for both of them.

She collected her drink – a latte – and moved to a table where she could sit and look outside, even though the vista was only the car park. She admired the colour of a car that she saw turn into the car park, a blue Mazda, she thought, not being particularly smart at recognising car brands.

Her own car, a black Focus that she had parked near to the entrance, looked old in comparison to the blue car, and she sighed heavily. The Focus would be with her for a long time; having twins meant cutbacks in other areas of her world, and a new car definitely wasn't on the list. It was only when she saw Andrew get out of the passenger seat that her breath caught in her throat. She half stood, intending to wave to him, but then sat without raising her hand. The driver door had opened.

The car driver appeared to be a blonde woman, wearing jeans and a top that revealed a perfect figure, someone Chantelle didn't recognise. Had Andrew said he was out of the office? She shrugged. Andrew rarely spoke to say anything to her, although he was the same old Andrew with their girls.

She watched as he disappeared inside the Currys' store, following behind the blonde. A wave of irritation washed over Chantelle – to her it looked as though the blonde was there to pick something up for the office, but she needed a gopher to do the fetching and carrying for her. Andrew, meek and mild Andrew, who never said no to anybody. Except her.

She took her time with the latte, watching the Currys' door whenever it opened. Her phone was clutched in her hand, the camera app already activated. She would take a photo of him and show it to him that evening, just a little bit of light relief in an otherwise-stressful home life.

Finally her husband and the woman came out, neither of them carrying anything that required muscles to carry it. Andrew's muscles were employed in holding his right arm around the waist of the woman. They laughed as they approached the car, and he held her for a moment before bending to kiss her lips, then both of them got in the car and disappeared from the car park. Chantelle had caught the kiss on her phone, albeit through the window of Starbucks, and she checked the quality of the resultant picture.

Good enough, she thought, as she stared hard at the photograph. But instinctively she knew it had to be withheld for the moment – she needed to share it with the others first. Andrew couldn't talk himself out of this one. But why didn't she feel angry that she appeared to be married to a cheating, lying scumbag? Shouldn't she at least be feeling tearful, or even bewildered?

* * *

Lily and Daisy excitedly helped their mother ferry in the multiple bags from the car, eager to find the one that held sweeties of their choice, but she shooed them away from her with a laugh. 'Let me get through the door!'

'Anybody would think they'd never had jelly babies before,' Jess commented, watching the bedlam two three-year-olds could create, and in such a short space of time.

'They're like this every night when I mention bath time,' Chantelle confirmed. 'They love playtime in the bath, but my bathroom floor is awash with water every evening. Peace descends like magic after I've tucked them in for the night – they know they're not allowed out of bed once I've got them settled.'

'They've been brilliant while you've been out. Much better than me at Tiddlywinks, but I beat them hands down at Snakes and Ladders.'

'You'll stay for a meal? And you only beat them at Snakes and Ladders because they've never even heard of it before, let alone played it,' Chantelle said, as she reached up to the top of the fridge to move things around and create some space.

'Love to, if that's okay. I want to talk to you anyway.'

'Oh? That's odd. I've something I want to chat about with you as well. But can we talk before Andrew comes home, and not after?'

'We can, but I thought he always disappeared after his meal these days?'

'He does, but it's only to the guest room. I don't want him to hear what I'm going to tell you, not yet, anyway. I'll get this lot put away while you make us a coffee. I'd say wine, but I know you're driving.'

'A wine-sized discussion then? Sounds serious.'

Chantelle shrugged. 'It seems ages since we all sat down together here and had a long chat. Group chat on the phones isn't the same, is it?'

She began to stack tins of beans and spaghetti hoops into the cupboard designated for such necessities, while Jess sorted out the fridge and freezer, after switching on the kettle.

Lily handed Jess a small pink plastic teacup. 'Cup of tea, Aunty Jess?' she asked.

Jess smiled down at the tiny girl. 'I'd love one, thank you, Lily. Do we have cake?'

Lily nodded. 'Cake,' she repeated, and disappeared back to the lounge.

She returned as Jess was closing the freezer door, satisfied that not even an ice cube would find a place in the large appliance.

This time Lily was carrying a small plastic plate with a very small piece of plastic pizza on it.

'Cake,' she said and solemnly handed it over before returning to help Daisy cook an egg on their little wooden stove.

'Simply adorable,' she said slowly, watching as the door closed following Lily's departure.

'I know,' Chantelle said, giving a quick wipe to the work surface now everything was suitably installed in its rightful place. 'And they're not even tiring to bring up. Know what I mean? I couldn't consider going to work, partly because who in their right mind would want to childmind three-year-old twins, but I consider it's my job and my life at the moment, certainly for maybe the next five years. They seem to come up with something new every day, a true joy to have. I don't actually recommend having two at once, but at least it gets all the difficult stages over in one go, so to speak. So come on, let's have a proper drink out of a real mug, instead of a plastic cup, and leave them to their baking while we have a chat. I may need to talk further with Mel in her paralegal role eventually, but while you're here and captive, I can start to sort out my head with you first.'

Jess stared at her. 'You need Mel in her paralegal role? Have you murdered somebody?'

'Nothing so easy. I saw Andrew kiss another woman in the car park in the retail park, outside the Currys store, about an hour ago.'

3

'Andrew? Another woman? Is he mental?' Jess was horrified, and Chantelle smiled, albeit more of a wobbly grin than a smile. She took her phone from her bag and clicked on the Photos icon.

She handed the phone to Jess, with the picture so recently taken open, and sat back.

Jess stared at it. 'What the fuck is he playing at? He has two beautiful children, a stunning home, and more than all of that, he has you.'

'Well,' Chantelle hesitated for a moment, 'two out of three ain't bad.'

Jess frowned. 'Two out of three?'

'He doesn't have me. We've sort of drifted apart. I've tried to keep it from the three of you, though I think Erin may have clocked on. She called in last week for a cuppa and to see the girls, and brought with her a dress she'd picked up in that second-hand designer clothes shop. She went upstairs to change into it so I could see it, but she went into the guest room. Andrew's room.'

'And is it obvious it's now his room?'

Chantelle nodded. 'It is. He's even got a little desk in it. I tried saying it was the room he uses as his office, but there were clothes on the bed, toiletries on the bedside table, that sort of thing, so she wasn't fooled. I managed to change the subject, feeling I wasn't ready to talk about it, but after seeing that kiss this afternoon, somebody has to start talking.'

'You need a full meeting? All of us?'

'Sooner rather than later, I'm thinking.'

'What caused it? The split, I mean?'

Chantelle shrugged. 'I don't really know. It was a slow thing, that started with a jokey conversation about our sex life not being what it was, because either Daisy or Lily would be guaranteed to wake up in the middle of it. You had to get there quickly to stop twin one from waking up twin two. It certainly puts a dampener on orgasms.'

'And now you both want out?'

'I kind of thought we'd get over it, I must admit. But seeing that kiss today has made me change my mind. It's made me query if I want to "get over it". I think the phrase that's running around my head is more "get it over with".'

'Big decision, Chantelle. Think of the girls...'

'Why? The girls would hardly notice he wasn't there after a bit. He gets home around six and they're in bed by seven. During that hour he has his evening meal, then goes out for his evening bike ride, which usually lasts around half an hour, during which time I've bathed the girls, read them their story and loaded the dishwasher. The girls call him Daddy, but honestly, I think he'd be quite happy to be an "every other weekend" kind of father. He's a career man, and that's always come first.'

Jess sighed deeply. 'Everything you're saying all makes sense, but – with that in mind – maybe give yourself time to think this through. Don't suddenly stick your phone in front of his nose when he walks through the door. You need to prepare things for you and the girls. And talk to Mel, she'll either give you advice, or connect you with someone who will see that you come out of this with what you want, and not what he wants.' There was an initial silence that ended with a short bark of laughter from Jess. 'Sorry, I'm just finding this a bit unbelievable. Andrew? The man who chased you around the country until you gave in?'

Chantelle nodded. 'That's right. That Andrew.'

Jess exhaled, a long, slow drawn-out breath. 'Well, I know you wouldn't joke about this, but is there a possibility you're mistaken?' She picked up the phone again and stared at the picture of Andrew clearly kissing the unknown woman. 'He works with her?'

Chantelle shook her head. 'I have no idea, I certainly don't know her. The question is, do I want to know who she is? Or do I just tell him to get on that blessed bike and piss off? The relationship's been dodgy for a while, but I thought we were simply drifting apart. It didn't occur to me there might be some other woman in the picture, but this tells me there is.'

The kettle clicked off; Chantelle stepped to the side to make their drinks and she filled the teapot. It amused her that they always spoke of having a coffee, but given a choice, both she and Jess preferred tea, while Erin and Mel chose coffee.

'We definitely need to bring Erin and Mel in on this, especially Mel with her ability to think things through. Shall I text them?'

Chantelle nodded. 'Ask if they can pop round for a drink tomorrow night. Andrew has to go to Edinburgh tomorrow and he's staying overnight. I'll knock up some nibbles. Make sure you tell them so they'll know I'm feeding them.'

Jess pulled her phone towards her and clicked on the Messenger group chat they had laughingly entitled the Coven.

Calling all my witches. Can you make time to
meet up at Chantelle's tomorrow night? 7–7.30?
She's feeding us. It's important.

The replies pinged back almost instantly, telling Jess that Erin wasn't currently dealing with a book-buying customer, and Mel would probably be staring out of her office window wondering why she'd chosen law as her profession. Both women said yes, and Mel asked if they needed her to bring anything in addition to a couple of bottles of wine.

She read out the replies to Chantelle, who smiled. 'Strange how we always turn to wine, isn't it? Even though none of us ever have more than one glass.'

'I'm not convinced I like it,' Jess acknowledged. 'Alcohol, I mean. As you can probably remember, I got very drunk when I was sixteen at that party we all went to, and it's never happened since. In fact, don't tell the others because they'll think I'm a wimp, but I'd rather have a glass of milk.'

Chantelle grinned at her friend. 'Think we don't know? We all make sure we have milk in the fridge if we know you're popping round. Does Mike drink much?'

She shrugged. 'Not at home, but he's not home that much, is he? I've no idea what he does when he's in the hotel.'

Chantelle caught the stressful tone. 'Problems, Jess?'

'Nothing I can't deal with, and I don't think for a minute it's the same sort of problem you have with Andrew, but sometimes I feel I could just walk away and never look back.'

Chantelle placed her cup carefully back on the table and stared at her friend. 'I know you're the quiet one of the four of us, Jess, but for God's sake, talk to us.'

Jess allowed Chantelle's words to wash over her, and to her

horror realised she couldn't stop the first recalcitrant tear rolling down her cheek.

'It's not that I've stopped loving him, or anything, it's more I've lost me. I don't know who I am other than the wife of Michael Armstrong. And... I want a baby,' she suddenly wailed, sank her head down on to her hands and sobbed.

Chantelle stared for a few seconds. This was completely out of nowhere. Then she jumped up and moved around the table to get to Jess. She wrapped her arms around the woman she would die for, and sobbed along with her.

The two women pulled apart as Daisy wandered through to the kitchen carrying a small plastic saucepan in one hand and the handle in the other. 'Broke,' she said, and waved both items at her mother.

Chantelle took the two pieces, promised they would be mended in five minutes, and sat down with a thud.

'I didn't expect that,' she said to Jess. 'The baby bit, I mean. Have you told Mike?'

'Half-heartedly.' It was clear Jess was seriously upset. 'He's not interested. Says he doesn't need kids, we have everything we need. But I don't,' she sobbed. 'I don't have everything I need. I need what you have, what I've had this afternoon while you've been out. I need to play Tiddlywinks with my *own* child, Chantelle, and I'll never do that.'

Anger bubbled over inside Chantelle. 'Okay, so he doesn't want to be a father. My darling Jess, find another feller. Then have your baby. And tell that control freak to go to hell. We see what he's like, how you can never do anything without checking it out with him first, how he watches every move you make. You could be so much happier, Jess. Go out to work, have your baby, but for heaven's sake do it without him.'

4

Erin Chatterton turned around the shop sign on the front door and smiled exactly as she did every day. Her business made her smile. The sign now showing to the outside world read:

Fully Booked is now closed.

The side facing her read:

Fully Booked is OPEN and welcomes you inside.

Chantelle, Jess and Mel had bought her the sign as a gift for opening day after the long night of discussions had ended with them choosing Fully Booked for the name of the newly refurbished bookshop, hence the smile every time she looked at it.

She stared into one of the antique mirrors on the wall by the side of the door, inspecting her almost non-existent eye make-up. She ran her lipstick around her lips, muttered a brief, 'That'll do,' and picked up the tub of popcorn. Having already locked up the entire front of the shop, she left by the back door, and walked towards where her car was parked, by the side of the recently built office building.

The text message inviting them all round to Chantelle's had been like a little gleam of light in a somewhat fraught day, and her response had been swift and emphatic. It was only later that she had wondered if something was wrong, and which one of them had the 'something wrong' going on. Hence the popcorn. Popcorn had always been their comfort food, the go-to food, especially toffee popcorn. It had also meant travelling by car and not by bike – no way could she balance a tub of popcorn with any safety, if she went on her bike.

Erin heard a ping as she turned on her engine, and she fished out her phone. It was a query about her success or otherwise in tracking down an old book for Alistair Jones, the man who spent more money in her bookshop than any other customer, and she returned the query by saying she thought she had tracked down the signed copies, and she would have more details the following day.

The reply came swiftly, with three kisses attached, and once again she felt uneasy. He had caused more than a little discomfort in her life over the past few weeks. She dropped her phone deep into the recesses of her bag, and put the car into drive, headed out of the large rear yard and pulled up on the road outside. She quickly closed the gates and locked them, jumped back in the car and headed towards Chantelle's house.

She wished with all her heart that her grandfather could see what she had made of his business. The shock of it being willed to her and not to her mother had been huge for both of them initially, but as Suzanne, her mother, later explained, it hadn't really been such a surprise the more she thought about it. Leaving home at sixteen to live with Erin's father had devastated the whole family, and although she and Jake had eventually split up, the hurt had always remained.

Although the rift had lessened, especially following Erin's birth, it had never entirely healed. Though everyone had seen the love between the old man and his granddaughter, the will had confirmed it.

His death had changed everything. Suzanne had helped her bring the old bookshop into the new century and now continued with that help one day a week just because she loved books. And her daughter.

They had reworked the entire ground floor, and completely changed the upstairs flat which was now Erin's beautiful home. They had also introduced the antiquarian department for the serious collectors; the room on the left at the top of the stairs had been fitted out as a shelved-out library, then antique furniture had been installed. Only special customers saw the inside of this room, and it facilitated sales of truly expensive tomes, tomes that were of such importance and quality that she insisted on them being handled by white-gloved hands.

The library room had initially been her grandfather's office, but now she had a new custom-built office in the large rear area outside the back door, and Erin felt everything was perfect. Chantelle, Jess and Mel had been so supportive and now she had something to discuss with them that she would like help with.

She had taken time out earlier in the day to get a cut and blow-dry in the hairdresser's next door, and Livvy, the owner, had revealed her plans for selling up.

'I can give you first refusal,' she said to a suddenly bright-eyed Erin. 'You've talked so many times about having a coffee shop for your clients that's a bit bigger than the cubby hole in the corner they currently have.'

Erin had laughed, albeit a little tremulously, making some inane comment about gaining a coffee shop but losing her hairdresser, but she promised she would get back to Livvy within a couple of days.

And that thought was the main one in her mind. She needed to talk to her friends, discuss the pros and cons, get their thoughts on it, not to mention work out the finances. But inside her heart and her head she could already see the coffee shop layout, the shiny new hot drink machines, the old-fashioned furniture that would blend in with the dark wood used throughout the bookshop.

Sometimes in your life things happen at exactly the right moment, and with exactly the right end result; Erin knew this was one of those times, and she sent a virtual hug to the grandfather she had loved, and who had given her the world he had loved.

The second ping emanated from her phone as she switched off her engine outside Chantelle's home. It was confirmation that the signatures in an antique book collection she was considering acquiring had been checked and authenticated; also the additional letter that came with the set. She responded with her offer for the entire collection and the authenticated letter. The instant reply said they would contact the seller and send the answer the following morning.

She smiled at the speed. It was good to work with this small business; they never tried to drag out discussions, just got on with it and delivered genuine articles. Now all she had to do was decide how much she would take as a minimum offer from Alistair. 'Job's a good 'un,' she said to herself, and locked the car before heading up the front path.

She quietly opened the front door, smiling to herself that she had remembered the no-knocking rule after seven o'clock. It was an ever-present threat that they must never wake up the twins, and it was a sort of pain of death threat.

Jess was already there, sitting at the kitchen table while Chantelle arranged plates of nibbles on the work surface.

They both spoke at the same time. 'Hi, Erin.'

She waved a hand towards both of them and sat by the side of Jess. 'We in here?'

Chantelle nodded. 'We are. This is the furthest point from the kids' bedroom, so I'm hoping they can't hear us. Not that it really matters, they won't understand anything of the conversation anyway, I'd just rather we didn't wake them up. And we can keep the wine chilled in the fridge.'

'And the milk,' Jess laughed.

They heard the front door open and Chantelle smiled. 'She's here, witch number four.'

'I heard that,' Mel said, moving to sit by Erin after putting two bottles of wine into the fridge. 'I'm starving. Hope the sausage rolls are big fat ones.'

'You've not been home yet?'

'No point. It's much too quiet and there's no food in my fridge. I've had a heavy day with being in court almost the full afternoon, so I wrote everything up, stayed a bit later and came straight here. It'll be an easy day tomorrow now, unless any of you are planning on getting arrested or anything.'

Chantelle began to transfer stuff to the table, and there was a brief lull while they filled their plates.

Mel bit into her sausage roll and sighed. 'Awesome. I've had nothing since my cornflakes this morning. So, who has the problem?'

'Me.' Chantelle spoke quietly. 'I didn't know until yesterday just how much of a problem I had, but this is a print-out of my reason for getting you all here tonight.' She reached behind her and took three pieces of computer paper from the work surface, then handed one to each of the women.

Mel's hand was heading towards her mouth ready for a second bite of the sausage roll. Her hand stopped in mid-air. 'This is Andrew.'

Chantelle nodded. 'It is. I don't know who the woman is, but I'm guessing it's someone from work, because they came out of Currys. He brought some ink home for both our printers, so that's why they were there, presumably. They are quite clearly on excellent terms.'

Erin picked up a fork and speared a pickled onion. She held it up. 'That's what I'd like to do to his balls.'

The tension was broken, as laughter rolled in waves, backwards and forwards between the four women.

'So can I take it from the lack of tears and anger that you're not that bothered, Chantelle?' Mel asked. She felt strangely troubled by Chantelle's reaction, or lack of one.

'I took this photo yesterday, so I've had time to think things through. I haven't spoken to Andrew about it, if that's what you're asking. And you're right, I am strangely unperturbed by it. I suspect anger may be the next feeling that overwhelms me, but at the moment I feel more dead to it than anything. So tell me what you all think. Apart from cutting off his balls, I mean.'

Erin stared at the pickled onion still impaled on her fork. 'So you're spoiling our fun before we even get going?'

'I'd rather none of us ended up in prison because of this,' Chantelle said, 'but if you can think of a way of doing it without ending up locked away, then be my guest.'

Mel was still staring at the photograph. 'How did you manage to get this? Are you having him followed?'

'No, it's much simpler than that. If I'd thought I needed to follow him, if I'd had any suspicions at all, I would have approached you, Mel, because I know you know the right people. But this was purely accidental. Jess had the girls while I went to do a big shop, and I treated myself to a Starbucks at the place on Drakehouse retail park. He arrived with her and they went into Currys. I actually thought nothing of it, just assumed he was doing something for work, but then they came out. I picked my camera up to photograph him, thinking I would make a joke of having spotted him, but then he kissed her as I was focusing on the pair of them. Perfect timing for the perfect shot, but it was definitely a lucky picture, not a planned one.'

Jess gave a slight laugh. 'I think I was more upset than Chantelle. She showed it to me when she got home, and I knew we needed a meeting.'

Erin put down her fork after popping the pickled onion into her mouth. 'It goes without saying, Chantelle, that whatever you need, we're here for you. Do you know what you want to do?'

'I've not thought it through fully, but I need you to sort out an appointment for me, Mel, with your colleague who handles divorces. I'm just going to carry on as normal, not let him know I have the photo, because first up, I need to secure this house for me and the girls.'

'Consider it done,' Mel said. 'Can you switch off from it?'

'Oh, I can.' Chantelle's tone was forceful. 'I even sent him off this morning with a kiss and a smile. I almost asked him where he was staying tonight, but decided against it because I don't really want to know if he's there with her. This picture is proof they're together, so I don't need to concern myself with further evidence. A woman scorned and all that, but I do need to know who she is. He's giving everything up for this woman – his babies, me, this house. And hopefully by the time I'm finished with destroying him, he'll have lost his sanity as well.'

'And the children?' Mel spoke, knowing the answer really. Andrew had never shown much interest in the girls.

'Andrew's career comes first. I can't even see him wanting shared custody, but of course I'll have to agree to it. However, it will weigh heavily for me keeping the house if I get full custody. But that's not for me to think about; I'll have discussed it all with your colleague, and will follow her advice.'

5

The evening continued in a slightly lighter vein, although Chantelle was quieter than usual. Erin lightened the atmosphere by talking about the news that her hairdresser was closing down and she had first refusal on the shop next door.

She ran through her preliminary plans and thoughts, and Jess listened until she had finished speaking, before asking if she would be looking for additional staff to work in the new tearoom area.

'I definitely will. My love is books, not making cups of tea and selling scones.' She let her glance linger on Jess's face. 'You interested?'

'I am. I've been talking about getting a job because not working is driving me crazy. It's not about money, it's about needing something in my life other than Mike. I've been offered the chance of a job in the charity shop, on a voluntary basis, but if you think I can work for you too – or instead – that would be awesome.'

'It's very early stages, Jess. You'd have to continue as you are for a bit, but if the plans which are running around my head all come to fruition, I'd love for you to come and manage the tearoom for me. I will be knocking through from the bookshop, it won't be a separate establishment, just an extension of the book area. If you've time, pop round tomorrow and we'll go and talk to my lovely ex-hairdresser. She did say she wants a quick sale; it closes as a hairdressing salon in three weeks. I want to move as fast as possible on this, bring in the feller who created my antiquarian room for me and have it up and running by late October.'

'You have the finances?' Chantelle let the question hang in the air.

'I barely touched most of the money Granddad left me when I did the renovations in the bookshop. And I'll go to the bank for the rest if I haven't enough. I won't let money stop me. This shop next door is perfect for what I want to do. And of course it will eventually pay for itself, unlike the free tea and coffee my customers currently get because they have to help themselves from the big samovar thing in the corner of the room. In the new place I'll be able to have small armchairs and coffee tables, as well as ordinary tables and chairs. It will attract more customers, help me grow the business even more.'

'It all sounds fantastic,' Jess said. There was a huge smile on her face, and she stood, walked towards Erin and hugged her. 'I don't give a shit what Mike says, I need to do this for me. I told you years ago that working part time in that Starbucks would help me one day. That day is here.'

'My God, I'd forgotten you did that. That was... what, fifteen years ago?'

'Okay.' Jess grinned. 'You don't have to rub it in that we're now an ageing population. But seriously, I'm happy to go on any courses we can get me on; this job with you has come at absolutely the right moment in my life.'

'Right, that's three of us with our problems sorted. Mel? You have anything you need help with?' Erin turned to Mel as she spoke, suddenly aware that Mel had been abnormally quiet.

'Not really, unless you can find me a job as well. But I'd be no good in the hospitality industry, I don't really like people. I've just realised I've reached thirty-five, there's currently nobody in my life, and I'm bored out of my mind with my job. I could progress, get further qualifications, earn a lot more money, but I'd rather be at home doing things I want to do, not things I *have* to do. Can you help with that?' She looked round at the other three women, and nobody answered.

'You want some even worse news?' Chantelle asked. 'Erin's the only one who's still thirty-four, the rest of us have tipped over to thirty-five.'

Mel picked up a pickled onion and threw it at Chantelle. 'Get stuffed, Mrs French.' She picked up her wine glass, drained the last few dregs from it and looked at it with disgust. 'It's empty.'

'Want another?' Erin waved the bottle around.

'Of course I do. But I'm driving. It wouldn't do to be arrested for drink driving, I'm in court enough without having to go with myself up on charges.' She looked and sounded disgruntled. 'I'm going to get off, if we've finished sorting everybody's problems out. Text if you need me, but I need to go home and feed Cat. Can I take some food, Chantelle? For me, I mean, not Cat.'

Chantelle smiled. 'You'll never change. I'm guessing there's nothing in your fridge?' She reached into the drawer and took out a plastic bag, then handed it to Mel. 'Help yourself. I can't eat this lot.'

'That's lovely. I hate having to go, but I hope I've helped. I want you to ring me about ten tomorrow, Chantelle, and I'll have an appointment sorted for you. Will you be able to get somebody to look after the twins so you can come in?'

Jess held up her hand. 'I'll cover that, don't worry.'

Mel filled what she referred to as her doggy bag, kissed each of them and headed back to her car. She was feeling more and more stressed as the day drew to a close and knew she had been right to leave when she did. Her work problems had no place in Chantelle's home, and it seemed the others had enough issues between them to keep them going for a while.

* * *

'What's wrong with Mel?' Chantelle had a slight frown on her forehead as she asked the question.

'Since that new bloke arrived at work, she's not been settled. It's not like her to take against anyone, she can usually see something good in everybody, but she definitely doesn't like this Charles feller.' Erin grinned. 'I asked her if she was secretly in love with him, but from her reaction it seems not.'

'Then she should leave. It's really not worth being unhappy at work, and with her qualifications she could go anywhere in the city and they would want her.'

'Maybe we've got it wrong,' Erin said. 'Maybe she wants a complete change, away from the law altogether.'

'She wants to be a criminal?' Jess joined in the conversation, carrying her glass of milk to the table.

'That's one way forward,' Chantelle agreed, 'but I feel she's a bit strait-laced for that career. But if that's what she wants, who are we to squash her? She need a uniform for it?'

'Maybe a balaclava, a black one,' Jess said.

'Well, my attempts at knitting are always full of holes, so I can knit one for her,' Erin offered. 'We can't have our Mel unhappy for the sake of a balaclava, can we?' She picked up her wine glass and drank the small amount left in the bottom. 'You have any lemonade, Chantelle?'

Chantelle stood and opened the fridge, took out a small can and handed it to Erin. 'If you want more wine, the beds are all made up. Jess is staying over.'

'No, I'll head home in an hour or so, I've some work to do before bed and a busy day tomorrow. My mind is buzzing with this next challenge, and I don't want to lose this opportunity. Jess, can you be at the bookshop for about nine?'

'I can. Looking forward to it. Daisy and Lily will probably have exhausted me by then, so I'll be glad to escape.'

'But they're adorable,' their mother said, her tone not altogether a convincing one. She continued to nibble at the little pile of crisps on her plate. 'We haven't really talked through what I do next.'

'What's your gut feeling?' Jess lightly touched Chantelle's hand.

'That it will be hard bringing up the girls on my own, but I also feel there's not much left of our marriage anyway. Although I must admit that the possibility of losing this house is worse than the possibility of losing Andrew.'

'You'll not lose the house, but you'll probably have to buy him out. Could you do that?'

Chantelle shrugged. 'I could go back to work. A good PA is always in demand, so I'm not too worried about the financial side, it's just I hadn't planned on leaving the girls for at least another four years. I wanted this time with them.'

Erin stood and moved around the table to hug Chantelle. 'Look, we'll manage. One for all and all for one with the four of us, and you'll not be on your own, whichever way you tackle this. But I personally don't recommend you let it simmer too long. When's he due back?'

'Tomorrow night. I've until then to decide how to play it. Do I pack his stuff and leave it in the hall for him? Or do I ask him for an explanation of the picture? I guess I could be heading for another sleepless night. And I can't blame it on the twins; it's all down to my overactive brain.'

'Want to know my take on it?' Erin asked, resuming her seat at the table.

Chantelle nodded. 'Go ahead, but don't joke about it. I need serious, not comic.'

'No jokes, I promise. I am with the other girls: I think you bide your time a little. This will be hard for you because don't forget we know you, know you don't have that much patience with anything and everything has to happen at hyper-speed, but I reckon you just bite your tongue. We have to work out how to get maximum benefit for you and the girls on this, and if you jump in with both feet it could all escalate pretty quickly, and it will be out of your control. Go see this person that Mel is going to find for you, listen to her advice, find out exactly what you are entitled to, then deal with the philandering idiot. Don't pack his bags ready for him coming home tomorrow night. Carry on as though you don't want to actually stab him, let it play out and when the time is right you can act with conviction, knowing you're taking the right steps for the three of you.'

Erin sipped at her lemonade and waited.

There was a temporary silence, and then Jess spoke. 'Sometimes, Erin, the stuff you say makes perfect bloody sense. And for once it seems we're in agreement!'

'And sometimes, Jess, you use a swear word and we all stare at you as if you've suddenly grown two horns,' Erin responded. A smile flashed across her face. 'I think, in all these thirty-odd years we've been sisters, I've only heard you use a swear word maybe three times. Of course I'm making perfect bloody sense, woman, and while I might want to throw him under a bus or something, I do recognise Chantelle is going to have to get this absolutely right, and then we can pick up the pieces and be here for her. Okay?'

6

Jess stared around her as Livvy showed them every nook and cranny of her hairdressing salon. It was the first time she had been through its doors, and she could immediately see the benefit the space could have on the bookshop next door.

Erin had come armed with a drawing of sorts showing where the door or an archway could be knocked through from Fully Booked to the hairdressers, an indication of where the ordering and serving area would be, and everything else that had crept into her tired brain the previous evening.

None of what had been in her head throughout the night bore much resemblance to the reality, and she was hurriedly adjusting any notes she had made as they toured the entire premises, pointing things out to Jess but not really wanting a response at that time.

They thanked Livvy, and at ten o'clock, following the arrival of Livvy's first client of the day, returned to Fully Booked, where Suzanne Chatterton was packaging a book for a customer. She smiled as the two women entered the shop. She could tell from their animated chatter that things had gone well.

'So?'

'Mum, it's perfect,' Erin said. 'I'm going to put an offer in, try and get it reduced by five thousand, but if I can't I'll pay the full asking price. I'd be stupid to let it go.'

'I've told her I'm not wearing a short waitress uniform, though,' Jess chimed in. 'My bum is too big.'

'Huh,' Suzanne snorted, 'there isn't one of you that's got a big bum. But maybe a short waitress uniform isn't quite what the tearoom needs.'

'Well, I reckon if I can get a builder in quickly, we could be opening by the beginning of next year. That gives us around four months, but Livvy is still in it for the next three weeks anyway, so we can't do anything yet. Except buy it.'

'You okay for the money?'

'It might flatten me, but it's a sound investment. Livvy says she has no objection to me taking a builder round to get an idea of costings, but I'm going to contact the feller who did my library room upstairs. He did an amazing job of that, and what's more, he turned up every day.'

'So is that it? Can I go now?'

'Of course, and thanks for standing in at such short notice, Mum. I know it's not your normal day in. You going out?'

'I'm meeting a friend for lunch, and we're taking our credit cards along for the ride.' She leaned forward and kissed her daughter on the cheek. 'Let me know how everything goes. Oh, and a courier-delivered book arrived, so I took it up to your flat for safety reasons, rather than leave it down here. I want to talk to you, though, so when you've a spare ten minutes ring me. I'll be in all night.' She locked eyes with Erin. 'Ring me,' she repeated.

There was a whoosh of air as the door closed behind her, and Erin moved behind the counter. 'Let's have a cuppa and a chat, shall we? Sounds as if Mum has some serious points to make as well. Why don't our parents accept we've grown up and can make decisions? Strange, isn't it? Wonder what she wants me to ring her for? I'd best remember, or she'll be round here to talk in person. Think she's okay? I thought she looked a bit grey, tired, I suppose.' She laughed. 'I need to stop worrying about her. She's supposed to worry about me.' They all knew what Suzanne was like.

'I'll go and make the drinks, you stay here in case you get a customer.' Jess grinned at Erin as she headed towards the tiny staff kitchen hidden away in the back of the shop.

Erin gave a huge shiver which she recognised as excitement, and picked up her phone to ring Danny Harrison, the man who had used all his creative skills to produce the room that she used to entertain her important clients. The ones who came to inspect the antiquarian books she collected on their behalf, paying vast amounts of money for the privilege of owning them. Her special people.

Danny promised to call round the following evening, explaining he couldn't make it any earlier unless she could do ten o'clock that night. She laughed and said the next day would be fine.

Jess returned with two mugs, and they sat quietly, each lost in thoughts of the changes that they hoped were to come.

'Should I ring now and put in an offer?' Erin asked.

'You mean you didn't do it while I was making our drinks?' Jess teased.

'No, my initial thought was I should wait to hear how much it will cost to knock through, and then transform it into a tea shop. But I don't want to miss out on the chance of having it by not offering a price now. God, I hate doing grown-up stuff. Life was a lot easier when we did all this kind of thing with Barbie dolls and Ken.'

'Happy days,' Jess agreed. 'But at some point you have to make

Barbie decisions of your own, and today could be the day. It's not officially on the market yet, so I think you should do it. You'd be devastated if you didn't get it because you'd procrastinated.'

Erin stood. 'You're right as usual. I'll go outside to the office to make the call; it'll feel a bit more formal then. You okay to hang on in here?'

'You mean serve customers?' Jess looked and sounded horrified. 'Tea and cakes I can do, but I've never sold or talked about books in my life.'

'Jess, there's nobody in. And I'm sure you'll cope if we actually get somebody in.'

Erin smiled all the way to the back of the bookshop, through the rear door, then into her interconnected prefabricated office building. Time to put her money where her mouth was. And time to get Jess standing on her own two feet, away from the controlling Mike Armstrong, who wanted her doing nothing but waiting on him hand and foot and keeping their home immaculate.

Suddenly it seemed that her sisters needed help, and she stopped for a moment before picking up the phone. Something wasn't sitting right with Mel, Chantelle obviously had big issues with Andrew, and Jess was... unhappy.

* * *

With the offer in and accepted without having to go through any estate agents, Livvy promised to organise everything with her solicitor as soon as she could get an appointment. Having made the decision to sell up, she was keen to get everything moving quickly. She planned on vacating the business within three weeks, but guessed the legalities might take longer. She would give Erin full access as soon as she herself left Sheffield, though, in order to push forward with the changes that would be necessary.

And one day she would return for a cake and a cup of tea...

Erin spent the evening with a silly smile on her face, plans laid out on the coffee table, and a glass of Prosecco by her side. She had remembered to phone Suzanne, and had reluctantly explained the story behind the picture her mother had seen in her flat when she had taken up the couriered parcel. She had obviously recognised Andrew, just not the woman he was kissing. They had said goodnight, with Suzanne promising to keep it to herself that Erin had told her of the marital issues between Chantelle and Andrew. And yet Erin felt uncomfortable. The picture was now tucked into the pocket in the back of her diary – nobody else would see it accidentally.

Wednesday began with an early phone call. Chantelle picked up her phone expecting it to be Erin lighting up her screen, but it said 'MUM'. She always felt a slight panic if her mother rang unexpectedly, and answered it quickly.

'Mum?'

'Hi, love. Take that note of concern out of your voice, everything's fine. I just wondered if we could borrow the twins for a few days?'

Chantelle giggled. 'How many days? Fifty?'

'I was thinking three or four. Today's Wednesday, bring them home Saturday or maybe Sunday?'

'Course you can. You want me to bring them over?'

'No, we'll pick them up. We've been offered a caravan free of charge because my friend Sue has been let down by somebody who had booked it. They've paid for it, but swanned off to Lanzarote instead. It's in Whitby, so I thought we might take Daisy and Lily, if that's okay with you?'

'They'll love it. When do you want them?'

'We'll pick them up in about an hour, if that's okay with you. Get the car seats out of your car, and your dad can be fitting them in while I juggle the suitcases. Don't overpack, we're not driving a 4x4, don't forget.'

Chantelle laughed, and they disconnected. She looked at the twins, who were building towers with large building bricks before throwing balls at them to demolish them, and she sighed. Suddenly there would be peace and quiet, something unusual in this household, she reflected. Would it be welcome? She thought it might just be very welcome.

She clapped her hands to get their attention. 'Okay, my lovelies.' Two heads turned in unison. 'Would you like to go to the seaside for a few days with Nanny Laura and Grandy Samuel?'

'Take my bucket and spade?' Daisy asked.

'Of course.' Chantelle crossed her fingers that she could find them. 'Let's go upstairs and pack a suitcase, Nanny Laura will be here soon to collect you.'

The sound as they stampeded upstairs caused a picture of a herd of elephants to flash through their mother's mind; she followed them, loving the sounds of their giggles.

With promises of new buckets and spades from Nanny and Grandy as Mummy had no idea where they could possibly be, Chantelle brushed away a tear as she watched the brake lights of her father's car flash briefly at the end of the road.

She re-entered her home and dialled Mel's number. Mel spoke quietly, aware that Chantelle might not be alone. 'I was just about to call you, give you details. I have organised for you to see Caroline Martins tomorrow morning at quarter past ten. Can you make it for then? Maybe ask Jess if she can babysit the girls?'

'Not necessary. Mum and Dad have just taken them to the coast until Saturday. It's worked out perfectly really.'

'I thought it sounded quiet. God, what will you do with your-self? Is Andrew home tonight?'

'Expecting him around five. I won't be confronting him about the picture, though, I'll speak to your Ms Martins first.'

'Good girl. Let's not give him advance warning of the brewing storm. He'll find out soon enough. I just wish you'd spoken out sooner, you must have been so unhappy for quite some time if he's moved out of your bed.'

'Oh, Mel, don't worry about that. I think we'd grown apart anyway. The thing that's upset me most is the deviousness. If he'd been open about it instead of blaming it on having to work into the night and other such rubbish, I could have handled it, I think. But he's going with another woman, and that's not on.'

'Couldn't agree more. If you need me, ring me. I'll probably see you tomorrow morning when you keep your appointment with Caroline. She's nice, so don't get worked up about it. She's not only nice, she's smart as well. She'll help you get what you want from the settlement.'

7

Erin and Jess sat on the floor in Erin's lounge. The large coffee table held several cartons of Chinese food, and the two women dibbed and dabbed between the different offerings, as they attempted to make drawings of how they envisaged the tearooms eventually looking.

Jess pulled the sketches closer as Erin reached across for some chicken balls. 'Can I make a further suggestion you haven't considered?'

Erin shrugged and dipped her chicken ball into the puddle of sweet and sour sauce on her plate. 'Suggest what you want. It's definitely a blank canvas.'

'Well. I know you've always said in the past you didn't want to deal in second-hand paperbacks and I know it's been an issue around not having enough room to stock them, but we could have a wall of shelving in the tearooms that would cater for the second-hand book market. I could make it my job totally, so it didn't put added work on your shoulders, and we can either sell the books and count it as profit for the tearooms, or we can make it a charity thing. All proceeds to a different charity every six months.'

Jess stopped talking for a moment and scooped up some rice. 'Just consider it. Once word gets around, people will donate the books. We don't need it to be massive, just enough to bring clientele in who wouldn't normally buy from a bookshop because of the price of new books, but who do use cafés. By opening this annex, you're widening your client base, giving them an option to buy a book, and second-hand ones in charity shops always sell well.'

'And where would you put these bookshelves?'

Jess hunted through the sketches and held one out towards Erin. 'This is the entrance door. The wall on the right could have bookshelves, as long as we leave enough room for people to get past the tables.'

'And you're definitely up for making this part of your job? You'll keep it well stocked?'

'I don't think I'll have to. People always want to donate used books. I'll make it known we're seeking second-hand books, and there'll be no shortage, I promise you.'

'Then I agree. I just don't want anything to do with it. We'll make all proceeds for charity, so it will involve keeping a separate set of accounts for it, but I'm sure I don't need to tell you that. What will Mike say about you working?'

'He'll begin by being caustic and sarcastic, then he'll move on to hilarity, then he'll turn nice and try to talk me out of it.'

'And will he?'

'Not an earthly. This project has woken up my brain. You've done that with your wonderful offer of a job, and I'm buzzing with ideas for it. But first we need to work out what we want from your feller with the saw and drill.'

* * *

Andrew arrived home around half past four, and Chantelle jumped at the sound of his key in the lock. She put down the magazine she was looking at but not reading, and went to meet him in the hall.

'It's very quiet,' were his first words.

'Hello, Andrew, welcome home,' she responded. The sarcasm was very evident.

'Oh, sorry. Hi. I was just a little taken aback by the absence of tiny feet running around.'

'Mum and Dad have taken them away, probably until Saturday. Sudden acquisition of a friend's caravan until the weekend, so they asked if they could take the girls. They've just gone out for food, so don't ring them yet, give them time to get back to the caravan.'

'I'll do it later. I'll take my suitcase upstairs, then I'm going out for a spin on the bike. I feel as if I've been sat down for two days solid, so I'll stretch the muscles with a bike ride. Then I'll have something to eat, ring the girls before they go to bed, and get an early night.'

'Your meal is already done and in the fridge. I've made us a salad, because I'm having some time out as well. I'm eating, then having the longest bath ever before going to the bedroom with my Kindle and reading until I fall asleep. I'll see you tomorrow morning.'

He stared at her. 'You okay?'

'I am. I just want to take advantage of a child-free environment.'

Andrew gave a brief nod, then disappeared upstairs. Chantelle went back into the lounge and shortly afterwards heard the door leading to the garage open and close. She heard a brief but loud 'damn and blast' from the garage and hoped it didn't mean he had a puncture but then she heard the garage door rise and knew it couldn't be that.

She felt a sense of relief that she had been in control of her emotions, and she smiled, and walked through to the kitchen. She would eat later, she decided, as she wasn't feeling particularly hungry, then the bath was waiting for her. But first she had something else to do, and she switched off the kitchen light.

* * *

Her thoughts seemed to be chasing each other around her head. Planning her life, or trying to. And if she stayed in bed the following morning, she wouldn't have to see Andrew until the evening. It was all about getting through the next few days on her terms and not his.

Her parents rang because, despite the lateness of the hour, the twins wanted to speak with her. They gabbled excitedly about having been down to the harbour, and they were going to see a church the next day, which Chantelle presumed was Whitby Abbey. They all blew kisses to each other down the phone, said 'love you' numerous times, and she eventually lay back with a smile on her face. No matter what happened in the future, these girls were her life, and she wouldn't change a thing about them.

She relaxed for some time in the bath, slipped on a thin cotton nightie as the heat in the bedroom was overwhelming, and began to read. Her eyes slowly closed, and the Kindle fell to the floor with a thud.

She slept, sporadically.

* * *

It was around four when she woke for what seemed to be around the tenth time. Two cats appeared to be starting World War III in the back garden, and she got out of bed to investigate. The animals in question were circling each other, screaming as only cats can scream, and she leaned out of her bedroom window to shout down at them. For a moment there was silence and then they continued their battle for supremacy. She turned, picked up her glass of water and launched the liquid in the general direction of the cats. They ran, jumping over the garden fence in their panic to get away from the water that had evidently found its target.

Chantelle shook her head, and headed downstairs to get a glass of milk. It was only as she reached the bottom of the stairs that she realised that the security chain and the bolt on the front door hadn't been used after Andrew's return from his cycle ride.

'Thoughtless,' she said under her breath, and secured both items. She headed for the kitchen, and poured herself a glass of milk, then enjoyed the coolness of it as it trickled down her throat. She opened the fridge door and replaced the bottle, closed it then immediately opened it once more. The cling-film covered plate of salad was still in the fridge.

She frowned, still sipping her milk, and continued to stare at the plate of salad. She took out the plate to check he hadn't had any of it, then replaced it, aware she was being stupid. The obvious place to look for him was his bedroom, not the plate of salad in the fridge.

She carried the rest of the glass of milk upstairs with her, and opened the guest room door. Even now she couldn't bring herself to think of it as Andrew's room; it was, and would always be, the guest room.

It was, of course, empty. The clothes he had arrived home in were on the bed, and the drawer where he kept his cycling gear was partially open. The bed was exactly as it had been earlier in the day.

Maybe, she thought, he was with her. The woman. Or simply

lost on the moors, but that was hardly likely. He had an extensive knowledge of the Derbyshire Peak District.

Chantelle returned to her own bed, plumped up her pillows and opened up her Kindle. She didn't read it, simply stared at the page, her mind on what Andrew thought he was playing at.

Slowly her eyes closed, and she slid back down the bed, finally sleeping once again. Her dreams were of her girls, and when she woke it was to the sound of hammering on her door.

She glanced at the clock, noted it was half past six, and scrambled out of the sheet which had been over her, but was now twisted around her legs, holding her prisoner on the bed. So he'd returned, was her thought as she headed downstairs, returned and been unable to get back in because she'd put the chain and the bolt on.

She slid back the bolt, removed the chain, and unlocked the door, opening it to let Andrew in.

'Mrs French?'

Chantelle nodded. She stared at the tall man in front of her, and at the woman who was standing slightly behind him.

'Who are you?'

Again he repeated, 'Mrs French? Is your husband Andrew French?'

'He is, but he isn't here,' she said slowly, her mind moving into first gear.

The man held out his identification. 'DS Joe Royce, and this is PC Kathryn Spencer. May we come in?' He stepped forward at the same time as Chantelle opened the door a little more, and they edged past her, remaining in the hall until she directed them towards the lounge.

'Where is he? Where is Andrew? I realised at four o'clock this morning that he hadn't come home, but I assumed...' Her voice drifted away. Her mind was fast approaching second gear. These police officers weren't here to tell her they'd found Andrew with some girlfriend.

'Please sit down, Mrs French,' DC Spencer said.

'I don't want to sit down. Where's my husband? Have you arrested him or something?'

'No, we haven't,' Kathryn Spencer said gently. 'Did your husband go out for a bike ride last night?'

Chantelle nodded, already knowing what they were trying to tell her. 'He's dead, isn't he?'

'I'm sorry to have to tell you that his body was found this morning by a group of hikers. It seems he came off the road on a bad bend, and hit his head. He doesn't seem to have been wearing a cycle helmet.'

She stared. 'Wasn't wearing it? You're sure it's my husband?'

'His bank card was in the pocket of his shirt. Would he normally wear a helmet?'

'Always. If he wasn't wearing it, it will be hung up on its hook in our garage.' She stood, as if determined to prove them wrong. 'I'll show you.'

She led the way into the hall, and through the door connecting the hallway to the garage. She stepped through, with Kathryn close behind her. They both stared at the blue and white cycling helmet hanging on the wall. Joe moved around them, walked across and lifted it down. He showed it to Chantelle, shaking his head. 'The strap is broken where the buckle was. He took a risk instead of cancelling his ride.'

'The idiot,' Chantelle said, and finally the tears came.

Kathryn took a quick photograph of the helmet, then gently led the distraught woman back to the lounge. She gave a brief nod to her colleague, and excused herself. 'I'll go and make us a cuppa,' she said.

Joe helped her sit down, then sat himself. Leaning forward, he took one of her hands. 'I'm so sorry, Mrs French. It's a very hard part of our job, and not one we enjoy doing, as I'm sure you realise. May I call you Chantelle?'

She nodded and took a tissue from the pocket of her dressing gown, dabbing at her eyes as she tried to stem the tears.

'Can we call anyone for you?'

'My friend Melissa,' she said. 'It's no good calling my mum and dad, they've taken our twins away for a few days, so they're in Whitby.' She handed her phone over. 'It's under Mel. She can be here in a couple of minutes, she's one of my best friends.' She wanted to babble more, to tell them about her friends, but knew it was grief speaking.

He dropped her hand, and dialled. Chantelle heard him say the words out loud once again as he spoke to Mel, and he disconnected. 'She'll be here as soon as she can.'

8

'Where?' Chantelle finally asked. 'Where was he killed?'

'On the B5577 – or the so-called flying mile – it's a fast road with lots of bad bends. You know it?'

She nodded. 'It was a favourite run of his. He would turn round halfway down the hill, and then start to head back home. Did he skid or get a puncture or something? Or did someone hit him?' She screwed up the tissue in her hand, and Mel put an arm around her shoulder, giving her a gentle squeeze.

'We don't have those details yet. Our traffic people are there now, taking measurements. The road will be closed for some time. Initial reports are suggesting no third-party involvement. In other words, he wasn't hit by another vehicle, but we'll confirm that later.'

He placed his cup on the coffee table and stood. 'We'll be in touch as soon as we have further information, Chantelle, and we will need a formal identification.' He looked at the woman in front of him, who was clearly in shock. 'It doesn't have to be you – maybe a relative?'

She shook her head. 'No, I'll do it. He's my husband, and I can do this for him.' Her eyes filled with tears yet again, and she dropped her head in a vain attempt at hiding them.

Mel walked with both police officers to the front door, and watched as their car disappeared before firmly closing the door behind her and heading back to the lounge. Chantelle was staring into space, clearly lost in her thoughts. Mel touched her shoulder and she jumped.

'Sorry,' Mel said. 'Do you want a real drink now, or are you okay?'

'I'm fine. I need to keep a clear head. I have to ring Mum and Dad now. I know they'll want to come straight back to be with me, but I'm going to ask them to stay there with the girls, not to tell them anything, and just bring them home Saturday as arranged. It will be a help if I don't have to worry about them while I get through the rest of the week. Will I have to identify Andrew tomorrow, do you think?' And then she wailed. 'And how the hell do I tell my girls their daddy is dead? They don't even know the word, let alone the concept!'

Mel moved to sit by her side, and hugged her. 'I have no answers at the moment, but do you want Erin and Jess here?'

She nodded, and Mel made a phone call cancelling Chantelle's appointment that morning with Caroline Martins, followed by two very brief calls to Erin and Jess. Within half an hour, all four women were together.

They remained in the lounge, comfortable in the deep armchairs and sofa. Little was said initially because nothing like this had ever come into their lives before. All four still had parents, and in Jess's case even grandparents, so death hadn't particularly touched any of them, other than on a peripheral basis.

This wasn't peripheral. This was real, and right at the very heart of their lives.

'I spoke to Sandford's,' Chantelle said. 'It seems they were on the point of ringing here, because they hadn't been able to contact him on his mobile phone. I imagine that's still in its holder on the bike. They asked if I needed anything, and told me to ring them if I did. The CEO, James Sandford, was lovely, said how much they would miss Andrew, both on a personal level and in the workspace.'

'And are your mum and dad okay?'

'They are. And Mum agreed it was a good idea to keep the girls in Whitby – they're going to stay until Sunday, they've now decided, and she's promised to say nothing to them. I'll do that when they get home, although God knows what I'll say. But it gives me a few days to come to terms with things. I know I'd reached the end of the line with Andrew, but he was still my husband and I've loved him for a long time now. It's hard.' She reached for yet another tissue and dabbed at her eyes. 'Very hard. And I knew he wasn't home, but I thought he'd gone to be with that woman overnight. What if he was still alive, and I could have saved him?'

'Don't think like that,' Jess said. 'If he recovered consciousness to the point where he could have been saved, he would have used his phone. He didn't, so I suspect he didn't come round at any time. Try not to read stuff into anything, Chan, I'm sure the police will keep you fully informed once they have all the facts. In the meantime, will you come and stay with one of us for a couple of nights? It won't be good for you to be on your own, and we've all got a spare room.'

'No, I'll be fine, honestly.'

'Then one of us will stay with you. We're not leaving you on your own.' Jess was adamant. 'I'll nip home and pick up some clothes, drop Mabel off at Mum's, and be back here in an hour. You two will stay with her?'

Mel and Erin both nodded. 'No need to ask,' Mel said. 'I put lots of food and water down for Cat this morning, and she comes and goes as she pleases through the cat flap, so I don't have to worry about her.'

'And the shop is closed.' Erin reached across to squeeze Chantelle's hand. 'I put a notice on the front door as I left that said it was closed due to a family bereavement. I can stay as long as you want, Chan.'

Jess left them and jumped in her car. Her first stop was at her grandparents' home, where she checked they could have Mabel overnight.

'Oh, such sad news,' Nora said. 'I'll tell Arthur when he wakes up. He's gone for a nap. And of course we'll have Mabel. Bring enough stuff for a few days, then if Chantelle needs you, you'll not be worrying about a dog on top of everything else. Please give her our love. And go get Mabel now, then it's something off your mind.'

* * *

Within half an hour, Jess was back with Nora, surprised to find Arthur was still having a nap. Immediately she began to worry that something was wrong, that there was something her nan wasn't telling her.

'Grandpops not up yet?'

Nora shook her head. 'No, when he needs a nap I just leave him to wake naturally. Don't go worrying about him, he's fine, just getting a bit old. You've enough on your plate with Chantelle and her twinnies, at the moment. I promise I'll give a shout out when, or if,' she hurriedly corrected her words, 'I need you to be here for me.'

Jess stared at Nora. Then she gave a quick nod. 'Okay, I believe you. We maybe need to have a talk, though. I'll go get Chantelle through this awful time, and then I'll sort you out. Anyway, a bit of good news – I'm definitely going to be working for Erin, starting in a couple of weeks hopefully, so I'll let the charity shop know what I'm doing so they don't keep expecting me to turn up there.'

'Working for Erin? I thought her mum worked for her, along with that little lass who's just left school?'

'They do. That won't change, they work in the bookshop. Things have moved on, and there's going to be a tea shop attached to it now. I'll not go into details yet, but I'll be running the catering side of the business. Erin is only interested in books, but can certainly see the benefits of having a separate tearoom, bringing additional funds in. Hearing about Andrew has put a bit of a dampener on things, but we'll all get through it.' She reached down to stroke Mabel. 'Be a good girl, sweetie, no eating Grandpops's slippers, and do as Nan tells you. I'll be back for you as soon as I can.'

She kissed Nora, gave her a hug, and headed out of the kitchen door.

Nora stared after her, wondering how she would react when they had to tell her what was really wrong with Arthur. When the chemotherapy started, she would have to tell her, but until then their beloved girl could get on with supporting her friend.

* * *

Jess drove away feeling oddly out of sorts. Two days earlier, it seemed the only stress in her life was wanting a baby, and living with a husband who didn't want one. Now her mind felt as though there was a touch of turmoil in it, and she hoped she was strong enough to sort it. Mike Armstrong was most definitely a controlling man, something she had always accepted, and she could only imagine what he would say when she told him she was going to work. He would hate her having any sort of independence.

Would the situation be bad enough for her to walk away? Because she knew in her heart it was coming to that. The clock was ticking. At thirty-five, she had to make decisions about the child she desperately wanted, and if it wasn't with Mike, it would have to be with someone else. She glanced in her rear-view mirror and grinned at herself. David Beckham? Rob Lowe? Lionel Messi? The thought made her laugh out loud. She wanted a baby so badly that even Jimmy behind the bar of the Golden Plover might be next to be considered.

She pulled in to the kerb at Chantelle's home. With all four of their cars there, it made that short stretch of road look a bit like a parking lot, but she didn't care. She got out and collected her small suitcase from the boot of the car. She'd packed enough for three days, but was prepared to stay for as long as Chantelle needed her.

The silence as she went through the front door was almost impenetrable. The other three were all in the lounge, nursing mugs of tea, and Chantelle was mopping up tears.

Mel was quick to fill in the details for Jess. 'The police have just rung. I'm going in tomorrow with Chan to confirm it is Andrew. It appears there is some spoke distortion to the bike rear wheel, but they are of the opinion it was damaged as it left the road and hit the rocks in the field.'

Chantelle lifted her head. 'They say cause of death was a massive bleed in the brain, because he didn't have his helmet on.

His head hit a rock and they say he probably died instantly. You know, I always worried about a car hitting him when he was out on the bike at night, but he always said his helmet and reflective gear was enough to protect him. It turns out he was simply going too fast on a bend he's taken a million times before. I just don't understand it. He *never* went out without his helmet. Surely he knew the strap was broken. None of this makes sense.'

9

Friday was a rainy day. Not a cold day, but definitely a wet one, with quite strong winds, and Erin glanced up and down the road as she opened the front door of the shop. She carefully peeled off the notice advising customers the shop was closed due to family bereavement, and turned the normal sign to 'OPEN'.

The greyness outside made it dark inside, and she went around switching on her overhead lights as well as the small lamps dotted around the shop in the nooks and crannies she had created for the comfort of her customers. She heard the front door open and Tia's voice filled the air with its usual call, "'S me!'

'Hi, Tia. You may get some queries today about us being closed yesterday, so we'll start off with a cuppa and I'll fill you in. If customers do query the closure, just say you don't really know anything, but I'm going to tell you anyway, as I may need you to work a couple of extra days, if you can do them.'

Tia smiled. She liked Erin, loved the work in the bookshop, and would definitely jump at the chance of working extra days.

'I'll put the kettle on. Coffee?'

'Yes, please, and we'll go into the kitchen. We can hear if anybody comes in.'

Tia tousled her dark, curly hair as she tried to get rid of the rain, hung up her jacket and followed Erin through.

She quickly made Erin's drink, put her own water bottle on the table, and sat down. 'I'm ready.'

Erin began to talk, telling her the story of Andrew's death, what was happening with the police, and everything else that was relevant to the events of the day before.

'My God, I'm so sorry,' Tia said, her hands clasping her bottle of water as if it could offer comfort. 'Those poor babies. They were such a pleasure to be with when she brought them in to choose some books. But if you'd asked me to come in yesterday, you know I would have done. We could have stayed open.'

'I couldn't think straight yesterday. There's also something I haven't really discussed with you yet, but we're going to be expanding into the hairdressers next door.'

Tia looked baffled, then laughed. 'I can't cut hair. Don't put me in there.'

For the first time that day, Erin smiled. 'We're buying the shop, not the business. I'm going to knock through and make it an extension of Fully Booked, but it will be a tearoom. Though we're looking at having a sideline of second-hand paperbacks in there, with all proceeds going to a designated charity. My friend Jess will be running it, but there's going to be a bit of disruption once the work starts.'

The surprise on Tia's face was clear. 'But I've only just started going to Livvy for my hair. Now I'll have to find somewhere else. Is all of this imminent?'

'It is. Livvy is leaving Sheffield, so wants out as soon as possible. She's accepted my offer, and I've asked Danny, who did my upstairs room, to give me a quote for the work. I may have to ask you to increase your workload to five days a week. Would that be a problem?'

'You know it wouldn't. I can't think of a better job than working in a bookshop. And it will mean I can cut back on working with Mum. I'm not saying I hate cleaning other people's houses, but the days I work with you are much better than the days I work with her. Fortunately she knows I'll drop the cleaning if I ever get the chance of more hours with you,' she said, with a slight giggle. 'So there'll be four of us working for you?'

'That's right, although I think Mum is ready to stop. I don't pay her, she does it because I'm her daughter and a bit of it is in memory of her dad, despite their falling out in her earlier years, but she seems less enthusiastic lately when I ask her if she can come in, so I'm going to make it more formal with you and ask for five days a week. I'll then know what I'm doing without feeling guilty for having to ask Mum and knowing she won't accept any pay for it. Does that make sense?'

'It does. So are we still going to be closed Mondays?'

'We are. Opening hours won't change, and we're still going to close at three on Saturdays, although that may change once we see how this new tea shop performs.'

'And when do you want me to start the increased hours? It gives Mum something to work towards if she knows when she's losing me.'

'Can't give you a definite date, but...' Erin hesitated. 'Oh, sod it, let's go for it. Let's make it from next Tuesday, if your mum can sort her cover for you not being there. Then if I have to do things with the purchase or seeing equipment and suchlike, I can just go and know you're here to take care of things. It's more responsibility for you. You up for it?'

Tia's smile lit up the room. 'I'll ring her as soon as we've finished talking. Is this a promotion?'

For the first time in twenty-four hours, Erin laughed. 'It is indeed. Assistant manager sound good?'

'It sounds perfect.' They both lifted their heads as the shop door pinged.

'Customer,' Tia said, and stood up. 'I'll go in there.' She took her bottle of water, and left Erin to finish her coffee.

The man was negotiating the doorway with a sack barrow, which in turn was holding a large cardboard box.

'Can I help?' Tia asked, hoping he would say he was okay.

'No, I'm good.' He was breathing heavily as it finally shot into the shop as if jet propelled. 'I'm insured if it falls off and breaks my leg, you're not. I do need a signature, though.' He handed his clipboard across to her, and she wrote *one box* after her name.

Passing it back to him, she smiled. 'Thank you, I'll carry it upstairs now.' He stared at her, not sure if it was a joke. He gave a slight nod and left to walk back to his van, pushing the sack barrow with a little more jauntiness.

Tia stared at the huge package. Books normally arrived by the back door – only specially couriered ones arrived directly into the shop, therefore it followed that this was something expensive. She headed back to the kitchen, where she caught Erin wiping away tears.

'Sorry,' Erin sniffled. 'I was just thinking about Chantelle and the way her life has completely changed in just a couple of days. I suddenly felt overwhelmed...'

'Not a problem,' the new assistant manager said, and went to hug her boss. 'That was a delivery and it's in the middle of the counter area. I don't know what to do with it.'

Erin's eyes widened. 'Oh, good grief. Is it Friday?'

'All day.'

'It's those mega-rare books I've been sourcing. I'd not given them a second thought. I need to get them up to the antiquarian room. Carefully.'

'They're not just any old books, are they?'

'No, it's a complete set of Sherlock Holmes, in immaculate condition, but they're all signed by the author and they come complete with a letter from him to the original recipient of this set, who just happens to be a member of the Royal Family.'

Tia stared. 'And that delivery driver brought them in on a sack barrow?'

Erin finally smiled. 'He probably couldn't pick them up. But we can carry them one at a time using the white cloth and wearing gloves. I need to place them on the viewing table. These are the most special books I've ever received, and need all the care we can give them. The new owner will probably come to view them tomorrow, then we can arrange transportation for them. You think we can push the box between us? Bring it in here? I need it out of the shop.'

'We have muscles, boss. Let's give them a workout.' She wedged the kitchen door open and Erin cleared the table and pushed it over by the window, leaving space for the books to reside until the box could be emptied.

'We'll be getting a separate courier delivery today that is only small – it's the letter authenticating the signatures in all the books are genuine, as is the letter written by Conan Doyle, plus the letter itself. Until the bank transfer has taken place, these smaller items will remain in my safe. I'll remove them when the books are safely with our customer.' She shivered. 'Sorry, it makes me judder inside just thinking about it. This is a massive day.'

* * *

The second couriered package was locked away, and the books displayed on the viewing table. The room was immaculate and at just the right temperature as always. The antiquarian room wasn't just about imminent sales, there were many other first editions and ancient books which were added to at least once a week, and it was only known about by very few people, genuine collectors who made appointments to come and view every six weeks or so, in case she had managed to acquire something they absolutely couldn't live without. Erin had gained a reputation for this side of her work that was second to none, and it was the part she loved so much.

But this set of books was for one man, and one man alone. Alistair Jones was a much-valued customer and had been her first point of contact when she had been offered the books. She had known what his answer would be and tomorrow would be cause for a glass of champagne after the transaction. She felt it was such a pity she didn't like him very much. He made her feel just a tad uncomfortable, and she hated having to bite her tongue in case he took anything she said as a come-on.

She laid a fresh pair of white gloves on the table, then covered them with a small piece of white tissue paper. She gathered up the gloves she and Tia had used, then put them with the white cloths they had covered the books with to transport each one individually up the stairs. Every book was immaculate; leather bound with gold embossing, and Erin knew it would hurt to let this set go. She doubted any had ever been read, they had clearly been stored under glass to give them maximum protection from either the sun or people.

Finally she covered the whole set with a pristine white cloth; gold embroidery was all around the edges, and the linen cloth covered the entire set of books.

She gathered up the used gloves and carrying cloths, glanced around the room with an immense feeling of pride, then locked the door carefully behind her. She replaced the key around her neck, went down to the kitchen and put the white items into the washer.

So much preparation for this one sale, and she knew it would go through because she knew this particular man wouldn't be able to resist them once he saw them. Combined with the additional letter that detailed the previous owner, it was definitely a slam dunk.

Erin walked through to the shop and smiled as she observed Tia, in her element with the four or five customers all wandering around the place, chatting with her about different books. The girl had once merely been a customer, but a very regular one, and when Erin finally recognised she needed a part-time assistant, and that Tia had no intentions of leaving school and going on to further education, Erin decided it was a no-brainer. She offered her a job with an immediate start.

And now here she was, needing a name badge that said 'Tia Scanlon, Assistant Manager'.

10

Mel and Jess didn't know how to handle the situation. They had both accompanied Chantelle to identify Andrew, and she had simply fallen apart once they had returned home and closed the front door behind them.

Cups of tea weren't helping, so they stopped making them. Speaking to her mother made everything worse because she couldn't talk to the twins in her present tearful state, and she admitted to having had no sleep during the long Thursday night. She ate a biscuit because she inadvertently mentioned having had no breakfast, and within one minute was being violently sick.

The weather wasn't helping. It was raining; it was grey, exactly how all of them felt. They had all got on well with Andrew until they had seen the picture of him kissing the other woman, and so they all grieved as a unit.

Erin arrived once Mel informed her they were back from the mortuary. She had given her mother, Suzanne, instructions concerning collection of any pre-orders, but Suzanne had asked her to be back at the shop by four o'clock because she had a medical appointment. It seemed life simply went on, no matter what awful things were happening.

A huge bouquet of flowers was delivered in the afternoon from Sandford's, and around three o'clock Andrew's boss rang Chantelle to say he had started the claim for Andrew's insurance policy, and he would keep her informed. Once again, the tears started.

'What's that all about?' she wailed, and once again Mel pulled her close.

'I have no idea. Possibly a death-in-service insurance policy. When you get above a certain level with some companies, that kicks in. It may give you some breathing space before you have to start thinking of how you're going to manage financially. And Andrew was quite high up, wasn't he?'

Chantelle sobbed again. 'And who is that bloody woman? Is *she* in bits because he was part of her life, or is it just me?'

Ever-practical Mel put her ever-practical head on. 'Forget about her, she's nobody now. She can never have him, and in a very short time your life will look a lot clearer. You need your kids back with you, and they're your primary concern now, not this stupid bitch who thought it was okay to fool around with your husband.'

Chantelle blew her nose, took a deep breath and sipped at her glass of water. 'You're right, of course. I know you are, but the whole damn thing hurts so much. To see him this morning...'

'Hey.' Jess knelt in front of her. 'We all cared about Andrew as well, you know. We're all in this with you, and will have to learn to be without him, but I promise you, Chantelle, you won't ever need to feel you're on your own. We're still the gang of four, and always will be. Now, have you done anything yet about the life insurance you have on Andrew? The personal life insurance, nothing to do with his work life.'

'God, no. I haven't even thought about it. I remember when we bought this house he said we'd taken out considerable cover, but that's as much as I know. He saw to the finances, I saw to the normal everyday stuff. It worked well,' she said, and mopped yet more tears from her cheeks. 'I don't have to do anything like that immediately, do I?'

'No, but you will have to think about it at some point.' Jess stood, and walked across to the window. She stared outside, taking in the raindrops running down the windowpanes, the puddles spreading towards the middle of the road from the kerb. 'It all looks so normal, but everything's changed, hasn't it? In the space of a couple of days life has changed, certainly for three of us. There's only you, Mel, who seems to have settled on stability.'

'Maybe,' Mel said. 'Maybe.'

Chantelle stood. 'I'm going to jump in the shower, see if I can liven myself up. I couldn't even face showering this morning, I just wanted the day to be done, but look at me.' She held her arms out. 'I'm a wreck.'

The other three moved as one, and enclosed her in their arms. Nothing was said, they simply hugged.

* * *

When Erin's phone pinged, she fished in her bag to find it. Seeing the name Jones on her screen, indicating there was a message from him, she felt angry. And she knew it was an unreasonable reaction. The man was about to pay her a lot of money for a set of books, and he was wanting to view his potential purchase.

She opened the message to see that he was asking her to notify him when the books would be ready for viewing, and she took a deep breath. She felt a little calmer and messaged back that she would be available at ten the following day, and she looked forward to seeing him then.

The next ping confirmed that he too was looking forward to seeing her, and the message ended with three kisses.

Again there was that flare of anger. She squashed it as quickly as it started. Text kisses would never develop into real ones. She glanced at her watch and saw she had to go. She headed upstairs to give one last hug to Chantelle, and found her fast asleep on the bed.

She told the other two after quietly creeping back downstairs, hugged them both and left.

* * *

Suzanne walked back from the doctor's surgery, pleased that she had stuck to her guns with regard to treatment, and returned to Fully Booked. With her car booked in for some work with a garage, she had chosen to walk to her appointment. It was only a fifteen-minute stroll, and despite the now drizzly rain, she had enjoyed the journey.

The shop was busy. They had often talked over the phenomena of Friday-afternoon book buying, and neither Erin nor Suzanne could come up with an answer as to why it happened, but every week was the same.

She moved behind the counter to stand by her daughter, then took the book from the next customer waiting patiently to be served. She rang it into the till, popped a shop bookmark inside it, then put it into one of the paper carrier bags Erin had bought in with the Fully Booked logo on the front. She added a flyer advertising a special late-night opening with 10 per cent off everything bought on that evening, and handed it to the customer, who was waving her credit card over the card machine.

'Enjoy,' Suzanne said with a smile as she handed the receipt to the woman. 'He's such a good writer. He's got a new one coming out in a few weeks, so keep popping back to check if it's launched.'

Twenty minutes later, they both stood back with relief. The little queue had cleared, and although there was still quite a crowd in the shop, nobody at that moment required their attention.

'How did you know that author had a new book due out? Have you been reading the *Bookseller* on the quiet?'

Suzanne laughed. 'I didn't know. But she'll keep coming back until he does have one, won't she?'

'You're a wicked woman, Suzanne Chatterton. You need a lift home when we've finished here?'

Suzanne shook her head. 'No, the rain is dying away a bit, so I'll walk. Tell me a bit more about tomorrow.'

Erin's face changed. 'Alistair Jones is coming to look at the beautiful set of Sherlock books upstairs. You want to see them before they go?'

'They that good?' Suzanne was curious.

Erin gave a brief nod. 'They are, and I know I'm being unreasonable not wanting them to go to Alistair, but I can't keep them for myself. I need the money. And they actually need to be in a properly air-conditioned environment where they can remain in the condition they're in now. Alistair has the right conditions. He keeps every antiquarian book he's ever bought in a beautiful room in that awesome house of his, and it's been properly set up to ensure the books aren't in a constantly changing environment. But these books are so special, Mum. Every volume in the entire set is signed by the author, and we have a letter for the provenance of where they've been up to this point in time.'

Suzanne sighed. 'You have to let them go, sweetheart. I imagine they're going to be worth a whole chunk of money that is going to help massively with the building works you're about to undertake, so think about that and wave bye bye when the courier company come to pack them on Monday. Is Tia coming in?'

Erin nodded. 'She is, she volunteered even though it's not a day when we would normally be working. I'll be supervising upstairs. I've asked that they be packed in two separate boxes; they're heavy and I don't want them to be damaged by being dropped or anything. This is by far the biggest sale I've ever had to deal with, and I kept expecting it to fall through, but I've paid my suppliers, and even if Alistair says no after he's seen them, I have two others waiting on the sidelines to grab them. But I know Alistair, and I know what his reaction will be as soon as he sets eyes on them. At the moment it all looks a bit ghostly because I've wrapped every book in a white muslin cloth, but he'll inspect every single book, I know he will.'

'I'm a bit like that with bottles of gin,' Suzanne said, then laughed. She reached across the counter and took a book from a young boy. She scanned it and smiled at him. 'I love this series as well, and this is the new one.' She passed the card machine to his mother, then put the book into a paper bag. She also dropped in the Fully Booked bookmark, and a lollipop kept for children who visited. 'Don't eat this at the same time as you're reading the book,' she advised, and he smiled at her.

'I won't,' he promised, and they watched mother and son walk out the shop door, the boy excitedly chattering about the contents of the paper bag.

'That's what makes this such a good job,' Suzanne mused. 'Nobody ever brings anything back because they're unhappy with it, and everybody enjoys their purchases.'

Erin laughed. 'I remember Granddad once saying that he'd only ever had one book brought back, and that was because the last three pages simply weren't there. He exchanged the book for a new copy and the customer sat in the back corner and finished reading it because they couldn't wait to know the end. It's a wonderful thing to be a reader, isn't it? Everything stops for books.'

Suzanne's phone pinged, and she fished it from the bottom of her bag. She looked at the text.

'Certainly does. Do you need me any longer? That's the garage saying my car is ready, so I need to go now or else it's tomorrow. They're ready for closing.'

'No, I'm fine. You go. What have you had done to it?'

'Bit of a scratch. Shopping trolley height, so they've fixed it. It was a Waitrose shopping trolley that did it, so I suppose that's a positive. At least it wasn't Aldi.'

'Mother, you're a snob,' Erin said. 'Go on, go and get it back and let those lads get off home. You going out tonight?'

'No, I'm having a lazy lie in the bath sort of night, then getting in bed with a good book. Might even have a completely lazy evening and send out for a pizza. Hope everything goes well tomorrow with your Alistair.' She leaned across and kissed Erin's cheek, picked up her bag and walked around the counter.

It was as she reached the door that she heard her daughter say, 'He's not *my* Alistair. He's simply a customer.' The anger was evident in Erin's voice, and Suzanne winced.

'Ouch,' she said. 'My bad.'

11

Alistair pulled up outside the shop and felt a shiver of anticipation course through his body. Not only was he about to see a spectacular collection of Conan Doyle books, he was also about to spend quality time with the spectacular seller of the books.

Erin Chatterton fascinated him. She had so much knowledge of the literary world, and a reputation that was second to none in the trade. He had collected rare books for many years and he blessed the university professor friend of his who had spoken in glowing terms of the ex-student who owned her own bookshop, specialising in antiquarian books. He trusted her implicitly and knew that whatever provenance had come to light with this set of books would be verified to the nth degree.

He locked the car and headed towards the shop front. Pausing for a moment, he looked at the beautifully set out display of British crime books and knew he would be picking a couple of them up before leaving the premises. He was a sucker for a good crime novel, preferring British writers, and stored the thought away in his mind to discuss it with Erin once they had completed their business.

She was waiting for him, dressed in a stunning royal blue dress that emphasised the colour of her eyes, and he drew in a breath.

'You look wonderful,' he said, speaking quietly.

'Thank you,' she responded, and wondered if she should have worn jeans. It had just seemed like a special occasion, a dress occasion rather than a jeans and T-shirt one. 'Would you like a coffee or a tea before we go up to see the collection? As you know, we can't have drinks in that room, but we have a tiny kitchen in which we can sit,' she said, smiling at him.

'I'm good, thanks. Maybe after we've completed our business?'

'Then let's go up to the antiquarian room. Everything is ready for you.' She had done a last-minute check a little earlier, switching on the lights and also the electric fire, to give the room the atmosphere that her buyers always commented was absolutely perfect.

Alistair stood back. 'I'll follow you. I feel strangely nervous. I know I've bought lots of wonderful old books from you, but this time is different. I've had fun changing my own library around to accommodate them, and yesterday I had people in to add extra security. This set is going into the glass-topped desk. There is now a camera trained on it, and specialist locks. The books that were in it are now relegated to shelves.'

Erin gave a small laugh. 'Relegated to shelves indeed. I know those shelves are behind glass doors. I must say, Alistair, you give the best care possible to your books. When I meet new buyers of first editions and such like, I quote your room and the displays you have as something for them to think about. There's no point spending hundreds, or even thousands, on a book and not protecting it from the environment. Or burglars, if it comes to that.'

They reached the door and Alistair stood to one side while Erin focused her eye on the small glass in the door. It gave a small clink as it acknowledged the owner of the eye could enter, and they walked through into the room.

She heard Alistair draw in his breath, and she knew she had got the presentation right. None of the books were immediately viewable; she had left them still wrapped in the white muslin covers, and each one would be carefully uncovered and inspected by Alistair. He walked to the table and picked up the white gloves, smiling as he put them on.

'I have a whole drawer full of white gloves. In fact, I spend most of my time wearing white gloves. I often think it must be lovely to just pick up a book and look at it, feel it with your fingers properly, but I wouldn't dare risk doing it.'

'Neither would I,' Erin agreed, and reached across to the first book on the left. 'That is the first – *A Study in Scarlet*. I'm going to sit in the leather armchair and not trouble you until you're ready to speak, but if you have questions then please do ask.'

He gave a brief nod, and thanked her before tentatively touching the muslin cloth. She knew he was already lost in the wonderful world he inhabited, and she sank into the armchair and picked up the latest Robert Galbraith, placed there earlier for exactly this moment.

The very audible sigh of contentment occasionally drifted across to her, yet he asked no questions, simply lost in the moment. As he reached for the last book, she stood.

The safe opened easily at her command, and she removed the letters proving provenance, along with the confirmation that the signatures in all of the books were genuine Arthur Conan Doyle signatures. She crossed to her own desk and placed the items on it, ready for Alistair to inspect them before doing the bank transfer. She had no doubt he would want the books.

* * *

Finally he was done. She had explained the different documents, he had pored over them with more than a degree of fascination, and she had carefully placed each one back in its own envelope. The one that confirmed current ownership was in a Buckingham Palace envelope.

'The documents will be in a sealed envelope, and transported in the special boxes designed to carry the books. I'm using Chamberlain's for the courier service, the people I always use when any of my clients buy a set of books. They have scheduled Monday morning at ten for collection from here, and the books can go directly from here to your home.'

'So efficient as always,' Alistair said. His face was wreathed in smiles. 'These are wonderful, in perfect condition. It's my guess they've never been read, never been touched really, and have lived for all of their lives behind glass doors.'

She nodded in agreement. 'I'm sure you're right. So, we have a deal?'

'Indeed we do.' He pulled out the chair placed opposite her, and took out his phone. 'Is it the usual half now and half upon delivery on Monday?'

'It is. And thank you for never quibbling about the prices, Alistair. I have two more people interested in these books, and they're battling it out to get them, but that's not the way I work. This is a fixed amount, you either want them sufficiently to pay it, or you don't. I've always worked like that. One of them rang this morning upping his offer by four thousand, but I've explained several times my client had first call on them.'

He tapped on his phone, then shut it down. 'That's done. I'll complete as soon as Chamberlain's deliver them. It's an absolute pleasure working with you, Erin. Now, are you free tonight to go out for a meal to celebrate?'

She suddenly felt sick. Her brain went into overdrive, and

finally gave her the answer she needed. 'I'm sorry, Alistair, I can't. My friend's husband was killed Thursday night. She's devastated, and I'm staying with her to give her support while she comes to terms with it. I can't even think about myself while all this is going on with Chantelle.'

'I'm so sorry, Erin. Forgive me for even suggesting it. Maybe some time in the future?'

She tried a smile. 'Of course. But my friend needs me at the moment. She has twin little girls, so things aren't good.'

'I completely understand.' He stood. 'I need to pick up a couple of the crime books displayed in your window, so I'll head downstairs. Thank you for your time as always, Erin.'

She watched as he walked back to his car, and breathed a sigh of relief. Nicely swerved, she decided. She really had no intention of going out with him. Or any other man.

'He's nice,' Tia said. 'Now go and have your coffee break, relax for a bit, and I'll shout if I need you. It's been a good morning. We're selling a lot of the ones you're displaying in the window. I've been quite surprised by how many people have bought them because it's British crime. They're not big fans of US crime. One or two mentioned guns not being a big feature of British crime, yet it was all about guns in other parts of the world, especially the US. I hadn't really thought about it before. It's a proper education working behind this counter.'

'Good, we aim to please.' Erin headed for the kitchen, still clutching her book. It was a rarity that she read a print book, but this particular one had proved impossible to read on her eReader. She sometimes felt a little guilty owning a bookshop and yet reading from a Kindle, but she loved the convenience of the little machine, loved that she could read it in bed without having to switch on a light, and thought it was brilliant that she didn't lose her place when it fell on the floor as she drifted off to sleep. She always kept her thoughts to herself in front of her customers, though.

She made her coffee, and opened her book. Her concentration was wavering as she tried to follow the convoluted plot, so she closed it again.

She sat for quarter of an hour, thinking about her morning. It was her biggest sale ever, and she knew she had been lucky to acquire the books. She would send flowers to Sandy, who had initially contacted her to tell her about them. It had been an easy transaction, and Erin hoped that it might just have opened the gates for future purchases from Sandy's company.

But her bread and butter came from the books in the shop, and she stood to go back in. Tia hadn't had a break, and deserved one.

It didn't happen. It was as if a coach had pulled up outside, disgorging its passengers who all wanted to buy books. It hadn't, but suddenly the shop was full, orders were being taken for books they hadn't got in, and sales were swishing through the till as if there was no cost-of-living crisis.

By the time they closed the doors at three, they were exhausted. They looked at each other and burst out laughing.

'I'm knackered,' Tia said. 'No other word for it. What happened?'

'No idea. I'm just glad it's our early closing day. You going out tonight?'

'Not likely,' Tia said. 'No, Saturday nights Mum and I have a Chinese takeaway, watch a film and usually fall asleep while we're watching it.'

Erin walked across to the till and took out a twenty-pound note. 'The meal's on me. You've been an absolute star, Tia, assistant manager. Have a good night, and I'll see you Tuesday. I decided it wasn't fair to ask you to come in just for an hour on Monday, so it's Tuesday as usual.'

'You sure you'll be okay, though, with the packers coming?'

'I'll be fine. I'm not opening the shop other than to let them through the door. Mondays we're closed, and I mean to stick to that. Now get your coat, and go home. It's still raining, by the way. You need a lift?'

'No, I'll run. It's not far. You going out?'

'Probably back over to Chantelle's. The twins are coming home tomorrow, so she wants to talk with us, decide how best to get them to understand that they've no longer got a daddy.' Erin's voice caught in the back of her throat and she gulped, struggling to contain her emotions in front of her young employee.

Tia zipped up her coat, and Erin let her out, then re-locked it as she watched the girl start to jog down the street. Definitely puddle jumping, she mused, wondering how many *Peppa Pig* books had been sold that day.

She sighed. Speaking of Chantelle had brought the horror of the situation back to her, and she headed upstairs after setting the alarm for the shop. She would go round to her friends, and they would share a bottle of wine.

And talk of Barbies, and play ovens, and other things that made them happy. Not just about the death of a husband.

12

Arthur Wheeler lay on the floor of his shed, wondering what the hell to do. He was in pain. Unbelievably massive pain. He had been sitting in his chair, musing about his life; how it had been so far and how it seemed to be fading away now. And how much he hated to be leaving his ladies, his loves. But it was happening and they had intimated at his last appointment that it wouldn't be months, more likely weeks.

He had stood, and an unbearable pain in his back had catapulted him forward. He'd tried to grasp on to his workbench but missed it and went down to the floor, and cracked his head. Mabel was snuffling at his face as if trying to bring him round, but he couldn't even get to the shed door to open it. She would possibly have gone back up the garden to find Nora if he had. His phone was on his work bench, completely out of reach, and he reached his hand up to touch his head. It came away red with blood.

'Mabel,' he croaked. The dog gave a tiny bark. 'No, sweetheart, I need you to bark a lot louder than that.'

And the door opened.

* * *

Jess immediately rang for an ambulance, feeling so relieved that she had chosen that moment to go down to the shed and collect Mabel to take her back home. The blood was frightening, but so was the fact that Grandpops wasn't able to move his legs, or speak with anything approaching clarity.

She had tried calling for Nora but ended up having to ring her. They had been reluctant to move him, making him comfortable with blankets until the ambulance arrived, then Nora had accompanied him in the vehicle. There had been a very brief conversation where the words cancer, bones and lungs had formed parts of the talk, and Jess had held her tongue, not wanting to upset the elderly couple even further.

But this would mean changes. Nora would need help to deal with a man unable to move. Jess locked up the house, took Mabel home to be in the care of Mike, explained the situation to her husband, and shot off to the hospital.

Mike hadn't been helpful. They were meant to be having guests over for a meal. She had snapped. 'Either fucking cook it yourself, or cancel it,' she said.

Leaving him standing with his mouth open, and saying, 'You swore!'

It was busy in A&E, but Jess was shown through to the treatment bays where Arthur was being cared for. He appeared to be asleep. Nora looked grey with worry, and patted the chair at the side of her. 'I was going to tell you this weekend but when all that happened with Andrew I decided to wait a bit. Your grandpops is having chemotherapy, but the cancer is in his bones, which I'm assuming is what's caused the pain in his spine. They're taking him for an X-ray and a scan to see what's going on, but at least he's had some painkillers.'

Jess clutched at Nora's hand. 'I wish you'd told me. I knew there was something wrong, but this is more than something wrong. This is advanced, isn't it?'

'I don't know, love. Probably, though. This hasn't happened before with his back, or I wouldn't have let him go down to that shed on his own. They haven't said how advanced it is, but they have said it's terminal. I had to come to terms with that before I could tell you, and I'm sorry you've had to find out like this. I promise I was going to tell you this weekend, but this has forced the issue.'

'How long's he been asleep?'

'They gave him pain relief as soon as we got here, and he closed his eyes and drifted off straight away.'

'Shall I go and get us a drink? I think we'll be here for some time.'

Nora nodded. 'Please, love. But only water for me, not a hot drink.'

She watched as Jess walked away, and dropped her head onto Arthur's arm. He didn't move, and she kissed the back of his hand.

'I'm sorry, love. I shouldn't have let you go down to the shed. We know this can only get worse, not better, and I should have thought of that.'

Arthur's eyes opened for a second and he looked at his wife. 'Anna?'

'She's not here, Arthur. She left home, remember?'

He closed his eyes and went back to sleep.

* * *

Jess returned with four bottles of water, and still her grandpops slept on.

The two women he loved most in the world stayed by his side through that long Saturday night, only returning home at just after four on Sunday morning. They had seen him settled on a ward, made arrangements to be there for two o'clock that afternoon when a doctor would speak to them with any results they had garnered, and Jess finally closed her eyes around five.

Mike woke her five hours later with a cup of tea and an apology.

'I'm sorry, I didn't know he was so ill. I should have been there with you. When you rang last night to tell me the state of what was happening, it threw me. I had no idea, and you've told me nothing.'

She sat up and pushed her hair out of her eyes. 'That's because I knew nothing until I got to the hospital. I knew he was getting older, but had no idea we were dealing with cancer. Nan was trying to work out how to tell me, and would have done so this weekend, but Grandpops threw the spanner in the works by collapsing in his shed. We're going back to the hospital for two o'clock, and we'll be meeting a doctor to find out how serious everything is, and whether they can do something to help with his spine. From the bits we've managed to get out of him, he stood up to take Mabel up to the house, and felt a dreadful pain shoot up his back. His legs didn't support him, and he ended up on the floor unable to move, or reach his phone, which was on his workbench. This all happened a few minutes before I arrived to collect Mabel, so I found him. There was a lot of blood because he banged his head, and they've done several scans and X-rays to see what exactly he has damaged, and what is a result of the cancer.'

'And Nora is okay?'

'Far from it. This is all very new to her, he was only diagnosed officially two weeks ago. He wouldn't see a doctor, said his pains were arthritis. She didn't want to tell me until she had all the facts, but it all escalated yesterday afternoon.'

Jess sipped at her tea, then handed the mug back to Mike. 'Thank you, that was welcome. I'm going to grab a shower now, then I need to ring the others and tell them where we're at with it. I phoned them from the hospital last night because I knew they were expecting me round at Chantelle's, so we had a FaceTime chat about everything. Grandpops isn't just my granddad, he's a grandpops to all four of us. As you know, we all call him that, even you.'

Mike stood and looked down at her. 'I'm sorry I was such a bastard yesterday. It was unforgivable, now I know the full circumstances. Can I do anything to help?'

'Not really. I'll ring you when I know more. I'm going around one to pick Nan up, so you'll have to get your own lunch. Visiting is apparently all day until eight, so we'll just stay there until they throw us out. We'll probably go on how he is. If he's still sleepy, we'll come away, but if he's recovered a bit, we'll stay with him until he starts to droop. Either way, I'll let you know.'

* * *

Erin drove home from Chantelle's that Sunday morning, thinking only of Grandpops. Beloved Grandpops who had been a wonderful grandfather to all four of them, treating them all exactly the same, taking them to gymnastics, football training, and even ballet when they once thought they all might like it. The ballet was soon dropped in favour of an extra session of football training.

Mel had stayed over with Chantelle, and would remain with her for as long as she was needed. She would be there when

Chantelle explained to the twins about their daddy, and would ring to let both Erin and Jess know how they had reacted, and whether they seemed to have understood or not.

Erin was finding it difficult to be around Mel. Ever since they had kissed. It had been partly accidental, partly intentional, and very enjoyable. But now it felt like they daren't be alone together, and Erin found it a very strange state of affairs. She knew they needed to talk, but it had been a few weeks now, and she somehow didn't even know how to be alone with the friend she had loved all her life.

As far as she was aware, neither Jess nor Chantelle had realised that something was different, but Erin knew she was battling against the quiet, unassuming nature of Mel. But unless they were considering causing a rift within the gang of four, something had to be sorted. She needed to talk to Mel.

There had been a spark. It had been there all their lives if she thought about it, because if ever they needed to be two-sided for anything, such as their football games with Grandpops as referee, it was always Mel and Erin against Jess and Chantelle.

But since that kiss on the day that Mel had called in to collect a book she had ordered, things had changed. Mel had arrived at the same time as Erin took a two-package delivery of old books, so Mel had helped her by carrying the second package up to the antiquarian room.

She had stared in awe at the beauty of the room, the gleaming, highly polished furniture, and the array of books. While Erin emptied the two crates of books, Mel walked around the room admiring the books on the shelves.

'Love Agatha Christie,' she said. 'Very clever writer, and you've got nine on this shelf.'

Erin walked over to her. 'They're all first editions. Three of them are already ordered and will be packaged up later today. I rarely advertise them, it's more that I'm contacted to see if I've got any.'

'I think this room is amazing. It wasn't quite finished last time I was here, but I can see it is now. And look at that desk, it's superb.' She moved across to it, and sat in Erin's chair. 'Perfect,' she breathed. 'What are my chances of getting one like this at work?'

Erin laughed. 'Absolutely zero, I would say. Let me show you the pen tray,' and she reached across Mel to press the hidden button. Mel turned her head, and they kissed. When they pulled apart, they remained with their eyes locked.

'Oh my God,' Mel breathed, and tried to push the wheeled leather chair back from the desk. 'Oh my God,' she repeated. 'We shouldn't have done that!'

'Seems we should. I enjoyed it, would quite like to do it again.'

'But... but we're friends. Sisters, even. We can't...'

'We did.' Erin stepped back, straightening herself. It had felt good to be laid across Mel, but she could do without her mother walking in and catching them in some compromising position. 'We maybe need to talk.'

And that had been basically the whole of the conversation. Mel had never mentioned it again, and yet Erin desperately wanted the discussion.

She was thinking about Mel, and how to initiate a dialogue when her phone rang. 'Hi, Mum. Everything okay?'

'I was just checking on how Jess's grandpops is.'

'I won't know any more until Jess and Nora have spoken to the doctor this afternoon, but I'll give you a ring as soon as I do know anything.'

'Okay, sweetheart. Give them all my love, and my prayers are for them.'

'Will do.'

* * *

The phone number was under 'shop'. This call had always been a possibility one day, but now it seemed it was a necessity.

'Please ask Anna to ring Sheffield,' the voice said, when the call was answered.

13

Arthur kept his eyes closed. He didn't want to see any more expressions of love, fear, worry and pain on the faces of the two women who had cared for him for around fifty years of his life – Nora and Jess had been there most of the day, but acknowledging their presence meant acknowledging just how poorly he was. He had hidden the pain and discomfort from them for so long, until he had reached the point when he knew he would have to see a doctor. Even when he had fallen in the shed, he doubted that his wife knew how bad things were, how far the cancer had developed. But he knew, and she knew now.

They chatted quietly, talking about outings and holidays they had enjoyed as a family, discussing Jess's beautiful wedding, even talking about Mabel. He could hear their words but they seemed to hover around him like butterflies. He tried in vain to remember all the consultant had said, but his understanding wasn't too good these days. He vaguely heard something about tumour markers, and the cancer in his bones had spread into his spine, and he knew he wouldn't see another Christmas.

Nora would be lost. He had to talk to her, to tell her he knew how things had been all those years ago when Anna left Jess with them and he was sorry he hadn't spoken of it then. The truth was he couldn't bear to lose her, but he knew she had loved Graham Barker. She would visit without Jess at some point, and he would talk to her then, tell her he was sorry for ignoring the situation back in 1987, but he never stopped loving her so he couldn't do the brave thing and let her go.

He drifted off to sleep once more, and didn't hear the nurse saying he was responding to the increased dose of morphine and he would doze most of the time now.

* * *

It was a long weekend for all four friends. Suddenly, in a matter of days, their lives had been disrupted in a way that could almost be described as volcanic.

With the twins arriving home on the Sunday full of tales of playing on the beach and going on roundabouts, Chantelle knew she would have to tell them without the back-up of their favourite aunty, Jess. Mel would be a welcome stand-in, thankfully. Fortunately, her parents said they would stay for a few days with her until things had calmed down a little, so Nanny and Granddad were on hand alongside Mel when she broached the subject of Daddy not coming home any more.

As Chantelle expected, the girls simply didn't understand. 'So where is Daddy living now if he isn't living here?' Daisy asked, the ever-practical one of the two girls.

Flighty, fickle Lily simply asked if he'd found some new twins to live with.

Chantelle looked towards her mother, and both women

shrugged. They had known it wouldn't be easy, but to explain death to two three-year-olds was almost impossible.

Chantelle tried once more. 'It's just that Daddy had an accident while he was out on a bike ride, and he hit his head when he came off the bike. It stopped his heart from beating, and that is what happens when you die and can't live with your family any more.'

She felt she wasn't handling it at all well, and the twins reacted to the strange story by simply wandering off and playing with their kitchen. Mel went with them, leaving a sense of emptiness in the lounge as they disappeared into the playroom.

Laura moved to sit by her daughter, and they sat with their arms around each other. 'I don't know what to say, my darling,' Laura confessed. 'This is way beyond anything in my experience. But Dad and I are staying here for a few days. We can keep the twins occupied while you deal with other things. We can't do much to help, but that we can do.'

'Can you watch them while I just go into the guest bedroom? Mel has to go home soon. She'll be full up with plastic pizza, I imagine. She did say she had to do something for work before tomorrow, so I'll release her from her duties now, then I'll nip upstairs. It's where Andrew kept all our financial stuff, and I need to check everything is okay and I don't need to do anything – or at least find out what I have to do to get everything in my name. I can't afford to ignore it as finances are going to be a bit tight until I know what I can and can't do. Mel said something about checking Andrew's life insurance, so I need to actually find the paperwork to check it. We never seemed to talk about things like that, he dealt with it all and just told me when it was done. And I'll be honest, it's one of those things you tell yourself you'll never need to know about.'

'If you think you're up to doing it, go ahead. Of course we'll look after the girls. In fact, we'll take them for a McDonald's then call round at ours to pick up some extra medication and any clothes we'll need for a few more days, then we'll bring them back for bedtime. Is that okay?'

Chantelle nodded. 'Thank you. I couldn't have better parents, you know that, don't you?'

Her mum smiled. 'We try our best.'

Chantelle watched as both Mel's and her parents' cars disappeared then headed upstairs. It wasn't only the financial stuff she was concerned about – maybe Andrew had something up in that room that would solve who the mystery woman was. Even his death wouldn't let it go from her mind and she opened the bedroom door and looked around. She stood for a few seconds, almost dreading entering the room.

Was that bike ride so important that he had felt he should risk going without the cycle helmet? He could have bought a new one the following day, yet he had to go there and then. Where was he headed after his ride? She knew the accident had happened on his ride out, not on the return journey, so the accident details would give her no help at all.

She sat at the small desk and opened the centre drawer. He kept two diaries; one in his briefcase, the second he left at home. He said his work life was so convoluted he needed back-up for his appointments. He preferred a physical book because he could make notes – he hated using technology to keep track of his life.

She opened the diary, and went through every day, even the pages leading up to the end of the year that held very few annotations. He always had used a page a day type of diary, and she read every note, every comment. He had even noted the day he had moved out of their bedroom and into the guest room. There was no explanation. Just a simple 'first day in guest room' was all he needed and she supposed it told him something that she knew nothing about.

She hoped she hadn't missed anything, and decided at some point when she wasn't feeling so emotional she would do a repeat run-through of the small book. She replaced it in the drawer and rummaged around, gathering up receipts and other bits of paper that were lurking towards the back of the drawer. It seemed Andrew wasn't as tidy or organised as he had expected her to be.

The receipts were mainly for petrol, evidently being saved for when he submitted his monthly expenses claim. Maybe she should just put them in an envelope and give the whole job lot to his boss. She opened the top drawer on her right to seek out an envelope and saw her. The woman.

The booklet was obviously a Sandford's advertising strategy, and when she opened it, it told potential customers of everything the company offered in the way of technical help for small businesses. The picture on the front showed their small team of staff members, and she was there, standing right beside Andrew.

It seemed her name was Olivia Hardwick, and she was the Accounts Director. Chantelle stared at the picture for some time, feeling an anger building within her that she struggled to control. The tears finally came once more and she dropped her head onto her arms that now rested on the desk, sobbing uncontrollably.

* * *

It was only later that she realised what her next course of action would be. With receipts now in an envelope, she would take them to Sandford's. She felt sure she could just go without an appointment, and she would ask to see the Accounts Director. Once she told the receptionist who her husband was, she knew she would get access to anybody she asked to see, and their faces would all express sorrow, as they said words of condolence.

Once she was face to face with the woman who had thought it was okay to kiss somebody else's husband in a public car park, she would know what to do next. Right now, Chantelle had no idea what she would say or do, but something would come to her. It was quite possible she would stuff the envelope of receipts down the cheating, deceiving bitch's cleavage. Or even her throat, if that would give more satisfaction.

And she would make sure everyone at Sandford's knew about it.

* * *

Chantelle made herself a sandwich, feeling no inclination to cook anything. She sat in the lounge staring at the plate, and picked up her cup of tea, not convinced she could actually eat anything without throwing up.

She heard the car pull up, and waited for the clatter and clamour as her girls returned home, clutching whatever McDonald's toy had been in their Happy Meal box. She knew the girls would have had different meals, they always did, and she would be expected to guess who had eaten what.

Easy. Daisy would have had a cheeseburger and Lily would have had McNuggets.

The front door opened and the girls rushed in singing 'Old MacDonald Had a Farm'. Chantelle guessed her dad would have instigated that particular song – he was the one who had taught her to sing it and perfect all the animal noises. It seemed as if it was the farmer's pigs who came into the lounge, throwing themselves at her.

'Oink oink,' Daisy said.

'Oink oink,' Lily repeated, then both of them giggled hysterically.

'You've had a good time then?' She smiled at them and gathered them into her arms.

They both nodded. 'And we had a milkshake,' Daisy announced.

'What did Granddad have?'

'A huge beefburger,' Lily said solemnly. 'Huge,' she said, to emphasise just how big it was.

'It was a Big Mac,' Samuel chuckled. 'It wasn't that big.'

'And you, Mum?'

Laura shook her head. 'I wasn't hungry. I just had a flat white while my little family of pigs munched their way through their meals. Did you find what you were looking for?'

'I think so. And if I'm reading it properly, Andrew's life cover will pay off the entire balance of the mortgage. I'll let Mel check it, and then put things in motion. I can't handle it at the moment, but it's taken a weight off my shoulders.'

'Well, that's a relief.' Laura smiled at her daughter. 'But knowing Andrew, I can't say that I'm surprised. His head was always screwed on properly.'

It quickly flashed across Chantelle's mind that it was a pity his helmet hadn't been screwed on properly, but she kept the thought to herself. Her parents didn't need to know of the problems between husband and wife.

Laura ushered the twins upstairs to get them ready for bed, and Samuel sat by his daughter's side. 'If there's ever anything you need, or even just to talk, I'm always here,' he said gently. 'Anything.'

'Thanks, Dad.' She leaned into him. 'And thank you for feeding my two little horrors, I needed time on my own to think things through.'

'No problem, my love. No problem at all. And I had two Big Macs.'

14

Erin was in the antiquarian room before eight o'clock on Monday morning. Sleep hadn't come easy during the long Sunday night and as a result she had given up at seven and hoped a long hot shower would put some life into her.

Breakfast was a simple coffee; she would eat once the books were safely on their way. It was comforting to her that the rain had stopped, and a glimmer of sunshine was showing through the clouds. The wooden crates could be transported without having to be covered in plastic sheets.

The large roll of bubble wrap wasn't heavy, but it was difficult to manoeuvre. She knew she should find some way of keeping it in the antiquarian room, but there wasn't a space large enough to accommodate it. So it lived in the small spare room where all her junk lived, and had to be fetched and carried for each sale.

She measured the first book carefully, then cut a piece of the plastic. It fit perfectly, so she cut all the matching pieces and prepared to get the books ready for packaging into the crates when the couriers arrived. The white muslin sheets already around the books were tidied and sealed with a label bearing the name of

Fully Booked, then she began to fold the bubble wrap individually around the books. Finally it was done, and she stacked them neatly on the display table before covering the entire collection with a large white sheet.

In the early-morning light, it looked quite spectral, bringing a smile to her face. Mel had said the room felt haunted... and memories of that kiss now haunted Erin.

The text arrived at half past nine telling her the van was five minutes away from the destination, and she went swiftly downstairs to unlock the back door. She waited, then watched as the driver carefully reversed up to where she was standing.

He jumped out, introduced himself as Carl and his colleague as Ben, and Erin nodded at them both.

'Ben and I have met before,' she said with a smile. 'I believe it was raining last time, wasn't it, Ben?'

'More like a monsoon,' Ben agreed, 'but we managed. Thank goodness it's a better day today. No rain promised at all.'

The two men followed her through and up the stairs to the unlocked room. Ben took out a tape measure and began to work out which crates they would need, and how many.

'I think three of the medium size,' he said to Carl. 'That makes them manageable for Erin's client at the other end. We could get them into two, but they'll be really heavy.'

Erin, as always, was impressed by their professionalism. She remained in the room while they went back down to their vehicle to get the crates, then watched as they expertly packaged the books in the containers so that there was no room for movement by the contents.

'Brilliant job,' she said. 'This envelope needs to go in one of the crates as well, but it's the authentication and provenance papers, so can we tuck it down one of the sides?'

'No problem.' Carl took the envelope from her and slid it carefully inside, then they fastened all the tops on by stapling the corners.

'Can I offer you two a cup of tea before you disappear?'

'No, we're okay, thanks, Erin. I'd rather get these delivered in view of the amount of insurance on this load, so we'll get one when everything is complete. When it's a high-value load such as this, we like to get it with the new owner as soon as we can.'

'You'll text me when they're in Alistair's hands?'

'We will. We know how good a customer he is for you. I think this is our fourth couriered delivery to him from Fully Booked, and I'm sure he'll have bought individual rare books that he'll just pop in a bag and ferry home in his car. Don't worry, we'll look after him, and Ben will message you as soon as we've left his premises.'

With considerable grunting and groaning as they worked their way back downstairs, the two operatives finally got the three crates into the back of their vehicle and securely locked inside.

Erin waved as they drove out of the large back gates, then walked across to secure them. No deliveries were expected today and she preferred to keep them locked.

She went back up to the room and tidied round, putting a brief spray of polish on the display table before covering it with the pristine white cloth. Finally she sank into the deep leather armchair and breathed a sigh of relief. She had felt a tug of the heartstrings as she saw the books disappear inside the crates, and felt once more that she understood her grandfather more and more every day.

Books had been his life, and he had particularly loved his own private collection of first editions. When she took the decision to create her antiquarian room, she had called in valuers from the two separate auction rooms. They had independently told her which to sell, and which to hold onto, and the result was total agreement from both sources. She followed their advice, and

Granddad's books financed the makeover of the room. The books she had been advised to keep were in pride of place on one of the top shelves, and were definitely not for sale.

She remained in the chair until the text came through from Ben.

> Books delivered safely, your client delighted.
> Thank you for your business.

She smiled, and thanked him in a return text, then finally left the room. The next text she received was to confirm the books were beautiful, were installed in their resting place, and the balance of the payment had been transferred. It ended with three kisses. A flash of anger flooded through her. She comforted herself by thoughts that the payment would go a long way to paying for the equipment that would be needed for the tearooms.

* * *

Mel went into work and handed in her notice, the missive that had been written at 2 a.m. that morning.

She sat at her desk, stared at the Starbucks coffee she had collected prior to parking her car, fired up her computer and pulled the Transom file towards her. The case was going to drag on for many months, and as she'd given them three months' notice in her resignation letter, she guessed she might never know the outcome of the money laundering claims.

She felt awful that she didn't care. She also felt quite bad that she knew at this point of her life she would be happier working in a garden centre or a fish and chip shop than in one of the most prestigious law firms in South Yorkshire. She picked up her coffee and took her first sip. She felt quite grateful it didn't burn the skin off her lips.

Her office door opened and she looked up, knowing exactly who it would be; the man who thought it was okay to just walk in. She touched her phone under cover of placing her coffee back onto her desk. Without being able to look at it, she hoped she'd pressed the right button.

Charles Errington stood in the doorway, a white envelope in his hand. 'What's this about?'

'I'm leaving. The 23 December will be my last day working here.' Her tone was icy.

'I don't think so,' he said, stared at her for a long moment and turned his back to leave her office.

'I do,' she said quietly. 'And I will be telling HR exactly why I'm leaving. Sexual harassment isn't welcomed in the workplace. I won't take it any further than this company unless I hear of it happening to anyone else who works here, but if I do hear of that situation, I will open my mouth so wide you'd better start running. I have you on voice recording, and I have you on video. So back off, leave me to get on with my work and I'll make sure everything is up to date ready for when I leave.'

His back was rigid. He slowly turned around to face her once more. 'You never complained once.'

'Back off. Stop it. Don't touch me. I'll report you. Don't you think these are words of complaint? I used "back off" only last Wednesday when you groped my breasts. I'm giving you a chance by not putting my reasons in that letter, but I can write a second letter if I have to, and enclose links to my recordings. And why the fuck have you got that letter? It's addressed to the CEO.'

'He asked me to talk you round, doesn't want to lose you. I think he would be talking pay rise if you agreed to stay.'

'I'm not working anywhere where I can see you,' she said quietly. 'You, and you alone, have turned my work life into a living hell, and I'm done. Now get out of my office, I have work to do.'

The slam as he closed her door reverberated down the corridor, and Pam, Mel's secretary, left the large communal office and tapped softly on Mel's door.

'You okay, Mel?'

Mel unclenched her fingers and clicked on her phone to stop the recording. 'I'm fine,' she said with a sigh. 'Come in, Pam, I need to talk to you.'

* * *

Pam felt overwhelmingly angry. She was about to lose the best boss she had ever worked for, and it was all because of the man who had gained a reputation for touching inappropriately, using suggestive remarks, and generally being a pain in the arse.

Her colleagues in the secretarial pool dreaded the call to go to his office but after listening to Mel's words she knew he had gone much further with her. It was time to take action, and she sat down at her desk and began to type.

* * *

The communal notice board, where items for sale, arranged theatrical visits and notifications of promotions within the company were generally the only things advertised, suddenly acquired a new notice.

It spoke of sexual harassment in the workplace, and the fact that it seemed to be more prevalent at the moment. It asked that anyone reading the notice that it applied to should contact HR with their issues, and it would be confidential.

HR, of course, knew nothing about it, but when they received their third complaint, it was realised that something had to be done. The initial action was to send an internal email to every employee, and this, naturally, provoked an even bigger response, considering that the company had almost one hundred and fifty members of staff on their books.

The CEO was horrified. It would only take a tiny leak to the *Sheffield Star*, and all hell would break loose. He attempted to close it all down by removing the original notice, and then he remembered the resignation letter from someone he had considered to be one of his most respected and well-loved members of staff, Melissa Marsden.

Was this why she was leaving? She had a close working relationship with Charles Errington. He sent a memo to Charles asking him to drop into his office, but the man was in court, so he wandered down to Mel's office and asked her directly.

She refused to confirm or deny the sexual harassment, quietly asking him to simply accept her resignation because she needed to leave the company.

And he knew. He could see from her demeanour. He briefly wondered how other CEOs dealt with the issue, but decided he could do the right thing. Charles Errington would climb no higher up any ladder at this company, and he could ease Melissa's problems by giving her three months of paid gardening leave.

* * *

Mel cleared out her desk, packing everything into a banker's box and taking it down to her car. She went into the secretarial pool, explained what was happening and wished everybody goodbye.

There were tears, and Pam walked back with her to her office.

'Did you do this?'

Pam nodded. 'I had to. I knew he'd done it with others, and he had to be stopped. Because of him, I've lost the best boss I've ever had. It's taken half a day to sort, but all credit to the CEO, he's not messed about.'

Charles returned from court to his office, his mind on Mel. It was a shame she was going. Nice boobs, great arse...

He opened his office door, crossed to his desk and saw the note on top of his keyboard. It was written on a piece of the CEO's personal notepaper, and simply said:

My office. Now.

15

Tia arrived for work and Erin stared at her.

'What is this I see before me?' she said.

Tia laughed. 'Are you quoting Shakespeare?'

'Almost. I remember Lady Macbeth saying something about "is this a dagger I see before me?" I was simply sounding bookish and educated. You look stunning.'

'When I told Mum about me being assistant manager, she made me go and buy some smart clothes. She said I can't come in jeans any more. I've bought three pairs of these,' and she pointed to the trousers she was wearing. 'And she says I can't wear my slogan T-shirts any more, I've got to be grown up.'

Erin shook with laughter. 'We are about to start knocking this place about. We'll be demolishing a wall for a start, so I'll leave you to guess what will happen to the dust and muck from that, so you might need to bring some jeans with you and keep them here. The biggest part of our job until all the work is done is keeping everything as clean as we can. However, we've just had a postal delivery, and I think this is for you.'

She handed Tia a small brown envelope and Tia looked at the address. 'It says your name,' she said.

'That's because I ordered it. Now open it, I'm pretty sure it's for you.'

The name badge inside read 'Tia Scanlon, Assistant Manager'. There was a sharp intake of breath as Tia realised what she was holding, and her eyes sparkled as she fastened it to her new white top.

'Mum was right. I can't wear this name thing and wear jeans.'

'Well, assistant manager, let me fill you in on how yesterday went, what's happening later this week, and just how busy we're likely to be next week.' Erin glanced at her watch. 'We've about twenty minutes before we need to open. Let's go and sit in the kitchen.'

Tia followed her, stroking her hand over the badge, and sat down opposite the woman who had opened up her world just a little bit more. A lot more, if she was brutally honest.

'Hopefully, by the end of the week, Livvy and I will have finalised everything. Her solicitor is pushing it through fast because Livvy wants to leave by the end of the month, so we can start to get things done within the next seven days or so, all being well. I've already had a word with Danny the builder and he can start Monday, although his co-workers will be a couple of weeks away from starting because this has all happened so fast. We're aiming for the beginning of November for an opening date, so nicely in time for the Christmas traffic.'

'Brilliant. I love Christmas here. Though I swear most of our customers come in for the mince pies.'

'We've a lot of hard work in front of us before we get to the mince pie stage. And although Jess is going to be running the tea shop, she can't be here to help us at the moment because her grandfather is really poorly. They're almost living at the hospital with him, but the news seems to get worse every evening. He's actually like a grandpops to all four of us, you know. Used to take us for football training. My God, we love that man.'

'I can't imagine Mel playing football. She's a lady.'

Erin laughed. 'She was the most tomboyish of the four of us. She only turned into a lady when she graduated from Sheffield University and went straight to work in a solicitor's office. Like you, she stopped wearing jeans overnight. Chantelle was our goalie, and the rest of us just kicked balls at her. But Grandpops was our coach, and when he dies, a part of us will die as well. And reading between the lines, I don't think he will be with us for much longer.' She felt a sob start in the back of her throat and desperately tried to control it.

'That's awful. I haven't got grandparents but I imagine they're just as important as parents.' Tia shrugged. 'Only got one of those as well.'

'I've only really got a mum. Suzanne divorced my dad when I was still little, and I don't really see him. Get a Christmas card but that's all. Jake, he's called. His father died, my mum had fallen out with my grandfather who left me the shop, so it made sense to have Grandpops for all of us. We grew up as sisters, the four of us. It was an awesome childhood really, because there was always some adult to step into the breach if we needed looking after. And we've all been there over the past few days for Chantelle, of course. Andrew was like a brother to us three, back in the day, as well as being Chantelle's husband. We were closer to him than we are to Mike, Jess's husband, but he's away so much with his job. Her life would be a lonely one, if we weren't so close as a foursome. Mel and I have managed to avoid permanent relationships, but to be honest this business takes all my time.'

Tia smiled. 'We've never talked like this before, personal stuff, I mean. Is this how assistant managers normally are?'

'Certainly is,' Erin laughed, and stood. 'And now we've put the world to rights, let's get the shop open.'

She walked through the shop, turned the sign around so the customers knew they were open, and unlocked the door. Mel was sitting on the step, her back to the door.

'About bloody time,' she grumbled, and climbed to her feet.

* * *

'You've left?' Erin's face was a picture.

'Well, not technically. I have gardening leave until Christmas, then I've left.'

'So what are you going to do?'

'I'm going to help my mate refurb her shop, I'm going to be fully there for my other mate while she loses her grandpops, and I'm going to get to know the twins better so I can help with them more, because Jess will have enough on her plate when Grand-pops goes. She's the one who normally steps in when Chantelle needs back-up. In short, I'm going to be a better friend. Or a better sister, depending how you want to see it.'

'And you're looking for a new job?'

'Not yet. I don't know what I want to do, but I'm sick and tired of a broken legal system that is so fucked up it doesn't even prose-cute rapists in case the police don't win the case. There are people walking around Sheffield who should be banged up for life, and they've got away with it. Well, I can't be part of that any more, so I quit.'

'And you've reached this decision on your own?'

'Kind of. What brought this spectacular piece of decision

making to a head was Andrew's death. It's been accepted it was an accident, and he paid the ultimate price because he didn't have a helmet. Nobody has looked any deeper. Have we been questioned? Have we heck. He could have been caught by a passing car, in which case it is accidental death, but it could have been somebody who thought he would be better off dead. Somebody like a wronged wife. This is obviously my legal training overthinking things, but this is what our legal system is like now, far too quick to write everything off as an accident. So, I'm out of it. And then there's you.'

'Me?' Erin raised her eyebrows. 'What have I done?'

'Kissed me.'

There was a period of silence, then Mel stood and walked around the table towards the kitchen door. She closed it, walked back towards Erin, bent down and kissed her firmly on the lips.

There was a further short hiatus until Mel spoke, softly.

'One day at a time, Erin, one day at a time.'

Erin couldn't speak. She couldn't remember how, wouldn't have known any words to fit the issue anyway.

'Have I upset you?' Mel asked with a smile.

Erin shook her head, searching for her voice. It croaked when she finally found it. 'I thought I'd upset *you* with that first kiss.'

'No, you woke me up. I finally realised what was missing in my life, and it was you. That doesn't mean that I knew in any way how to solve that problem. Then last Wednesday, before all this with Andrew happened, that bloody predator at work made a lunge for my breasts. The result of that was to hand in my notice at the first opportunity, which was yesterday morning, and the other girls at work have now sorted out the problem of Charles Errington, I do believe. But it doesn't mean I've changed my mind. I needed out. I have absolutely no idea where I go from here, but I have savings, I can live without a wage for six months or so until I decide what I want to do, but I'm pretty sure it won't be anything to do with the law. I'm on gardening leave, which means I get my full salary for the next three months. I guess they thought it was cheaper to do it that way than for me to sue for sexual harassment. I wouldn't do that, just for the record, but they don't know that.'

Erin listened. She hadn't heard Mel be as vocal as this ever before; it seemed as if suddenly the passion had erupted, and while she might not know what was to come next in her life, she knew exactly what she didn't want.

'And while you're thinking about what comes next as a career, what will you do?'

'I want to spend it with you.'

Erin waved her hands in the air, unable to find the right words.

'I mean I want to help you. What you have planned for this place is massive, and what you're so unselfishly doing for Jess in her new role is awesome. I'm sure I can be of help, and it will be unpaid help for you. I can paint, I can clean, I could even possibly operate a till, but I suspect Tia is much smarter than me at doing the complicated stuff, but what I'm saying is you can call on me, and hopefully depend on me.'

Erin stood and walked over to the sink. She filled a glass with water and took a long drink. Mel stood, waiting for a reaction. Slowly, Erin turned to face her and held out a hand. Mel grasped it and Erin pulled her close.

'I didn't know you knew so many words,' she murmured, and lifted Mel's hand to her lips. 'Did you say this feller's name was Charles Errington?'

Mel nodded.

'He deserves a medal. It's like he's freed you to be you, instead of the career woman you've been since you were about fifteen. If ever I meet him, I shall thank him. That, of course, will be after I've punched him in the nose for assuming he could touch your boobs.' She reached up to the taller woman and slowly kissed her. 'Thank you for waking up, Mel, and thank you for the offer to help. And... are we now a tentative us?'

Mel hugged her. 'I think so, don't you?'

16

Chantelle drove into the car park at Sandford's and slowly pulled on her handbrake, deep in thought. She had brought the girls with her to give her mum and dad a break from the endless game playing and story reading. The twins treated their grandparents as their own personal slaves, until even Chantelle began to feel guilty.

She had dressed the girls in matching outfits of jeans and pink T-shirts, one proclaiming 'I'm Daisy, the cute one', the other saying 'I'm Lily, the naughty one'. The girls had arrived home from Whitby at the weekend with the tops, and Chantelle couldn't help but think how accurate they were.

The twins stood waiting patiently for their mother to take a hand each, and all three walked calmly across the car park and into the reception area. The receptionist looked up, clearly surprised to see children in what was normally a child-free environment.

'Can I help?' she asked, smiling at how cute the twins looked.

'I'm here to see Ms Hardwick if she's available, please. My name is Chantelle French, Andrew's wife.'

Chantelle watched as shock swept across the receptionist's face. 'Mrs French. I'm sorry, we've never met and I didn't recognise you, wouldn't have known...' Her voice trailed away as she realised she was way out of her depth and with no way of recovering.

Chantelle smiled. 'Don't worry about it. If you can ask Ms Hardwick if she has time to see me?'

'Of course.' The receptionist was now in full recovery mode. 'Please take a seat on the sofas, and I'll tell her you're here.'

Chantelle took hold of the twins' hands and all three of them walked across, and settled onto the sofas. She removed two reading books from her bag, and handed one to each child, with a silent little prayer that they would sit and read, and not want to explore.

Daisy and Lily looked at each other, then opened their books. For the moment, they had decided good behaviour would be an excellent idea. Mum wasn't as easy to manipulate as their grandparents.

Chantelle looked around, and felt a lump rise into her throat as she spotted a photograph of Andrew on the wall with his title of Technical Team Leader underneath it. Olivia Hardwick's picture was also there, very attractive and with a smile that Chantelle suspected wouldn't be there for much longer.

Chantelle had taken extra care with her appearance. Her soft light brown skin never needed much in the way of make-up, but she had used a touch of gold on her eyelids to emphasise the beauty of her dark brown eyes – she always blessed Samuel for the gift of his eye colour. A hint of a pale lipstick enhanced the overall appearance, and she had put on a figure-hugging black dress to show her state of mourning. Something that Olivia bloody Hardwick couldn't do. Black high heels added to her height, and she waited patiently until she heard footsteps coming down a corridor.

Her palms were moist, and she wiped them down her dress.

She recognised the woman as she came into reception, veering across towards them as she realised where they were waiting for her.

'Mrs French.' She held out a hand, and Chantelle touched it very briefly. 'I'm Olivia Hardwick. I believe you wanted to see me? I understand the insurance claim is being processed and we should have news later today about that. Is there anything else we can do to help?'

Chantelle was now standing, and was easily six inches taller than Olivia. Olivia took a step back. Chantelle hoped she felt threatened.

The twins climbed down from the sofa, assuming wrongly that their mummy was getting ready to leave, but Chantelle wasn't quite at that stage. She opened her bag and removed the envelope with the receipts inside, then handed it to the other woman.

'I spent some time going through my husband's desk, and found the petrol and hotel receipts for this month. He hadn't got around to putting them in order so I've just put the entire collection of them into this envelope for you to sort out.'

Olivia took the envelope from her, and smiled down at the two girls, who by now had gone to stand by her side, to simply stare at her. They clearly didn't know who this woman was, but they sensed their mother didn't like her.

'So you are Lily and Daisy. Your daddy spoke of you a lot. He loved you very much.'

'Have you got Daddy?' Lily asked the question, and Daisy nodded.

Olivia glanced at Chantelle, who remained perfectly still.

'No,' she said finally, 'I don't have your daddy. I only worked with him. He was a very nice man.'

Daisy nodded once more.

Chantelle now spoke quietly, knowing the girls wouldn't

understand what she was about to say. 'The police notified me this morning that they are releasing Andrew's body, so I can begin to make the arrangements for his funeral. I'll let everyone who needs to know what the details are. In the meantime, please sort out the receipts, as I'm assuming Andrew will be getting his final month's pay and you'll need to know the expenses part of it.'

She reached out her hands for the girls to hold on to her, and Olivia spoke. 'We have already had a brief discussion about it, and on the day of the funeral we will be closing down the company as a mark of respect, and so that we can all attend. Thank you for bringing these in,' she tapped the envelope, 'I'll sort them as soon as I get back to my office.'

Chantelle began to move towards the doors, holding tightly to the twins. As she reached the large glass front doors, she turned. She said loudly enough for both Olivia and the receptionist to hear, 'Olivia, the invitation to the funeral doesn't extend to you. You will not be welcome, so don't embarrass yourself by trying to attend. Maybe you can think about not sleeping with someone else's husband while you're thinking about not attending my husband's funeral. Come on, girls, let's get away from here, we have much to do at home.'

Olivia watched them walk back to the car, and remained in reception until the small black Focus disappeared from view.

She looked at the receptionist, as if daring her to say anything. 'What a strange woman,' she said, and headed back towards her own office.

Within five minutes, she had opened the envelope, shuffled briefly through the receipts and discovered a folded A4 piece of paper. Opening it up almost stopped her breath. It was a photograph of her and Andrew outside Currys on the retail park, locked in a clinch that left nothing to the imagination about the state of their relationship.

And she knew that within the next half hour the whole company would know she wouldn't be allowed to attend Andrew's funeral. She had had worse days in her life, she just couldn't remember one at that moment.

* * *

Chantelle drove home holding back tears. Nastiness wasn't part of her usual life, and yet she couldn't have stood behind her husband's coffin knowing his mistress was one of the mourners.

'Okay?' Her mum, Laura, could tell from the subdued atmosphere that things hadn't gone smoothly. She was only taking in receipts, wasn't she?

'Mummy not like lady,' Lily said, and Daisy nodded in agreement.

Laura looked closely at her daughter. 'So it's not okay?'

'It was fine. I got my point across,' Chantelle sighed. 'I'll talk later, Mum. I just need to make some decisions now about how to arrange a funeral. I don't know where to start. It's okay for the police to say they're releasing Andrew's body, but where to? What's it mean?'

'You place everything in a funeral director's hands, my darling. They will do everything. They'll collect him and take him to their chapel of rest, and eventually you will be able to see him.'

'I don't want to see him. I identified him. I would have preferred to remember him as he was, not with the facial and head injuries I had to see, so I won't be seeing him again. They asked if I wanted the bike back, but I said no. So I choose a funeral director and basically that's it?'

'Kind of. If you intend having a wake for him, you'll organise that yourself, but really that's just a matter of finding the right venue, and they will do the rest. Stop worrying, Chantelle, Dad and I will help. We're not going anywhere until after the funeral. We can keep popping home to check on things and I've asked our neighbour to ring me if there are any problems. She has a key anyway.'

'That's such a relief. You staying, I mean. I know I'll have to be on my own at some point, but at the moment I'm wallowing around like a hippopotamus, not knowing where to turn. And I need to organise getting Andrew's car returned to them, it's a company car and somebody else could be using it.'

'There's plenty of time for that. Maybe mention it when they give you some details about this company life insurance. Andrew never mentioned there was one?'

'Not a word. Mel seems to think it will be a death-in-service type of policy but that means nothing to me. At some point I don't doubt somebody will explain it, and you're right, that will be the point when I can ask them to collect the car.'

'That's my girl, brightening up already. Let's forget about things for today, and start to make a to-do list tomorrow morning. Going to Sandford's has clearly taken it out of you, so enjoy your girls today, tomorrow is soon enough to get on the phone.'

Samuel came through from the kitchen, a child in each arm. 'They want to go feed the ducks,' he said.

'Serves you right for singing "Old MacDonald Had a Farm" with them. I heard you quacking like ducks. Of course they're going to want to feed them. We got any stale bread, Chantelle?'

'Probably. We haven't been eating much of anything. I may go and have a bit of a nap if you're taking them out, I didn't sleep much last night, and going to Sandford's this morning hasn't helped.'

'That's fine. We'll take them for some lunch, go find some ducks to feed, and head back in about three hours. Make good use of your time. Either sleep, or do something nice that's just for you.'

'Thanks, Mum.' Chantelle kissed her mother's cheek, and the girls climbed down from Samuel's arms. 'Ducks, ducks,' they yelled.

Five minutes later, peace had descended, and Chantelle took a bottle of water from the fridge. She took two paracetamol tablets, more in the hope they would help her sleep rather than as a painkiller, and headed upstairs.

She hesitated outside the spare bedroom and went in. It spoke so heavily of Andrew and she knew she had to revert it to its original status as a guest room as soon as possible. It was a bigger bedroom than the one her parents were currently using, and they would probably appreciate a move into the larger space. As a start, she carried all his clothes which he had transferred from their bedroom and put them back into their original places. He had been using the dressing table as a desk, by the simple act of removing the freestanding mirror. She replaced that, emptied the contents of the drawers onto the bed, and turned it swiftly back into the empty dressing table that had been used for visitors. She brought in a suitcase and filled it with the desk contents for going through in some detail before throwing away anything she could, but that could wait.

She lay on the bed for a moment and could smell the unique aftershave that Andrew had used. She had always loved it, and sank her nose deeper into the pillow, letting her thoughts drift to happier times. And she slept.

17

Jess sat by her grandfather's bed, trying to decide what day it was, eventually settling on Tuesday, and holding his hand. He would be moving to a hospice later, where he would receive personalised treatment with one-on-one care. Nobody had actually used the term 'end-of-life care', but both she and Nora knew.

He was hardly awake now, yet when his eyes did open, he recognised them. He would say 'Nora,' she would say, 'Yes, love,' and he would drift back to sleep, secure in the knowledge that she was there.

Jess stayed all day and every day, going home at night to spend time with Mabel. Fortunately Mike had departed for a two-week trip to Japan, so she had only herself and the little dog to think about, but he rang every night to see how things were going. He seemed like a different person, and she wasn't sure how to handle it.

He knew Grandpops had been more of a father to her than a grandfather, but maybe, like her, he had assumed Nora and Arthur would be there forever. It was a sobering thought for Jess that if Arthur was nearing his end, then how far behind could Nora be?

The thought coincided with the opening of the room door, and Nora entered carrying coffees for them.

'Sandwiches in my bag,' she said. 'I got ham and tomato. That okay?'

'It's fine. Has anybody said what time they're transferring Grandpops?'

'Just said this afternoon. He's going to St Luke's. Jess, you know what this means, don't you?'

'Stop worrying, Nan, of course I do. We both know he can't carry on living on massive doses of morphine, and the pain he would be in if he didn't have the drug would be unbearable, so let's just accept what the future holds, and give him our time while we still have him. Okay?'

'Okay. It will be a strange world for us, won't it?'

'It will, but we have each other.'

'I think we'll not go to St Luke's today, we'll go tomorrow morning. They'll be settling him in, sorting his medication and stuff, and we'd only be in the way.' Nora handed Jess a sandwich.

Jess stared at it, trying to remember when she'd last eaten. She opened up the cellophane wrapping, knowing she had to eat whether she wanted to or not. Making herself ill wouldn't help anyone.

She watched Nora stare at the package in her own hand, and then put it down on the bedside table. 'I'll have it in a bit,' she said, picking up her coffee instead.

Arthur slept on for another hour, only opening one eye when he sensed something different was happening. The transport had arrived to ferry him across the city to the hospice. By the time the ambulance left the Northern General Hospital, he was fast asleep again.

* * *

Everyone gathered at Jess's childhood home that Tuesday evening, because FaceTime updates were no longer enough. Jess, Erin, Chantelle and Mel were all losing their beloved grandfather, and the meeting happened almost accidentally. Mel and Erin arrived together after Erin had closed the shop for the night, to find Chantelle had left the twins with their grandparents before jogging the half-mile journey to ask for an update.

Jess had decided to collect Mabel, then stay at her grandparents' home for the foreseeable future. If any middle-of-the-night phone calls were received, she needed to be with her nan. They would face the uncertain future together.

Nora went to bed around eight o'clock, saying she hadn't slept the previous night and was feeling wiped out. Jess followed her up half an hour later to check she was settled, and she was fast asleep, so she re-joined her friends downstairs.

'This is bloody awful,' she said, sinking into an armchair. 'She's asleep, but the way Grandpops looked today, I don't think we will have him for much longer. I always thought cancer was a pretty drawn-out illness, but this has been so quick.'

'Has it been quick?' Mel asked. 'Or is it that he kept it to himself? They wouldn't want you worrying, Jess, and I suspect he's been having symptoms for quite some time.'

'Let's talk of other things,' Chantelle said. 'Let's pretend for one night that all is right with us, and the four musketeers are living life the way they want to live it.'

Erin gave a brief snort of laughter. 'If only we could do that. I think we've all fallen apart in various ways over the last couple of weeks, and our lives are changing. But we're still us, still have each other's backs, and we can still talk. And actually I have a little good news... If everything goes well, I will own the shop next door on

Thursday. Or at least I'm paying the money to the solicitor on Thursday. Danny can begin the structural changes next week, so although it's all change, it's good change.'

'Crikey,' Jess said. 'I thought Livvy had clients booked in for the next month!'

'Livvy is in love,' Erin responded, as if that answered everything. 'She doesn't want to hang around here, she wants to be gone. She's been in touch with the few bookings she had and cancelled them.'

'Well, that's a relief,' Mel said. 'I'm happy to help out with cleaning and rearranging books, but I draw the line at hairdressing.'

Erin reached across and squeezed her hand, smiling at her. 'Well, now you have all this free time, you'll be looking for things to do.'

'Free time?' Jess looked at her two friends, sitting side by side and quite close. 'Am I missing something? And why are you nearly on each other's laps?'

'I thought that, but it's always been Erin and Mel, Mel and Erin. What's going on?' Chantelle stared at the others as she spoke.

'Nothing.'

'Nothing.'

'You're lying.' Chantelle stood up and moved to stand over them. 'Melissa Marsden, swear on Cat's life that you're not keeping anything from us.'

Erin was trying desperately hard not to laugh. 'On your cat's life, Mel. Best tell the truth, then.'

Mel gave a deep sigh. They should have known their 'take it slow' secret would be obvious to Chantelle and Jess. 'Okay,' she said, 'on my cat's life, we might have shared a kiss.'

Chantelle was still hovering over them. 'Only one?'

Mel frowned. 'Maybe.'

Chantelle and Jess looked at each other. 'How long is it, Jess? Fifteen years?'

Jess nodded. 'It's about fifteen years since we first predicted it. What the hell took you two so long?'

'It's Mel's fault,' Erin said. 'She's a bit on the slow side. I kissed her a couple of weeks ago, but she didn't kiss me back. Not 'til today, anyway. You two do know this is all top secret, don't you?'

'Why?'

'It's all very new.'

Jess laughed. 'Not to us, it isn't. It's been obvious you're meant for each other for years. You two are the only people who don't know it. Bet Suzanne's not surprised when you tell her.'

Mel and Erin looked at each other. 'Shall we go away for a little holiday? A six-month-long one?' Mel said.

'Can't. I'm buying a shop on Thursday. We've got some building work to do.'

Jess stood. 'Well, I for one think it's wonderful, that you've finally taken that step. And Erin, I'll come to help as much as I can, but a lot will depend on Grandpops.'

'Don't worry about it, Jess. You take care of Nan, make sure she can visit him and such like. Mel is going to be helping anyway, now she's a jobless vagabond.'

'Oops,' Mel said. 'Yes... I kind of forgot to also mention I'm kind of unemployed. You three may have to keep me in food and wine until I decide what I want to do next.' She then went into details of the activities of Charles Errington and the general support from the rest of the staff, which had resulted in three months' paid gardening leave.

'So,' she finished with a casual wave of her hand, 'I shall be working as an unpaid skivvy at Fully Booked for the next few months.'

Jess and Chantelle stared at her. 'Will you stay in law?' Jess asked.

'Not if I can help it. I was watching how many customers came to the bookshop today, and it occurred to me I could write a few bestsellers given my experiences with the criminal faction in Sheffield, and earn lots of money. Though I've got a friend who's written three books now, and she doesn't seem to earn very much, so maybe I should rule out that option. To be perfectly honest, I have no idea what I'd like to be doing in three months' time, but I'm sure something will crop up. I'm really quite fancying doing a complete re-train in something totally different. My degree will probably give me a head start, so there's a possibility I could end up as a mature student back at uni, which is all well and good if I can settle on something I'd like to do, and it needs to be for the rest of my life.'

'I think this is awesome,' Chantelle said. 'After the week I've had, first with finding out about Andrew and Olivia Hardwick, then Andrew's death, then Grandpops's hospitalisation, your gardening leave situation almost sounds like good news.'

Erin, Jess and Mel all turned as one. Jess spoke first. 'Olivia Hardwick? We have a name for the bitch?'

It was now Chantelle's turn to impart all her news, and she told her tale of discovering the woman's identity, meeting Ms Hardwick, and ultimately banning her from the funeral.

'And do you think she realises why she's banned?' Jess asked.

'She does now. The envelope that contained all Andrew's petrol and hotel receipts also contained a print-out of the picture I took of them kissing. I think as soon as she saw that she would know.'

'Oh, Chan.' Erin stood and put her arms around her friend. 'I'm so sorry this all had to happen. You know we're all behind you with this, and if there's any sighting of her at the funeral, she'll wish she'd never woken up that morning.'

'And this has reminded me,' Chantelle continued, 'I have found Andrew's life insurance policy, so will you have a look at it tomorrow, Mel, and see what I have to do? It seems he also had another policy through Sandford's, but I don't have to do anything about that, it's all in hand, according to Ms Hardwick.'

There were further discussions about what was to come next in all of their lives, as the horror of Chantelle's situation sobered them. She tried to explain how she truly felt about it – that she would miss Andrew no matter what had happened with 'the bitch', as she was now called by all of them. She and Andrew had loved each other for too long to lose that, and they had the twins as the strongest link of all, but the love that had been there for so many years had now died. And that, Chantelle said, was the hardest and the saddest part. They had lost each other without realising it was happening.

They left the Wheeler house quietly, not wanting to wake Nora, and Jess locked the front door after watching them leave. So much love, so much heartache at the moment, but they were strong women and strong women could survive anything. The news of Erin and Mel finally realising they could have a future together had been a welcome highlight of the evening, even though the rest of it had been a mixture of doom and gloom. She climbed the stairs after checking on Mabel, confirmed her nan was sleeping, and put on her Mickey Mouse pyjamas. Her comfort pyjamas.

She said a brief prayer for Grandpops, and winged her own thoughts to him across the city to St Luke's hospice. 'See you tomorrow, Grandpops,' she said. 'Love you.'

18

Wednesday was hot and sunny, and the front door of Fully Booked was wedged open to let in the welcome fresh air. It was a busy morning. Erin took several orders for obscure books required by university students, and directed other students towards the more commonplace books they needed. It was only after she had received a third request for journal planners that she began to realise she was maybe missing out on something. She needed to investigate further. She wrote 'JOURNAL PLANNERS?' on a piece of paper, and slipped it inside the till.

She checked her phone, not wanting to miss any calls. There had been an early-morning message on the Coven account from Jess, saying Grandpops was settled in but had slipped into a coma with palliative care only as a way forward.

Erin hadn't come to terms with the loss of Andrew, and now it seemed Grandpops was in his last few days in her life. How she would miss his sparkling eyes, his banter, the way he always called them his girls, and how he hid the heartache of losing his own girl, Anna, thirty-five years earlier.

She slipped her phone into her back pocket and switched on

her smile as the woman in front of her handed over the three books she had chosen to buy.

'That one's good,' Erin said, tapping on the Robert Galbraith book. 'You just need a degree in technology. Don't give up on it, it's not an easy read in the way it's set out, but it certainly earned the number one spot in the charts.'

'I'm looking forward to it,' the woman said with a smile. 'I've read the others in the series, but I've been a bit slow in buying this one. They're all difficult to read because they're so heavy.'

Erin laughed and stroked the front of *The Ink Black Heart*. 'Well, trust me on this one, don't attempt it on Kindle. I read all my books on Kindle, but gave up on this one and bought the hardback. I'm sure you'll enjoy it but it takes some time to get through it. Definitely worth it in the end. A superb book.'

'You're the owner?'

Erin nodded. 'I am. Erin Chatterton. I've slipped our leaflet into your bag of goodies. I haven't seen you here before, I don't believe.'

'It's my first time visiting the shop. I'm pleasantly surprised. And it's very busy, so you obviously have a good customer base.'

'It's students. Almost ready for starting at uni, and getting books together. This time of year is good, much laughter, joking, but it can be exhausting. If you ever visit us again it will be different. We're opening through to the shop next door, and we'll have a tea shop attached. There's only room for the coffee and tea table in here at the moment, but we're hoping to open the tea shop before Christmas.'

'That will be wonderful. There's just you and Tia?'

'You know Tia?'

'Not at all, but I did see her name badge. She was very helpful, trying to answer three different queries all at the same time.'

Erin pushed the card machine towards the woman, but the woman shook her head. 'Cash okay?'

'Always. It's £36.97, please.'

The woman handed over two twenty-pound notes, smiled her thanks, and headed for the door carrying two paper carrier bags. Erin had put the Galbraith book in one on its own, and the other two books, much smaller in size, in the second one.

The door closed behind her and Erin turned to her next customer.

* * *

Anna walked away from the shop, pleased that she hadn't bumped into Erin's mother. She wasn't sure that Suzanne would have recognised her, but she didn't want their first meeting in thirty-five years to be one of shocked surprise that would probably have given away her identity.

Now she needed to see her father, so a quick word with the one person who had been her informant about her family for many years would hopefully tell her where he was right now.

She headed to a nearby phone box. The call was answered with a very tentative, 'Hi.'

'I'm here.'

'Where?'

'In Sheffield. I just called in at Fully Booked in case you were there. Had a lovely talk with Erin.'

There was a gasp.

'Oh, don't panic,' she continued. 'She didn't know who I was, and I paid with cash so she didn't see my name. Do you know where Dad is now?'

'I do. According to Erin, he's in St Luke's hospice, but you need to be aware things have moved very fast, and Grandpops is now receiving end-of-life care. All four of them are devastated, and I can't begin to imagine how your mum is coping. How are you going to handle it?'

'I have no idea. I need to see Dad, to say goodbye, but Mum was always the stronger one. She may not want to see me.'

'You won't know until you ask. And I've never heard her say a bad word about you, despite what you did. She has no idea we've spoken every year on Jess's birthday, so please don't cause a rift between me and Nora, she's my friend. And this isn't just about your mum and dad, you also have a quite remarkable daughter. She obviously has Mike to support her, but when you arrive into her life, she could quite easily fall apart.'

Anna's tone took on a hint of stubbornness. 'I have to see my father. He needs to know I came home for him.'

'Then remember Nora and Jess will be at his bedside when you stroll in. I can't imagine anything good coming from this, but I kept my promise to ring you if this situation was ever in the offing. I'll never understand why you stayed away so long, but now you're back in Sheffield, it scares me.'

'I won't be here for long. My home and my business – and my partner – are in Criccieth. Thank you for contacting me. I'll ring again when I have something, anything, to pass on.'

They said goodbye and disconnected.

* * *

A feeling of sickness eddied for a short while deep within Suzanne. The practice of Anna ringing on St George's day every year had seemed like one of those things that had to be done then forgotten about for another twelve months, but this was something different. This was deep involvement in a family that she cared deeply about, and she felt it was going to end badly.

Had Anna ever loved Jess? But Jess hadn't been the reason Anna had left, she had been the solution. Jess had only been a month old when Anna disappeared one night, leaving a simple note for her parents to tell them they could have the baby, or put her up for adoption. As if they would have ever considered that.

Jess had never known a mother's love, but she had certainly known how much her grandparents loved her. They had even kept Anna's name alive with Jess, hoping that one day their daughter would walk through the door once again. But it had never happened, and now she was back in her hometown and nobody had any idea she had returned, and certainly no idea what would happen next.

Except Arthur Wheeler would die, and after listening to Erin's report on his status that she had gleaned from Jess, she suspected Arthur would never know his much-loved daughter had returned to him, albeit temporarily.

* * *

Jess and Nora sat quietly by Arthur's bedside, watching the gaps between his breaths get longer and longer. A nurse was permanently in the room, and she explained this state of breathing could go on for some time.

'Nan, I'm going out for a little bit of fresh air,' Jess said. 'Shall I get us a drink or something from the machine?'

'That would be good, sweetheart,' Nora said, her eyes never leaving her husband's face. 'Don't be long, will you?'

'No, of course I won't. I just need to cry, I think. But not in front of Grandpops, he'd laugh at me and call me a soppy mare.'

Nora smiled. 'That he would. He called me that all the time.'

Jess stood and stopped at the doorway for a moment to look back at Grandpops. When she had found him on the floor of his shed he had been retching, the intense pain in his back causing him to vomit. His moans had reflected just how bad the pain had been, and she knew she wouldn't want him back to suffer that. Her only wish was that they had told her before it got to this stage.

She continued to the outside, wiping away tears that were falling down her cheeks in little torrents.

Memories kept returning of the upbringing she had had with this wonderful couple: the football training, the trips out to the coast, the bigger car they had bought so that all four girls could be ferried in the one vehicle, and the love. Always the love.

And now she recognised the accompanying emotion as anger. Anger that she hadn't been able to swaddle him in her love as the cancer unknowingly spread through his body, anger that he was leaving her and her nan to face a world without him. Their spider remover, their battery replacer, the man who always beat them at Scrabble, the man who could lay his hands on any type of screwdriver known to man, because it would be somewhere in his shed.

Thinking of his shed caused fresh tears to erupt, and Jess scrubbed harshly at her face. She couldn't go back in looking like this, she decided, and walked into the reception to go to the vending machine. She stretched the time out as long as she could as she tried to heal the red ravages on her face, bought two teas, but didn't even look at the food. She needed the sick feeling to go away, not encourage it by trying to force feed herself chocolate and crisps.

Even looking at the food compartments brought back the memories. A day trip to Whitby with a beach picnic thrown in, followed by a boat ride, had resulted in all four girls being sick over the side, and bringing up all the food so carefully prepared by Nora. This brought a smile instead of tears and she gathered up the two drinks and headed back to the third room on the left, occupied now by Grandpops.

She carefully eased the door open, balancing one cup on top of the other. She was surprised to see three people in the room, the nurse, Nora and a third woman who she assumed was a member of staff, as she was clearly not in nursing uniform.

She walked around to the side where Nora and the woman were standing, and placed the first cup of tea by the side of Nora, on her grandfather's bedside table. She moved around to the other side and placed her cup on the windowsill. It was only as she did that that she realised how ashen her nan looked, and she turned quickly.

Her first thought was that Grandpops had passed and it had happened while she wasn't with him. But her nan was staring at the younger woman.

Jess looked at Grandpops but his chest was still rising and falling rhythmically, if a little more spaced out than previously. But he was alive and she turned her face back to her nan.

'Nan? What is it? What's wrong?'

There was a silence and the nurse moved towards the door. 'I'll leave you alone for a few minutes,' she said, and closed the door as she went outside.

'Nan!' Jess was now worried.

'Jessica.' The woman spoke quietly. 'Jessica, it's me, your mum.'

Jess felt the room begin to spin, and she grasped onto the back of her chair. She caught her breath, and looked at the woman. 'No, you're not my mum,' she said. 'At best, you're just Anna. And I'd like you to go, please, you're not wanted in this room.' She spat out the words with some force, emphasising them by pointing towards the door.

19

Jess knew that for the rest of her life she would always consider this particular Thursday to be the worst day of her entire existence. Nothing could ever match up to it – her mother had chosen this day of all days to reappear in her life, and she didn't want her there.

She also knew Grandpops was too far gone to acknowledge his daughter, so why was she there? For her own selfish reasons? She could imagine the words. *'Oh, I've always loved my dad, even though I haven't contacted him for thirty-five years.'*

'Jess.' Nora's voice was weak. 'Jess, please don't make things worse.'

'Could they be worse, Nan? Anna, I've no idea how you found out about Grandpops, but I suggest you go back to where you came from and pretend you don't know anything. Just like you've been doing for the last thirty-five-odd years.' Jess, the quiet, laid-back one, could feel her anger growing. Anger because her beloved grandfather was leaving her, anger because Nora was looking distraught, and anger at this bloody woman who thought she could swan back into their lives at this particularly awful time.

Well, she couldn't, and Jess walked to the door, held it open and said, 'Get out.'

She saw Anna look at Nan, but Nan simply dropped her head and said nothing. The nurse was standing just outside the door, and she spoke quietly to Jess. 'Is everything okay?'

Jess shook her head. 'Do you have security? This woman isn't part of our family and we don't need her here. I've asked her to leave but she doesn't seem to understand.'

'I'm going back to the Premier Inn,' Anna said. 'But I'll be back. He's my father, whether you like it or not, Jessica.'

Jess responded by opening the door even further, and Anna brushed past her. The nurse pointed to the exterior doors. 'That's the way out.'

'And my name's Jess, not Jessica,' Jess called after Anna as she walked down the corridor. 'A proper mother would have known that.'

And then she cried. The whole situation engulfed her, and Nora took her in her arms. 'Oh, my love, I wouldn't have wanted any of this, not at this time.'

'How does she know?' The question left Jess's lips as a wail.

'I have no idea. We haven't heard from her since the day she left. If I had known of her whereabouts, or had any connection at all with her over these many years, I would probably have contacted her to give the option of seeing her dad for the last time, but I swear I didn't know, Jess. Quite apart from anything else, I would have discussed it with you first, you know I would.'

'I know you would.' Jess felt exhausted. They simply needed to be sitting with Grandpops, hoping he knew they were there supporting him on his final journey, and Anna had intruded.

'We need to calm down, Jess,' Nora said. 'Let's hold his hands. We have no idea if he's aware we're here, but I need to hold him, and I'm sure you do. We'll have our cuppas, talk to him just in case he is aware, and simply spend time with him. It's getting close, the nurse was saying, so this is our last chance to let him know how much we love him. We'll deal with my daughter later.'

Two hours and thirty-two minutes later, Arthur Wheeler exhaled his final breath.

* * *

Erin and Livvy walked out of the solicitors, excitement hovering around them like a million fluttering butterflies. Both women saw what they had just done as the beginning of a new chapter in their lives; Livvy was on her way to a new life with a new man, and Erin could now start to put into place the changes she had envisaged for the tea shop. They were both full of praise for the speed of the sale, which appeared to have worn their elderly solicitor to a frazzle. He, however, had smiled through the entire signing of the forms that lunchtime. He freely admitted that things didn't normally progress so fast but he had put in some extra hours and moved it along to accommodate Livvy, who was leaving the area. There would still be paperwork to sign eventually, but Livvy had authorised Erin's full use of the premises pending completion.

It was while they were celebrating with a Starbucks coffee that Erin received the phone call from Jess.

'No, it's too soon,' she said, trying desperately not to cry. 'Where are you now?'

'We're still with him at St Luke's, but Nan looks drawn and not really with it, so I'm going to get her home as soon as I can. We've said our goodbyes, but we'll be able to see him again at the funeral director's. I'm going to ring Mel and Chantelle now. I think Nan might want to see you, if you can do it.'

'Of course I can. I'll drop Livvy back off at the shop – she left her car there, and we came in mine. Then I'll close up, and Mel and I will come straight over. When you ring Mel to break this bloody awful news, will you tell her I'm on my way? She's holding the fort at Fully Booked under the guidance of Tia, until I return from the solicitors, but I'm just going to close for the day. Unless you want me to tell her?'

'No, don't worry, I'll ring Mel next. I guess she may need to steer people outside. They seem to spend hours in the shop, your customers. Then I'll ring Chantelle. I need you guys at the moment.'

'And we're here for you. We'll be with you by four,' she said after a quick glance at her watch. 'That okay?'

'If anything happens to delay us, I'll ring, but I'm hoping I can get Nan to go home soon. I don't want her getting ill.'

They disconnected, and Erin explained the situation to Livvy, trying hard not to cry.

'Come on,' Livvy said. 'Get rid of me, and you're free to get Mel and go to Jess. That's the important thing now.'

* * *

Tia was alone in the shop when Erin arrived.

'Mel's in the kitchen,' she said. 'I've sent her to make herself a sweet coffee, she's been crying. It's not good for customers to see tears this side of the counter, and I wanted to keep hugging her to make her feel better.'

'How many customers are in now?'

'Three at the moment, shortly two because one has gone to pick up a book they were undecided about, but then decided the moment they arrived at the counter.'

'Okay, when that one has gone, lock the door. We can let the other two out when they're ready, then we're closing for the day. I'll let you know about tomorrow once I've been over to Nan's and spoken with her and Jess. If they need me for anything, I shall be there for them. This should have been such a good day, and it's turned into a horrible one. He's gone so fast...'

'Go through to Mel,' Tia said, suddenly feeling she was the older person. These two women were floundering, needed direction, and she was the one to give it.

Erin left Tia to deal with getting the customers out of the door as quickly and as smoothly as possible, and walked across to wrap her arms around Mel, who was sitting at the little table, staring into space.

'I'm struggling,' Mel said. 'Really struggling. I saw him two weeks ago and there was no hint of this.'

'I suspect it's been kept from us by Nan. Even Jess knew nothing until she found him on the floor in his shed. But maybe Nan didn't realise how bad it was. If he's been telling the doctors he didn't want Nan to know the severity of everything, they would have to abide by his instructions. He's spared her and all of us from the pain of watching him deteriorate, but it certainly hits hard when you've no time to say goodbye.' Erin wiped away the tears that erupted as she was speaking. 'We need to head over to Nan's place now.'

'You closing the shop?'

'Tia is just serving the last two customers, but the closed sign is already turned so nobody else can get in. I've told her I'll let her know about tomorrow. If Jess or Nan needs us, the shop will stay closed. I can't imagine how Chantelle is feeling, she's lost two people in just over a week. Thank God she's got her mum and dad staying with her.'

Tia came into the kitchen, zipping up her jacket. 'All done, but I haven't touched the till. I'll leave that for you, Erin. You'll ring me later?'

Erin smiled through her tears. 'I will. Now get off home, and thank you for your support, Tia. It's very much appreciated. I'll come through and lock the door after you've gone.'

Mel remained in the kitchen, deep in thought. She should ring her own mum and tell her the awful news, but she wasn't sure she could do it at the moment. She felt raw inside. Erin returned to the kitchen, her phone in her hand. 'I need to ring Mum and tell her. Did you ring yours?'

'I was just considering doing that, but you know what, Erin? I don't want to say the words. It makes it real once you speak them out loud, doesn't it?'

'It does, but better they hear it from us than from some random neighbour.'

Mel sighed. 'You're right, I know you are.'

'Then let's get it over with, and we can head over to Nan's house, give Jess some support.'

* * *

Suzanne was in shock, and sat staring at her phone, dreading the next call she had to make. The news had wiped her out. Dead? How could Arthur Wheeler be dead? He'd only been in the hospice a couple of days.

And now she had to ring Anna to say her father had died. She dreaded to think how Anna would react. She picked up her phone but it began to ring, saying it was an unknown number. She said a cautious hello.

'Suzanne?'

'It is. You ringing from a call box? Did you get to see your dad?'

'For about two minutes, then Jessica virtually had me evicted. But I'll go back tomorrow, try again. I need him to know I'm there. And I decided not to ring on my phone, just being cautious.'

'No, Anna. Don't go tomorrow.'

'No?'

'He passed this afternoon. I'm sorry it's me telling you, I wouldn't have wanted this job for the world, but he's gone and you need to know it now. You need to leave them in peace to grieve, and you need to go back home to Criccieth.'

There was a long period of silence, then Anna spoke again. 'I'm going nowhere. He's my father, and I shall be staying certainly until the funeral, so my daughter and my mother had better get used to me being around.'

She disconnected, and Suzanne stared at the phone in disbelief. Anna was going to stay in Sheffield? And there was nothing Suzanne could do about it. How could she warn anybody that Anna was going to be hanging around, when nobody knew of their connection over the past three decades?

Losing Andrew had been difficult enough, but this was something on the next level. And having Arthur's daughter causing trouble wouldn't help at all.

She had to talk to somebody. Suzanne's biggest problem was she didn't know who that could be. How do you start a conversation by admitting you've always known the location of the missing woman, but kept it to yourself?

How do you say, 'Anna swore me to secrecy, but I'm here to tell you now that she's not going back to Wales, she's going to stick around for a bit and make your lives even more of a misery than they are right now'?

There had to be an answer somewhere. And she thought she might know what it was.

20

Chantelle walked round the corner and saw Erin's silver Renault parked outside the Wheeler house. She felt stunned by the news. Her brain was spinning – two deaths to handle was never going to be easy, but two deaths of people really close to her was proving very difficult to process.

Her own parents had been devastated – they had known the Wheelers for many years, and they had virtually pushed her out of the door with instructions to come home when she was ready and know the children would be in bed and cared for. She was to stay with her friends for as long as she needed to be with them.

It was as if a pall was over the room. Erin and Mel were side by side on the sofa, with Chantelle and Jess taking the armchairs. Mabel immediately settled herself on Jess's lap.

'I've made my nan go for a lie down, but I don't think she'll sleep,' Jess explained to Chantelle. 'This has been a whirlwind few days that neither of us expected, although I do think Nan knew more than she was letting on to me. But I'm not going to dwell on that, what I need to do now is be here for her. I'm going to go through Nan's Christmas book tomorrow and let all their friends know about Grandpops; that's one small thing I can do for her. I have got something I need to tell you, though.'

Erin sat up a little straighter. 'Nan's not ill?'

'Not as far as I know, but would she actually tell me if she was? I had no idea about Grandpops other than I suspected old age had arrived fast in his world. How wrong was I about that? No, it's nothing to do with Nan's physical health, but mentally we're feeling a bit hammered. Anna turned up at Grandpops's bedside. Apparently she's staying at the Premier Inn, of all things!'

All three began to speak at once.

'Anna as in your mother?'

'Anna? How bloody dare she?'

'That bitch, Anna?'

Their reactions brought a small smile to Jess's lips. 'Well, don't hold back, girls. Say it like it is. But yes, that Anna. I basically threw her out, and gained some satisfaction from it. Grandpops was slipping away. The nurses knew, and they told us he would be gone today and he wouldn't recover consciousness because the drugs they were having to give him to keep him pain free also kept him in a coma state. If he had been able to see her then it would have been a different story, because he always talked about her, always hoped she would return one day, but he knew nothing at that point when she turned up.'

There was a frown on Erin's face. 'How did she know?'

Jess shrugged. 'I've absolutely no idea, but I intend finding out. I don't believe she just turned up accidentally on the day Grandpops died. Nan was as gobsmacked as I was. I was out getting drinks from the vending machine for us, and when I walked back through the door she was in the room. I didn't know who she was, just assumed it was someone from the hospital admin team because she didn't have on a uniform, but I knew something was off when I saw how grey Nan looked.'

'Can we do anything?' Practical Mel spoke, but Jess could hear anger in her voice.

'A magic wand might help,' Jess said, trying to defuse the tension. 'We could wave it and whisk her back to wherever she came from. The worst part is this is the same house she walked away from, so I just know she's going to turn up here at some point. She only left the hospice because I asked that they get the security people to escort her out. And I'm pretty sure she'll hang around for the funeral now she's ventured back to Sheffield.'

'Has Grandpops left a will?' Mel asked.

'I've no idea, I never thought he would die so never gave any thought to anything like that. You think that's why she's turned up? She thinks she might get something? If so, that makes it all even worse.' Jess wiped away her tears that she couldn't stop. 'But even if he had left a will, and even if he did leave her something, Nan will still be living here until she passes. Whatever they have is in joint names, and always has been, that much I do know. It doesn't really make sense if she thinks she's likely to get anything at all.'

Mel was deep in thought. 'This almost feels like a set up scenario. Like... maybe she's in touch with somebody in Sheffield, and that somebody has told her Grandpops is ill. Would that be enough to bring her back? I think it would. Just because she dumped you, Jess, and walked away from responsibilities, doesn't mean she stopped loving anybody. And we all know from first-hand experience how easy Grandpops was to love. The man was a legend. The man *is* a legend.'

It was quite spooky the way the lounge door opened as Mel finished speaking. However, it was Nan who joined them, and she crossed the room to sit in Arthur's rocking chair. 'I'm sorry,' she said, 'I just needed a bit of company. Do you mind?'

'Nan, it's your home.' Erin smiled and stood. 'Tea? Hot chocolate?'

'Thank you, Erin. I'll have a tea. I was lying on that bed and my head was spinning. Everything's changed, and it's changed so fast. But it seems this happens a lot with certain types of cancer. They become very aggressive very fast, spread quickly and the organs begin to close down. It seems that was the way Grandpops went, and I know it saved him so much pain, but he's caused a lot of heartache, I fear.' She leaned back in the rocking chair and the familiar creak creak as it moved brought tears to Jess's eyes yet again.

'I'll help Erin and make drinks for all of us. Nan, when did you last eat?'

'I had a Weetabix for breakfast.'

'Can you manage a couple of slices of toast? I know you probably don't feel like eating anything, but you need just a little bit of something.'

'Do it, and I can either eat it or leave it. Thank you, Jess.'

She continued to rock until Erin and Jess returned with a tray of drinks and the toast.

Nan took a small bite, then looked around at everyone. 'You're good girls,' she said. 'Always have been. But Melissa, Jess has told me you've left your job. Now is that sensible?'

'Probably not,' Mel said, grinning at the others. 'But I've *always* been sensible, and now it's time not to be. My next job will be one I want to do, not one I've been shoe-horned into and expected to excel at.'

'But you're a paralegal.'

'I am, and I earn vast amounts of money for the company, not such vast amounts for me. However, I do like the law, so it's quite possible my next job will be within a law framework, but working on more pro-bono cases. I'd rather feel needed than used, I think is what I really mean.'

'Oh, well, that's okay,' Nan said. 'I just didn't want you frittering away your savings and doing nothing. As long as you've got a plan, you'll be okay.'

Chantelle, Erin and Jess were trying to keep their faces straight. It was obvious from Mel's face that she was floundering.

'I promise, Nan,' Mel eventually said, 'that by the time I reach the end of this three months of paid gardening leave I will have a new job lined up. And you'll be the first person I tell.'

Nan nodded at her words, and took a sip of her tea. 'Good girl. You've never been the irresponsible type, and I don't want you starting to be like that.'

And now Chantelle, Erin and Jess exploded with laughter. 'Consider yourself told, Mel,' Erin spluttered. 'If you could see your face...'

'Oh, shut up, you lot,' was Mel's retort.

* * *

By eleven o'clock, everyone had left for home, leaving Jess to check everything was secure, and to get her nan settled in bed. She took her a glass of water up, and a couple of painkillers in case she needed any during the night.

'I'm not in pain,' Nora said. 'Not physical pain, anyway.'

'I'm more concerned that your mind won't let you sleep, and a couple of paracetamols will help you drop off. Can I get you anything else?'

There was a quick shake of the head. 'I don't think so. It's been a long, difficult day, hasn't it, love?'

'It has, and there are more to come but we'll get through them.'

'You know we have to see her?'

'Anna? I don't, but I'll make sure I'm with you when you see her. I owe her nothing, Nan. I bet she only held me half a dozen times, if that.'

'She gave you life.' Nora spoke gently to this most precious granddaughter. 'And where would your grandfather and I have been without you?'

Jess wanted to respond with 'you would have been with the man you loved', but she bit her tongue. This definitely wasn't the right time to bring up ancient loves.

She leaned over the bed and kissed her Nan's forehead. 'Love you, old woman. Now take those tablets if you can't get to sleep, and I'll see you in the morning.'

'Hey, less of the old woman. And don't forget to leave on the landing light.'

'As if I'd dare turn it off.' Jess smiled. 'Night, Nan, love you.'

'And I love you, my darling girl.'

* * *

In the end, it took two tablets down Jess's throat to send her off to sleep. Her mind was racing round and round, as she tried to decide what to do about the arrival of Anna back in their lives. She wanted nothing to do with her, but that didn't mean her nan felt the same, and she didn't want to lose Nan because of a dispute over Anna.

She tossed and turned, her mind in turmoil. Added to the issues surrounding the arrival of Anna, of course, was the loss of Grandpops. She wished desperately he was still here; the upset she had felt when they had found out Andrew had died had been nothing in comparison to this. And yet she had cared for Andrew, deeply loved his girls as much as she had always loved their mother, but losing her grandfather was something way off the planet.

She eventually took the painkillers and drifted off to sleep, not sure how she would handle life the following morning, but hoping she could stay asleep long enough to get some reasonable rest.

Chantelle walked home, wishing her mum and dad would already be in bed. She suspected they would still be up, waiting for her to make sure she was okay, but the reality of the situation was that she wanted some time to herself to take in and digest all that had happened to her recently.

Her mum had been a godsend helping her through organising the funeral, but it had convinced her that when she reached the end of her life, she simply wanted to be put in a wheely bin, tipped into the council lorry and deposited on the local rubbish dump. She did not want her kids to have to go through what she had done today; forced into making instant decisions, ordering flowers, having to decide something she had never discussed with Andrew – cremation or burial.

And in the end they had decided on cremation. The disposal of his ashes was for another time; another decision to be put off until it was time to think about it.

She'd had her fill of death. She needed to go to bed. She quietly opened the front door, and instantly the lounge door opened, and her mother hugged her.

Chantelle sighed. All she wanted was sleep.

21

Fully Booked remained closed that Friday. Erin and Mel had talked far into the night, and at seven o'clock Erin messaged Tia to say she would see her Saturday, then turned over and slid her arms around Mel. She had tentatively suggested that as the hour was so late, and they both needed the comfort of each other, Mel might want to stay over, and not have to drive home.

Mel had smiled and said she had been wondering how to suggest it, she just wasn't quite as brazen as Erin.

It had actually been a night of intermittent tears as they had talked over old times with Grandpops; how he would never allow them into the sea without him being there as well, just in case they got into difficulties. He used to say he daren't go back home if he managed to kill one of them.

They had also discussed Anna. Neither of them had ever seen her other than in photographs, but they knew that Jess never spoke of her. Her nan was her mum and it would always be that way. But on one thing they were agreed. They would protect Jess from the woman, no matter what it took.

Finally sleep had claimed them, but some inner alarm clock

had woken Erin in time to stop Tia getting ready to head out for work, and she set a real alarm to get her out of bed at just before nine in order to put the same bereavement notice on the door that had been put there for Andrew's death.

She was thinking that she'd never experienced anything like this in her life before as she drifted off to sleep once more. This was when she realised Mel had disappeared, and she guessed she had headed back home quietly, not wanting to wake her sleeping love. Cat had probably needed food.

* * *

Ruby Potter enjoyed her job very much. For years she had worked as one of two cleaners in a small bed and breakfast place, but then her friend told her there was a vacancy at the Premier Inn. She had just completed a full week where she was the only cleaner because the other one, Zoe, had been off with Covid. She was knackered. She called into the large hotel as soon as she had finished her shift, was hired on the spot, and it had proved to be a blessing.

Now if somebody was off ill, or on holiday, their work was shared between all the other cleaners, instead of everything being on the one remaining cleaner. The routine was simple, the tips were good and her fellow members of the cleaning and maintenance team were helpful and friendly.

Most days she sang her way through her work, and being a huge fan of Rod Stewart, sang mainly his songs. Although rooms were no longer cleaned every day, if a room required a restock of the tea and coffee tray, the guests left the tray outside the room to indicate it needed attention. Room 124 on the first landing had a tray outside and she checked her list. Not scheduled for anything else, as the guest was booked in for three nights with the option of remaining further if required.

She restocked the tray, knocked on the door and called 'cleaning'. There was no response, so she used her smart pass to enter. She walked by the bathroom and entered the sleeping area, where she dropped the newly loaded tray, gave a small shriek of alarm and then began a high-volume screaming.

She screamed until somebody arrived and didn't stop until they placed their arms around her and turned her away from the sight of all the blood and an almost naked woman in the middle of the bed, her eyes wide open and fixed. Her throat area was covered in the blood, and an enormous gash bore some resemblance to a second mouth.

Ruby was led outside by someone – she couldn't tell who was holding her – and taken to an empty room next door, room 126.

'Sit here,' she heard the young man say, 'and I'll come and get you when the police get here. Just rest, Ruby, it's been a massive shock to your system and you need to sit quietly now. I'll get you some water, and I want you to drink it.'

She looked up for the first time and saw it was the assistant manager, Ian Ormond, and she nodded. 'Thank you, Ian,' she whispered. 'She is dead, isn't she?'

'I didn't go near enough to check,' he said, 'but with that blood loss there's no way she could be anything else. You didn't hear anything at any time?'

'No.' Ruby was still whispering. It hurt her throat to speak properly. 'You mean she's only just done it?'

'Done it? I think we'll find it's not suicide, Ruby. That's why I've moved you in here, we shouldn't risk contaminating what I'm pretty sure is a crime scene. I'll go get you a bottle of water. Just sit quietly, and let's see if we can find that wonderful singing voice again. It doesn't help if you scream yourself hoarse.' He smiled gently at her. He liked Ruby, she was a real hard worker, loved her job and was never late. An employee to be treasured.

He closed the door as he went out and Ruby sat. What she really wanted to do was lie down on that wonderful bed and go to sleep, but she guessed that might be a bit inappropriate, so she dropped her head onto her arms and leaned onto the desk.

Five minutes later, Ian returned. 'The police are in reception,' he said. 'I have to go to them, because Mr Ketteridge isn't here. Jonathan decided to take today off to go golfing. I've rung him, so I expect he'll become manager again any time now and come haring back here. In the meantime, I have to deal with them. So drink this, soothe that throat, and I'll be back when I know more. I'll tell them where you are, and I'm going to wedge this door open so they can get in and out if they need to speak with you. That okay?'

'It's fine,' she said. 'That poor lady. And thank you for the water.'

* * *

DI Paul Marshall watched as the body was transported out of the room, and waited patiently while the forensics team did all their checks, removing the badly blood-stained bedding as it was of primary concern to them. If there was going to be any foreign DNA it would be on that, because it was a definite that the bedding had been on that bed only for the duration of the guest's stay. It looked as though the woman was called Anna Wheeler, according to her driving licence and the hotel's own records.

There had been no weapon, but he guessed it had been a pretty hefty knife – the gash across the throat had been deep and very quickly fatal. He had already despatched uniforms out to check the hotel's bins, but didn't think for a minute the knife would be in one of them. It seemed these days that all criminals were a little bit too savvy from watching too many crime programmes on television, and nobody in their right mind would imagine it would be a smart move to get rid of a murder weapon in a bin at the property where the dead body rested.

'I'll be in the room next door,' he said to nobody in particular, and nobody acknowledged his words. They were too busy gathering evidence.

* * *

Ruby had moved her chair over to the window where she could watch the comings and goings in the car park. Her head was pounding, and she wanted a cup of tea. With sugar. Everybody said having sugar in your drink helped after a shock, and it had been the biggest shock of her forty-two years on this earth.

So much blood. Had the woman known her killer? Had it happened during the night, or, heaven forbid, had she almost walked in on such a brutal scene? She hoped the police would tell her a bit about what had happened, always assuming they hadn't forgotten she was sitting in the next room waiting for them. And she still had three rooms to finish...

Paul Marshall tapped on the door and walked in. 'Ms Potter? I'm sorry you've been waiting so long, but I'll just ask you a few questions and we'll let you get off home.'

'I can't. I've three more rooms to clean,' she said firmly.

'On this floor?'

She nodded. 'Numbers 122, 120 and 118. All the rest are done.'

He made a note in his book. 'Well, you'll not be doing them today. There's crime scene tape along this entire section of corridor, certainly for a couple of days, and I definitely don't want you entering any of the rooms you haven't already serviced. Are you okay?'

'Thumping headache, but I'll grab some painkillers before I go home. It was a massive shock, and I couldn't seem to stop myself screaming. I apologise for my voice, I think it's the screaming that's done it.'

He smiled at her. 'It will be back by tomorrow. Now, you say you've already worked your way down the rest of this corridor?'

'Yes. Five of them have had a full clean and bedding change, the rest I've maybe done towel replacements, or top-ups of drinks trays.'

'This full clean presumably involves emptying waste bins?'

'It does, and the large bag hanging on my trolley contains everything collected from today.'

He stood. 'Thank you – I'll be back in a minute, I'll just take care of that.'

He moved towards Ruby's trolley, slipping on gloves, lifted off the trash bag and took it through to where the forensics team were still busy. He handed it to them and returned to Ruby, who was dabbing at her eyes.

'I'm sorry,' she said, 'I just felt a bit overwhelmed. I've never seen blood like that before.'

'Don't worry, I understand. I have, and yet it still came as a shock to me. Nobody ever realises just how much blood there is in a human body. Did you know the lady?'

'No, I hadn't seen her. It was the first time she needed her tray topping up, and that's all I was doing. I wouldn't have known her name or anything, I just know people by their room number if I actually ever see them. But to be honest, most people are off out pretty early, and arrive back after I've gone for the day.' Ruby was aware she was babbling but seemed unable to stop.

Paul took Ruby's address down, and then looked at her. 'Right,

Ruby, I want you to close your eyes, and open your mind to going into that room. Try to shut out the bed area from what your mind is telling you is there, and just think if anything else was out of kilter, anything out of place, not right about the room, if that body hadn't been on the bed.'

Ruby felt that what he was asking was possibly the last thing she would ever want to do, but after a couple of seconds she took a deep breath and closed her eyes. She saw the desk, she saw the chair, the closed curtains, the suitcase in the corner, the body... and she put her hand to her mouth as if she was going to be sick.

'No,' she said. 'From what I recall, there was nothing unusual. Can I contact you if I do think of anything? It's all a bit raw at the moment and I don't think my mind is going to cooperate at all just yet.'

He smiled. 'Go home, Ruby. I'll give you a call tomorrow, just to check how you're doing. I have your contact details, so here's my card, in case you need me. Thank you for waiting so patiently. Now go and tell the manager you're going home.'

22

Sergeant Owen Donald sat in the car and stared at the shop that bore the address he had been given. South Yorkshire Police had asked him to make the death notification as soon as possible, as it wasn't a death by natural causes. He turned to PC Cerys Kitchen, who was sitting in the passenger seat, and asked if she was ready.

'Not really, this has got to be the worst job we're ever expected to do, death notifications. And when it's murder, it's even harder. Do we know anything at all about this Anna Wheeler?'

'Only that she's lived here for a number of years, and this is her shop. It sells crafts made by locals, and by her.'

'So who are we here to tell? We don't know if she has a husband, or a partner?'

'Not till we get in there and start asking questions. Come on, we're putting this off, aren't we?'

They exited the car and walked across to the shop. The door was open, and it was busy. The stock was eclectic, and Cerys briefly wondered why she'd never been here before in an off-duty moment. This was exactly her sort of shop.

The woman behind the counter was looking a little frazzled,

and there was a considerable amount of noise caused purely by chatter between the customers. Many of them had already filled one of the little shopping baskets that had been provided for the customers to use and Owen knew the next few minutes were going to be chaotic as they attempted to clear the shop.

As the two uniformed figures entered the shop, a hush descended and Cerys remained by the door while Owen walked up to the counter. He showed his warrant card to the petite lady in the midst of ringing in a sale, and asked if he could have a word with her.

Without really speaking, she waved her arm around as if to say look at the state of the shop, and all these customers.

'It's about Anna Wheeler,' he pushed.

Her face froze, and she spoke. 'Anna's not here at the moment, she's taken a few days off. Can I help?'

'You're close friends?'

'She's my wife. Life partners and business partners. Something's wrong, isn't it?'

'We need to speak with you.'

She came round from her own side of the counter and moved amongst the customers, who were watching what was happening with some curiosity.

'I'm sorry, ladies and gentlemen, I have to close the shop for the rest of the day. If I'm not going to be open tomorrow, I'll post it on the website. Please just leave your baskets and their contents on the table in the middle of the shop, and I'll sort them out. Thank you for your patience. I'm sure this is just a blip, but when two police officers turn up, I have to listen.' She smiled as everyone good-naturedly did as she had asked, and slowly the shop emptied.

She locked the door after helping one elderly lady out to her car, and turned to Owen and Cerys.

'Tell me.'

Cerys spoke first. 'Can we just have your name, please? As you're married, I'm assuming this is your address?'

'It is. We've been together for around thirty years. My name is Siân Jefferies. We've been married for nearly ten years now, but chose to keep our own names. We couldn't decide which one to use, and Wheeler-Jefferies sounded just as daft as Jefferies-Wheeler, so we stuck with the names we had. Why are you here?'

Owen took a deep breath. 'We've had a conversation with South Yorkshire Police this morning because someone called Anna Wheeler has died. Her driving licence and the address she used to register at the Premier Inn showed this as being her home. The SYP were keen to notify as soon as possible because it will be reported in the newspapers.'

'We're so very sorry, Siân. Can I ask when you last spoke to Anna?' Cerys said.

Siân's face was now devoid of all colour. 'About half past ten last night. She went to Sheffield because she heard from a friend there that her father was very close to death. She hasn't seen him for many, many years, but that didn't mean she didn't love him. It simply meant they were estranged. The second she got the phone call she packed a bag, gave me a kiss and went. Was it a road accident? Was she distracted? Her father died yesterday and I know she wasn't with him.'

The two officers exchanged a glance.

'Siân, I think you should sit down. In view of what you're saying, we may need to ask deeper questions than we anticipated asking.'

* * *

Siân locked the shop completely and lowered the blinds, then led them out of the back door, and into a courtyard. 'This is our home,' she said, and waved a hand at a house that was attached to the shop. 'We live and work on the premises, and the barn-like building is where we keep all our craft supplies, any machines we need, that sort of thing. Please, let's go inside and you can stop frightening me and tell me exactly what's happened.'

She led them through the pretty front door and into the lounge. All three of them sat down, and Siân waited patiently for one of them to speak.

Owen coughed. 'We only have an account of what's happened from a distance, as I'm sure you can appreciate, but it wasn't a road accident. It seems that your wife's throat was cut. I don't have many details such as when it happened, but I do know she was found by a member of the domestic team at the hotel. I'm pretty sure SYP will have to come down to see you, but they're starting the investigation from their end at the moment. I'm so very sorry to bring you this awful news, but it will very quickly be in the newspapers and our colleagues in Sheffield didn't want any relatives or friends finding out that way.'

'Does her mother know?'

'I don't know. We didn't know who she was beyond her name, and certainly the investigating officers will probably be unaware she has family in Sheffield. Cerys, can you make us all a cup of tea, and while the kettle's boiling give DI Marshall a ring and tell him that the deceased has a mother in Sheffield who lost her husband yesterday. Her name is Wheeler as well, but I don't know anything beyond that.'

Cerys stood and went to follow instructions in the kitchen, ringing the Sheffield policeman as soon as she had sorted out the kettle. He thanked her, and said it was a massive help, because they didn't know anything about the deceased lady. He asked that she keep him informed of any other snippets of information coming from the wife of the dead woman, and she disconnected. With three teas on a tray, she re-entered the lounge and handed the cups out. Siân was trembling, the reality of the situation suddenly starting to overwhelm her.

'What will I do without her? We're never apart, and only yesterday I booked two weeks in the Canaries for us this winter, once we've closed the shop at the end of the season. She left really early yesterday morning, said she wanted to see her dad before booking into the hotel. That didn't go too well because her mother had her thrown out, and shortly after that her dad passed. Somebody, possibly the friend who told her he was ill, must have told her when he passed, because she certainly wasn't there with him. That was why I rang her last night, offered some words of comfort, told her about the holiday booking and she was pleased to have something to look forward to. She's simply the driving force behind our business, our lives together, and I'll be totally lost without her.'

Siân sipped at her tea, not tasting it, but aware it was a hot drink. 'Should I go to Sheffield? I don't even know where her family live. All I know is that she has contact with somebody once a year, and that's it.'

'I wouldn't advise going to Sheffield. It's distressing enough losing a loved one, don't make a long journey and add to the stress of the situation. They will contact you, and you can discuss it with them. Is there someone we can call for you, to get them to come and sit with you while you digest what's happened?'

'Not really. I had parents here in the village but they've both gone now. I feel scared, but it's because Anna was my rock. It will be a long, lonely life without her.' She placed her half-empty cup on the coffee table, and sank back into the armchair. 'Would you mind leaving now?'

The two officers stood and headed for the door. 'You have my card, I left it on the counter in the shop. If you need anything, please do ring,' Owen said.

* * *

Owen and Cerys sat in the car and stared at the shuttered windows of the shop. 'Nice lady. How the hell will she cope without her wife? I got the impression Anna was the strong one,' Cerys said.

'Me too. This was a really shitty job, wasn't it? It's strange how she knows so little about her wife's early life, don't you think? They've been together thirty years, married for almost ten of them, and yet she's never met any of the Wheeler family. And she couldn't have thought they'd all died, because she knew that Anna had contact every year with somebody. Real puzzle, this one. I'm glad we don't have to solve it, and we can safely just type up a report and send it off to Sheffield, sorted.'

Cerys laughed. 'You reckon? What's the betting we end up with this one on our plates, with our bosses having set up a collaboration with South Yorkshire Police? You ever been there?'

'To Sheffield? Once. Fantastic place, to be honest. Very green was my overriding impression. Excellent nightclubs, loads of restaurants and two major football clubs. What's not to like?'

'The football bit?'

* * *

Siân watched them drive away from behind the blinds and shutters of the shop window. They had treated her well, she thought, but what should she do now? She knew she had to put something on the website, and fortunately Anna had taken the time to teach her how to add stuff, but she needed to tidy up the shop first. The central table that they used for displaying trending goods, and which was currently sporting Halloween ephemera, was also covered in the small baskets that people had been carrying around the shop, dropping in their articles they wanted to buy.

Everything needed putting back on the shelves, the table was desperate for a quick tidy up, and she blessed the customers who had been in the shop as the police arrived for leaving so quickly. Nobody had grumbled, or insisted they wanted their goods, and she hoped and prayed they would return in a few days to complete their purchases.

She quickly wrote out a sign that explained the shop was currently closed due to bereavement, and she stuck it on the outside of the door. That one small action suddenly made it real, and she slumped to the floor with her back against the shop door, sobbing. It was all too much; she needed the love of her life back with her, working together, planning together, living together.

Just too much.

23

Nora and Jess were both asleep, despite it being early afternoon, when the police knocked on the door. Neither of them had rested particularly well during the night, and Jess had watched her nan slowly drop into a deep slumber as she sat in the armchair with the raised footrest. She covered her with a throw, then grabbed one for herself and drifted away on the sofa. As a result, she almost fell off as she struggled to get her legs out from under the throw, before reaching the front door.

She knew it wasn't any of the girls. They would have gone straight round to the back door, and she peered through the spyhole in the door, to see a warrant card being held up to it.

She opened the door cautiously.

'Hello,' the tall man said. 'DI Paul Marshall, DC Ginny Keswick. Does a Mrs Nora Wheeler live here?'

'She does, but she's asleep. Her husband, my grandfather, died yesterday and we didn't sleep too well last night.' She suddenly realised what her hair must look like after an hour on the sofa, and she lifted her hand to flatten any errant wisps that were probably framing her face.

'Can we come in?'

She opened the door, and knew the puzzled expression must be showing on her face.

'If you do,' Jess said, her spirit starting to come back, 'you'll wake her. And then I might get pissed off. She's not far off eighty years old, she hasn't burgled anyone, hasn't murdered anyone, and hasn't knocked any senior citizens down on the zebra crossing. She just needs to rest after everything that happened yesterday.' Her tone softened. 'She's just an old lady.'

'I know,' Paul Marshall said, 'but we do have something we need to tell her. We aren't here to interrogate anyone, but we need to talk to you both. You're her granddaughter, you say?'

'I am. And you've just woken me up, as well as being about to wake Nan up. You're a brave man to tackle both of us when we're grumpy, DI Marshall.'

'I'll bear that in mind.' He couldn't help but smile at the irate woman in front of him, ferociously defending her nan. He turned to Ginny.

'Ginny, can you go and make us all a hot drink. Tea okay?'

Now Jess felt bewildered. 'Yes, we both drink tea. No sugar for either of us,' she said to Ginny, who wandered down the hallway looking for a kitchen.

Jess led the DI into the lounge, and Nan was slowly surfacing from her sleep. She reached down the side of the armchair and pressed the button to lower the raised footrest, then looked at the tall man looking back at her, compassion in his eyes.

'DI Paul Marshall,' he said, and handed her one of his cards. 'Please put that somewhere safe, and then if you need to contact me it's easy.'

She stared at him, weighing him up, and not finding him objectionable. At the minute. Time would tell if that would change.

'Why are you here?' she asked.

'I need to ask you a few questions before I can answer that, but I promise I will. Let's have a cuppa first, shall we?'

Nora looked up at Jess, and Jess gave a slight nod. 'My grand-daughter says that's okay,' she said. 'But if it's anything to do with me driving through that bus gate in the city centre, I didn't do it. Or at least, they shouldn't keep changing things and then I wouldn't have to do it.'

'That's perfectly true. But I'm not here about that. Ah, here's Ginny. She's good at mashing tea, and doesn't go through bus gates either.'

Ginny smiled at her boss, and placed the tea tray on the coffee table. 'There's no sugar in any of them, so just help yourself,' she said. 'That's a lovely kitchen, Mrs Wheeler. As you can probably imagine, I see some dubious ones, but yours was a pleasure to make these cuppas in.'

'My husband insisted I had a new one, so we've only had it about a year. He said we'd to spend some money so that he could die and know I would be okay with my kitchen. We thought he was joking. He wasn't. Is that why you're here? He died yesterday, peacefully and under the wonderful care of St Luke's. No accidents or anything.'

'No, and I'm really sorry to hear your husband has passed, Mrs Wheeler,' Paul said. 'Drink your tea, wake up properly and we'll talk.'

* * *

The DI waited until he was sure that she was fit and ready to talk. She seemed much brighter than when they had first arrived, and eventually he put down his own cup, took out his notebook and looked at her.

'Mrs Wheeler, forgive me for getting straight to the point, but do you have a daughter called Anna? Anna Wheeler?'

There was a sharp intake of breath before Nora could respond. 'Yes, yes, I do.'

'And can you tell me where she lives?'

'No.'

He was a little taken aback. The word was short, sharp and to the point.

'Why not?'

'Because I don't know. Until yesterday I hadn't set eyes on my daughter in thirty-five years. When Jessica was a month old,' she waved a hand in Jess's direction to indicate she was talking about the other woman in the room, 'Anna left her with us and walked away from all responsibility. There has been nothing since, until yesterday, during the morning. She arrived at the hospice where my husband was in his last few hours of life. I don't believe this was a coincidence, Inspector, I believe someone who knew where she lives now contacted her to tell her my husband was dying. I have no idea who this person might be.'

'I'm sorry to have to tell you this, Mrs Wheeler, but it seems your daughter, Anna, was murdered at some point late last night. We know she was alive at half past ten because her wife rang her to say goodnight. We are still awaiting forensic results to tell us when she died, but she was in the Premier Inn. A member of the domestic team entered her room this morning and found her.'

Nora's eyes were huge, as if she could see something really big and scary at the other side of the room. 'But she can't be... are you sure it's her?'

'She had her driving licence with her, and she checked in at reception under the name of Anna Wheeler. Her address was a house in Criccieth.'

'Where on earth is Criccieth?'

'It's in Wales.' Jess now spoke, her voice quivering. 'It's near Pwllheli. Mike and I went for a week's holiday there about three years ago, remember? I suppose on the plus side, I wouldn't have recognised her if I'd bumped into her, as I've never known her.' She turned to Paul. 'You said murder?'

He nodded. 'Yes, I'm sorry to be the bearer of such sad news, but she was cut across her throat. She bled out very quickly and wouldn't have suffered. As you haven't seen her for such a long time, we won't ask you to make a formal identification, Mrs Wheeler, we will ask her wife to do it. She will have to make the trip up from Criccieth but we can offer her transport in one of our vehicles to get her here if she doesn't normally drive long distances.'

'So she's married?' Jess raised her voice. 'And she didn't even let anyone know.'

'I understand they've been married for almost ten years, but have been together for thirty years. They own a small shop in Criccieth selling artisan wares made by themselves and other local craftspeople in the area, so I was told.'

There was a long silence and then Nora spoke. 'I'm finding it really difficult to get my head around this. We were nasty to her, Jess.' She held out a hand towards her granddaughter, and Jess grasped it.

'Of course we were, Nan. She turned up with no advance warning, and expected to be welcomed with open arms. I didn't even know who she was, I thought she worked at the hospice.'

Nora lifted her eyes to Paul, and he could see the tears.

He swallowed before speaking, hoping he didn't sound as upset as he felt. 'I'm so sorry we had to break the news like this, but there really is no other way. Do you need us to ring anyone, get somebody here to take care of both of you?'

Jess answered for them. 'No – we have a supportive network,

and I'll give them a call when we've finished here. Do you need to know anything else, because I think you've got the picture. We didn't know her. She was my mother, and I never had so much as a birthday card from her. Never a phone call, nothing. You'll forgive me if the grief I'm feeling is for Grandpops, not for Anna.'

The two police officers stood. 'I'll leave you to talk, I'm sure you must have a lot to say. We'll be in touch in a couple of days to tell you how the case is progressing. We have lots of checks to do, starting with CCTV at the hotel to see if we recognise anybody coming and going at any point during the night.'

'Where is she now?' Nora asked quietly.

'She's been transferred to our morgue, where they will perform a post-mortem. The forensics team will search for DNA transference, and we should have some results in a couple of days. We will look after her, I promise.'

Nora nodded. 'Thank you. Whatever else has happened, or whatever else she's done, she is still my daughter and we had a perfectly normal relationship of love and a lot of laughter, until she had the baby. I believe deep in my heart she developed severe post-natal depression that nobody spotted, or she hid it very well, until she reached the point when she had to walk away. And a mother's love never dies, you know, no matter what the child has done.'

He gave a gentle smile. 'My own mother says this to me at least twice a week. We'll let ourselves out and I'll speak to you early next week. Is that okay?'

'It is, and thank you for being so understanding.'

* * *

Nora and Jess sat side by side on the sofa, not saying much but holding hands. They needed the comfort of each other but they had very different feelings with regard to Anna's death.

Jess was feeling as though the unknown Anna had intruded on their grief, but Nora's feelings were completely at odds with her granddaughter's thoughts on the matter. Anna was her daughter, the one person she had loved above all others. And now she was gone.

She looked across at her most precious granddaughter, who was sitting on the sofa looking completely lost, bewildered by the events of the last few days. What could she say to help her? Very little, because nothing was going to bring either Arthur or Anna back, and she knew Jess would have to handle this in her own way. Where the hell was her bloody son-in-law? He should be here by Jess's side, or at the very least on his way home to be with her.

The anger briefly flared and Nora forced it back down. Getting angry with the world wouldn't help matters. What would help was getting Mel, Erin and Chantelle to come to her home and bring their own brand of comfort as they tried to digest this new turn of events.

She picked up her phone and sent text messages. The replies were swift and predictable.

MEL

Will be there in five minutes. Xxx

ERIN

Be there in five minutes. Will bring Mel. Xxx

CHANTELLE

Let me organise my parents / the twins. Ten minutes, Nan. Love you xxx

24

That long weekend seemed to drag on forever. By the time Monday morning came around, Jess had decided she wanted Mike out of her life. She needed a husband who put her above all else, and Mike hadn't even rung her, merely sent three texts. He explained he couldn't just drop everything and come home, and she thought herself into a reverse situation where, had he lost someone very dear to him, she knew she would have gone immediately to be by his side.

Everyone was going out of their way to help – Jess and Nora hadn't cooked a meal since the passing of Arthur. The girls had nipped in and out all the time, checking on them, delivering food, doing anything that needed doing.

Some things they had to do on their own, though, one of them being the organisation of a funeral, although Chantelle was able to point them in the right direction, towards the business she had used. And still Mike didn't come home.

Jess, along with Mabel, had taken up residence in her grandparents' house without thinking twice about it. She didn't want to be on her own, she wanted to hide away from the problems surrounding the death of Anna, which had now reached the media, and she guessed at some point they were going to have to meet the woman Anna had married several years earlier.

It was late afternoon on the Monday before they heard anything from the police. The same two officers arrived to see them, but it wasn't to give them anything concrete.

Paul Marshall looked quite grim; he would rather have been coming with some news, but all he could do was give them information following the forensic and the post-mortem results.

'I wanted to keep in touch with you, and we've just got the last of the results through that we've been waiting for.' He sat on the sofa, and Ginny remained standing near the door. He took out his phone and began to scroll.

'Okay, the post-mortem showed death would have been almost instantaneous and she wouldn't have really known what was happening. The blood loss was massive and the cause of death is officially exsanguination following the throat being cut. We believe she died in the early hours, possibly around one o'clock, and we've looked at several CCTV recordings but cannot link anybody being in or around the Premier Inn who shouldn't have been there. Only two people returned to their rooms between eleven and midnight, then there was no activity until guests started leaving around half past five the next morning. Every person on the hotel's CCTV has been accounted for.' He paused for a moment and Jess asked if they would like a cup of tea. She hoped it might remove the frown from his face. He was clearly unhappy at having so little to tell them.

'I'll make it,' Ginny said. 'DI Marshall can tell you what we know, I've already heard it.' She disappeared to the kitchen, and Paul continued.

'There is external CCTV on the car park to protect the guests' cars, and we have cleared everybody who showed on that. They were staff members who were legitimately there. It doesn't, of course, cover the entire area; CCTV never does get to all the little corners and in a hotel they tend to focus on the cars. In short, we have cleared everybody who was around after the last time we know for definite she was alive, and that was half past ten when she had a brief phone call with her wife. Now we come to an anomaly.'

Jess's head shot up, and Nan exhaled slowly.

'If the theory is right that someone contacted Anna to say her father was seriously ill, there's no evidence of that phone call. Her mobile phone was in the room, and it was showing her wife's call as being the last incoming call. There are a couple of calls that are attributable to her business, and a couple more from earlier in the week that were to her wife.'

The two women looked at him, waiting for him to reveal something, but he shrugged. 'The truth of the matter is that we don't know how she found out about her father's illness, or indeed who told her. We've requested a log of calls to the shop landline in case someone rang her on that with the news, but we're not really expecting a positive outcome on that.'

'Burner phone,' Jess muttered under her breath as the door opened, Ginny once again carrying the tray with the mugs on it.

'You could be right,' Paul said, showing that he had heard her half-hidden comment. 'I read crime books as well, you know. Seriously, it could be. Anna clearly never wanted to be traced, but would anybody bother with a separate phone just for the one phone call summoning her home to a death in the family? It's a real puzzle. And there was no second phone in that hotel room. That's what I mean about an anomaly. If a second phone is the answer, surely she would have needed it once she got here.'

'So you know nothing of why this has happened, how it's happened or anything else?' Nora looked at both officers, speaking very quietly and carefully. She actually felt angry, but didn't know why. It was very early days in the investigation, results were still coming in and it would probably just take one small item to reveal much bigger truths.

'Very little,' Paul admitted, sipping at his tea. 'The bedding was taken away and has been thoroughly tested, but it is only showing DNA from Anna, nobody else. We do believe whoever did it cleaned up in the bathroom, but even in there it is only showing Anna's blood, so the killer didn't damage himself. Or herself,' he corrected.

'You think it could be a woman?'

'I have a completely open mind on that. I'm off to Criccieth tomorrow to speak with Anna's wife, Siân, who we will be bringing back with us to formally identify Anna.'

Nora put down her cup. 'Please tell her we'd like to meet with her. Where is she staying? Or does she have to go back?'

'She's booked into the Hilton. She's taking today to close down the shop until next season, and that means she can go back whenever it's the right time. She did say that when Anna's body is released to her, it will be for burial in Criccieth, which is what both of them have spoken about in the past. We have a long journey back to Sheffield tomorrow, so plenty of time to talk to her, to tell her you'd like to meet her.'

'Thank you. That poor woman. Within two days we've both lost our life partners, and it's a confusing and shocking time. But to lose them when it's not natural causes is unthinkable. We didn't have long to get our heads around the imminent death of my husband, but he didn't die because someone else decided it was time for him to go. Anna must have been so frightened. That's the part that distresses me the most.'

'I'm sorry if talking about this part of Anna's life upsets you,

Mrs Wheeler, but when Anna left Jessica with you and simply vanished, did you never find out where she had gone?'

'No. She left us a note saying she couldn't handle motherhood without a partner to help, and we could do what we wanted with Jess, either keep her or put her up for adoption. The decision took no making. Jess was ours. We made it official by formally adopting her, but she's always called us Nan and Grandpops, rather than Mum and Dad.'

Jess felt it was time to interrupt. 'I had the best childhood ever. I certainly didn't need a mother, I had my nan. And I had my friends' mums as well, so life was very good, probably better than if Anna had stayed. Maybe I would have liked to have known who my father was, but it's not something of major importance. Not to me anyway, unless he's the one who tracked Anna down when she came back to Sheffield, then I suppose it is kind of important.' She realised she was being glib, and smart-ass clever, and held up a hand in apology. 'I'm sorry, ignore me. This is all getting to be too much to handle. I never really think about my mother under normal circumstances, but suddenly I now know what she looks like, and I've found out a little bit about her life.'

'Mrs Wheeler, she never said who Jessica's father was?'

'No. The only thing I did know was... I'm sorry to tell you this, Jess darling, but Anna was raped. I've never spoken of this before, and I'll never speak of it again, but she went out for a drink at the local pub and was attacked while walking home. She wouldn't let me contact the police, said they never believed the woman anyway, and I listened to her. I shouldn't have, because three months later she told me she thought she was pregnant. She didn't know who the rapist was, never seen him before, or so she said. We talked for many hours about her options, but she said she couldn't kill a child, no matter the circumstances, so we agreed not to tell her father the details, just to say the lad was no longer on the scene, and she was going to bring up the baby on her own. With our help, obviously.'

Nora's eyes filled with tears as she remembered the long talks into the night, the decisions made, and the beautiful baby who came home from the hospital with Anna. 'It lasted just a month, the mothering bit, and then she walked away.'

The two officers finished drinking, glanced at each other and stood. 'We're going to get off now. I just needed to tell you as much as we know, but I'll give you a ring after I've approached Anna's wife tomorrow about meeting with you. Is that okay? And thank you for being so open about Anna, for not hiding behind the truth, no matter how difficult it is to stir up your memory all over again.'

'Of course it's okay to ring. Please tell her how sorry I am, and that I never stopped loving my daughter, even if I never understood how she could do what she did.'

Jess stood and escorted them to the door, and thanked them as they left. It felt right that they should have come to update them on the investigation, but she also knew they didn't have to.

She went back into the lounge and stared at her nan. 'Would you ever have told me?'

'About the rape? Probably not. It was never relevant because I couldn't persuade her to report it. I never told Grandpops either. It was as if she just wanted to get on with her life and never think about that night again, but she was in a dreadful state when she walked in. I was starting to worry because she was so late and I knew she had work the next morning, and I heard the back door open. I can still remember that feeling of relief that she was home. Her face was a mess. He'd battered her to stop her struggling, and her clothes were ripped to shreds. He'd taken her jeans and panties so she was almost naked when she walked in. She must have been in horrific pain, there was blood down her thighs, and her eyes were... dead. No emotion. I helped her upstairs and I washed her down like a baby. She said she couldn't get in the bath, it all hurt too much. I rang her work next morning and said she'd been in a car accident and would be off work for a few days. It was a month before she went back, and it changed her completely. She never went out again, until the day she walked away from us, and gave you to us. I will love her forever, Jess, partly because you always love your child no matter what they do, but also because of that one massive thing she did leaving you with us, and to know how she died has broken my heart.'

25

'Shall we go away?' Mel spoke without lifting her head, while flicking through a magazine. 'I picked this up a couple of weeks ago because I knew I needed a break, but then, of course, I thought I would be paying a single person supplement.' She waved the magazine around. 'It's a travel brochure.'

'I can see what it is, numpty. It just seems to me that there are quite a few obstacles to our going away at the moment. Number one – I've just bought the shop next door, and as we speak there are at least three men in it starting to do things. Measuring up, mainly, I believe. Number two – it'll be Grandpops's funeral within the next two or three weeks. Number three – it now seems that we might have to attend a second funeral, this time for Jess's mum. Number four – we will have a third funeral in our diaries, for Andrew, now they've released his body.' Erin paused for a moment. 'Anyone would think we had a serial killer on the loose. And number five – I've just set Tia on as assistant manager, and I need to make it much more official and train her up properly, instead of it being a part-time job for a school-leaver. I can't walk away and leave her and my mum in charge of Fully Booked, not when there's all sorts of strange men in and out of the place.'

Mel's head never moved. She stared open-mouthed at all the words coming from Erin, then burst out laughing. 'Okay, we'll hang on a bit. I was lost on a beach in Rethymnon, could almost feel the heat from the sun, and could suddenly picture the two of us there. Skins turning browner by the second, wine by the bucketful, skinny dipping in the sea at midnight, and I got carried away.' She suddenly stopped speaking. 'I'm a cow. I'm trying to bury my head in any bucketful of sand, aren't I? Trying to forget what's going on. Just ignore me.'

Erin leaned over her and kissed her. 'Hang on to those thoughts. Next June?'

'Definitely. All I need to do is get a job, and I'm not in any rush to do that.'

'I've a couple of queries, though. Skinny dipping in the sea at midnight? And where the hell is Rethym... whatever?'

'Rethymnon. It's in Crete. Wonderful island, you'll love it as much as I do. And we can make it one in the morning for the skinny dipping if midnight is a little early for you.'

Erin shook her head, amazed at the change she had seen in Mel over the last few days. Since leaving work, she had bloomed. She grinned at the thought that it was to do with having gardening leave, but she knew it was because of the many hours of talking long into the night, confessing they could have been together much sooner, if only Mel hadn't been so scared. But the fear had now gone. And together was a wonderful word, as far as Erin was concerned.

* * *

Suzanne kept asking if they were a couple, and they refused to confirm or deny it, laughing at the frown on her face every time she hinted at secrets and tales.

She even tried quizzing Tia, but Tia had learned it was best to deny everything, usually by raising her shoulders as if to say, 'How the hell do I know?' But she did know. She had taken a parcel delivery through, and found them wrapped in each other's arms. Laughter had exploded from both Mel and Erin, and Tia had walked out after putting the parcel on the table. 'I saw nothing,' she said.

And that was her mantra from then onwards. If Mel and Erin wanted Suzanne to know, they would tell her. Besides, Suzanne was a pussycat. It was Alistair Jones who wouldn't be too happy that he'd missed out on the woman he'd been chasing for a couple of years; that was the thought that made Tia uncomfortable. Erin had told her he was pushy, so she always watched what he did when he came to the shop, and she knew Erin was right. But she also knew her boss could handle him. She'd kept him at arm's length for some time, and she'd carry on doing that.

Mel and Erin walked around to Jess's grandparents' house, hoping they would learn what the hell was going on. The newspapers had got the story, as had the local news programme shown after the main six o'clock news. Speculation was rife, and after texting Chantelle to say they were going round to make sure everything was okay, they opted not to take the car, but to add extra steps on to their Fitbits.

Jess was leaning on the front gate, staring into space. She moved to go back inside, then spotted her two friends walking down the road, arms linked. She waited until they reached her.

'Come in the front door, I've just let the police out of it.'

'Chantelle will be here soon. She wants to bath the girls tonight, to try and bring back some sort of normality, she said.' Erin leaned across to kiss Jess's cheek. 'You okay?'

She shrugged. 'Not really. I've stuff to tell you, but I'll Face-Time you after I've settled Nan in bed. I don't want her to know I'm talking about stuff that's been hidden for years. We can talk about what the police have told us, which actually is bugger all, but the deeper stuff I'll leave for later. Tell me what's going on with you first – take my mind off things. You want wine?'

'Sounds good. Not much, though. Some of us have work tomorrow,' Erin said. 'Speaking of work,' she continued as they followed Jess through the front door, 'the men have made a start. There's a huge skip outside currently with several sinks in it, and assorted chairs and suchlike. They've cleared the entire room, and there's lines drawn on the walls for the demolition of various bits of them. If you've time, I'd love you to see it and let the builder explain things, then we can be sure it will be as you want it for when you start work properly.'

'It'll certainly take my mind off all the horrible things that are happening at the moment. It'll have to be when Nan is okay to be left, because at the moment she's really tired, not wanting to know what's happening – I think she's overwhelmed by the whole situation. Just pretend she looks well, though, won't you?'

They both nodded and Jess opened the lounge door. 'We have visitors,' she announced.

Nora's face beamed. 'Well, thank goodness it's you two love-birds, and not those awful police people again. I've had enough of their nosey-parker activities to last me a lifetime. Jess, get these reprobates a drink, and I'll have a hot chocolate, please.'

'You're going to bed?'

'I am. It's been a long day, so excuse me, girls, but I'm

whacked.' She eased herself out of the chair. 'I'm going to read for a bit, try to take my mind off my worries and hopefully tonight I'll sleep.' She stood and her legs caused her to wobble slightly.

Erin moved to catch her, but Nora waved her away. 'I'll be fine.'

'No, you won't,' Erin said. 'I'll follow you upstairs, then I know you're not going to tumble back down them.'

The two left the room and Jess waited until they were out of earshot before saying anything.

'She's aged over the last week. I'm hoping it's just grief and not illness. The grief will eventually fade and I'll get my nan back, but at the moment I daren't even leave her.'

* * *

They didn't need a FaceTime chat later. With Nora deeply asleep, Jess began to talk. She told them about Anna's situation and how it was likely she would never know who her father was, and Chantelle pulled her close for a hug.

'I can't imagine how life must be not knowing who your father is. Though I know both you and Mel are in the same boat – thank God we have each other. It's made me more determined than ever to keep Andrew's memory alive for the girls. I've started little memory boxes for both of them, put some photos in and suchlike, because they'll need reminders like that when they reach adulthood.'

'I had a text message from Mum today,' Mel said and Erin looked at her in surprise.

'You didn't say you had! Where is she?'

'You were busy chatting about some part of the tearoom with the builders, and by the time you'd finished I'd forgotten about it. It's not really that important. I haven't even replied yet, it's only talking about absentee parents that's reminded me. I think she's in

Turkey with that waiter she met a couple of years ago while she was on holiday. It seems to have turned into her longest relationship, so if she's happy then I'm happy for her. I get the impression she's heard about what's happening here from some source, but the message was quite short. Just hoped I was okay, and sent love to all four of us. Let's face it, she was never the world's best mother, but she's not the world's worst either.'

The conversation continued pretty much along the same lines, absentee parents and present parents all discussed amidst differing degrees of admiration and scorn, and drifted into the main one of who could possibly have wanted Anna dead.

'Surely it was just a random thing?' Chantelle sounded puzzled.

'Nobody here actually knew her now, not after thirty-five years away,' Jess said. 'But it was at some early hour of the morning, so why would some randomer be in her room at that time? And it can't be anything to do with the hotel staff, because there's no record of any communication between her room and reception. I asked DI Marshall if a member of staff could be a possibility, and he told me they'd ruled it out. It seems to me that they're concentrating on finding out how she knew Grandpops was dying.'

'And how do you feel, Jess, knowing that the only time you've seen her, she was dead within about twelve hours? You can talk to any or all of us, you know.' Mel's eyes glistened with unshed tears. She hated to think of any of the other three having rough times, but suddenly Jess and Chantelle seemed to be immersed in problems way beyond their control.

'I think the word is numb,' Jess said, nodding as if agreeing with herself. 'I'm trying not to overthink it, but it won't leave my mind. You see, the thing that is tormenting me is she never lost the love for her family here. This is literally the first time there has been an issue, and she found out about Grandpops, however that may have happened. And she came. As it turned out, she was too late anyway, because Grandpops was in a coma when she arrived, and never opened his eyes again. I simply can't get away from the fact that it was always Anna with him, he missed her so much and always thought she would come back one day. But she didn't, not until it was too late and he didn't get to see her. Love can be a hard thing to live with, can't it? And Grandpops certainly lived with it for his Anna.'

Jess rarely opened up about feelings. To hear her, and to see the anguish on her face, tore the hearts out of the other three.

'My God, Jess, you have to talk to us. This is going to tear you apart if you bottle it up, and we won't let that happen.' Erin's eyes were like saucers as she stared at Jess. 'None of this is your fault. You took Anna's place, if anything, and I'm sure Nan will say the same thing. You meant just as much to Grandpops as Anna ever did. Never forget that.'

26

_____

Siân Jefferies had cried a lot since the Welsh police had delivered the news of Anna's death. Unhealthy, snot-running crying that had been behind closed doors and with nobody else knowing about it.

Sitting in the police car beside DI Paul Marshall was causing her to have palpitations. She'd never done anything quite so frightening as this before, and she knew it was going to be a long drive to Sheffield, where they would go straight to the morgue for her to see her Anna, and confirm it was her. She had no doubt it was her much-loved wife. They wouldn't make mistakes of this magnitude, wouldn't have even approached her unless they were absolutely sure.

She felt a hand touch her shoulder, and Paul asked if she was okay.

She nodded. 'I'm fine. Let's just get today over. Then I have to decide what to do. I will probably arrange to meet Anna's mother, but I kind of feel as though I'm intruding if she's just lost Anna's dad.'

'If it's any help,' Paul said, flicking on his indicator to overtake an extremely large articulated truck, 'she's a lovely lady. I'm pretty sure she wants to see you. Don't forget Anna walked away from Sheffield thirty-five years ago, and she's never seen her or any of her family since, or at least not till she turned up at the hospice.'

'So if she's seen Anna recently, couldn't she have identified her?'

'We did consider that,' he said, 'but she admits she didn't recognise Anna when she walked into that hospice room, so we couldn't ask her to do the identification because she would actually be identifying the person she saw by her husband's bedside. You don't want to do this?'

'No, I don't. I'm afraid of how she will look. She's beautiful, you know.'

Ginny again leaned forward from the back seat. 'Oh, Siân, you don't need to worry. You will only see her face, and that wasn't touched. You will still be seeing your Anna as she was, just very pale. I'll be with you, I'm not leaving you today until you're ready to be left. Later, I will just need to take you to get Anna's car from our compound; we've made sure it's had its checks completed so you can take it back with you. The forensic team found absolutely nothing in the car to connect it with the crime, so you've been cleared to take it back to Wales.'

Siân spun around to look at Ginny. 'Thank you, you've put my mind at rest. I should have asked you instead of waking up every five minutes and feeling overwhelmed about it. Once today is over I can begin to think clearly, and decide what happens next.'

'You jointly owned your business?' Paul asked.

'Yes. We met through attending a crafting course that was a week's intense stuff. By the end of that week, I truly believe we were in love, and yet before we met we both had boyfriends. Within a week of returning home we had dumped the boyfriends, got a flat in Criccieth where we figured nobody would be able to track us down, and settled there.'

'And bought a shop, presumably.'

'Not immediately. We began to make things. Anna was far more talented than me because she had an imagination. I had skills, I could produce anything from a drawing or a plan, but I couldn't come up with original ideas. No confidence,' she added. 'The items we made we sold in the shop that is now ours. When the owner told us she was selling up to move to bigger premises in Tenby, we scraped up every penny we had. Borrowed some from my parents as a last resort, and got the shop. Within a year, we'd paid back the amount we'd borrowed from Mum and Dad, and completely transformed what used to be quite a miserable shop. Anna loved colour, and when she started to change the shop's interior from "don't touch" to "touch everything", it was like magic. Other artisans approached us to sell their wares in the shop, and we take a small commission for that, but that little shop is the hub of the crafting community in that part of Wales.'

'And what will you do now?' Ginny's tone was gentle.

Siân sighed. 'God knows. Anna was our guiding force. Our star. I'm not at all sure I can do it without her.'

'Don't make decisions in a rush,' Ginny said. 'If you act on anything now, in six months' time you will realise just how wrong it was. It's now the end of the tourist season, so you have until next February to make decisions. But from what you've said, I think Anna would want you to keep her memory alive by carrying on with your business.'

Siân hesitated. 'At three o'clock this morning, I decided I was going to sell up. Thank you for showing me I'm wrong. Anna would be horrified if I did that.'

Ginny sank back into her seat, and watched as Siân leaned her head back against the passenger seat. She hoped she'd made her stop and think, prevented her from rushing into anything. It had only taken a couple of minutes for her to realise how insecure Siân was without the strength of Anna by her side, but she had a feeling that one day this terrified woman would take on Anna's confidence.

* * *

They reached Sheffield just after midday, and Paul drove them straight to the morgue. They stayed with Siân throughout the entire process, and she sobbed and turned to Paul's shoulder when she confirmed it was Anna.

Ginny then took over and they went to get some lunch, while Paul returned to the office to write up the morning's events and check if anything further had come in on CCTV. It hadn't, and he banged his hand down on his desk in utter frustration.

Siân and Ginny settled on sandwiches and a coffee, although Siân was by no means convinced she could eat. She managed half of it, but welcomed the warmth of the latte. Ginny tried not to talk too much about the case, knowing that when they approached the car that Anna had driven up to Sheffield, it would be yet another traumatic moment for the Welsh woman.

'My parents were from this part of the world towards the end of their lives,' Siân said, while trying to swallow some chicken. 'They lived in the Peak District, in Bakewell. Beautiful place. I started at Cardiff uni when I was eighteen, studying art history and art in general. Once I was settled and they saw I was happy doing what I was doing, they decided to follow their own hearts and leave Wales, moving to Bakewell. I'm an only child, so they'd only themselves to please, and they did. They're both dead now, sadly, but they loved this entire area. I used to come up and see them a couple of times a year, but Anna always said she would stay and mind the shop. I'm kind of guessing now that she simply didn't want to take any risks around her parents, didn't want to accidentally bump into them by the riverside in Bakewell, feeding the ducks! It's so sad now I know her parents are still alive – or one of them is, anyway.'

Ginny finished her sandwich. Once again, she could see a hint of tears in the eyes of this woman who was trying so hard to be brave.

'I think you need to get booked into the Hilton, then have a lie down and a rest. So, shall we go and pick up your car, then you know you have your transport. Did you two share a car?'

'We did. Anna was the main driver, though, because I drive if I have to, not when I want to. We simply didn't need two cars.' She finished her drink, and pushed the remains of her sandwich to one side. 'I don't seem to have much of an appetite, on top of everything else.'

'It's everything else that has reduced your appetite. It's the same for everybody when anything like this happens.' Ginny reached across and clasped Siân's hand. 'It will get better, but not for some time. You just have to keep going, then one day you will realise it doesn't hurt quite so much, it has almost become your norm. That time will come, you just have to get through this awful time. Draw on Anna's strength. It's still within you.'

* * *

Ginny completed the release form for the Range Rover at the compound then drove back to the Hilton in the squad car with Siân following in her own car.

They said goodbye in the car park. She gave Siân her card, and told her to ring if she needed her, before handing over a second telephone number. 'This is where you can make initial contact with Anna's mother, if you want to.' Ginny watched as Siân wheeled her small suitcase towards the hotel reception, before returning to the station to complete her own reports.

It had been an emotional day, with a very early start, and she had every intention of finishing early.

She spent some time making sure it was a complete and full report; she wanted nothing to be wrong on this case, it seemed suddenly to be so important that every little thing was annotated. She saved the file to the relevant folder on her computer and leaned back, allowing her tired eyes to close just for a moment.

'All done?'

She looked up to see Paul Marshall. 'Yes. You think she'll be okay?'

'I have no idea. She has both our cards?'

'She does. We got on really well, she seemed as if she needed to talk. And it wasn't about what's happened to Anna, it was just life stuff. Her parents used to live in Bakewell. She mentioned feeding the ducks, so she has memories of everybody's favourite market town. They're both dead now, and she did say she was an only child so I'm assuming she sold the house and inherited the money. Anyway, it's all in my report. Can I go home now?'

He looked up at the clock on the briefing room wall. He grinned at her. 'Part-timer. It's only half past five, you know.'

'Is it worth mentioning I was up at five this morning for this mammoth journey to a foreign country? And if I don't go home right now, I'm going to put my head down on my desk, close my eyes and sleep.'

'Foreign country? We went to Wales!'

'They speak a different language. Did you see the road signs? By the time you've read through the top part which is in Welsh, you've missed what they're really trying to tell us in English.' She stood, picked up her jacket from the back of her chair, and he laughed.

'Lightweight,' he said. 'See you tomorrow. We're going back to the Premier Inn in the morning. I don't believe in Harry Potter stuff like invisibility cloaks, so somebody managed to find a way to get to that room without being seen. We need to find out how.'

She stopped walking away and looked back at him. 'You don't believe in Harry Potter stuff? What sort of a DI are you, boss? How many of the books have you read?'

'Half the first one.'

She nodded. 'It shows.' She turned and walked away, muttering under her breath. 'Doesn't believe in invisibility cloaks. He'll be saying next that wands will never replace Tasers, but I saw what a wand did to Voldemort.'

She swung through the door and out in the corridor, heading down to the car park.

He was howling with laughter by the time she had disappeared from view. That woman had made a bad day into a much better one, but he would have to do something about the possibility that she might start substituting wands for Tasers.

27

Siân didn't bother with food. She made herself a cup of tea, changed into a nightie and slipped into bed. The day hadn't been quite as bad as she had spent all of the previous night imagining it would be; Anna had been pale, but had looked as though she was sleeping. In Siân's imagination there had been blood everywhere, she would have been able to see the gash across the throat, but of course none of that had happened.

Ginny had taken care of her, and had recognised the moment when Siân needed to be alone.

She finished her cup of tea, slid further down the bed and slept for the first time since the two Welsh Heddlu officers had turned up to inform her of Anna's death.

* * *

Nora woke early on that Wednesday morning, but wasn't convinced she wanted to get up. Her whole world seemed to be spinning out of control and it had started with Andrew's death. The funeral arrangements had been made and that was now only two weeks away, but she hadn't given any concrete thought to organising for her lovely Arthur to be laid to rest. That would really mean he'd left her forever, once that happened, and she knew she wasn't yet ready for that. And then, of course, thoughts of Anna wouldn't lie down.

It seemed that her only daughter was to be buried in Wales, and she had no idea if she would be welcome at the service or not. Jess was avoiding the whole subject of Anna, and not really wanting to talk about the funeral arrangements for Grandpops either. And then there was Chantelle. Since Andrew's death she had been so quiet, so subdued. Nora ached for her. It wouldn't be easy once Laura and Samuel returned to their own home, and the poor girl was on her own with the twins.

There was a gentle knock on her bedroom door, and it opened slightly. 'Can I come in?'

'Only if you're bearing gifts.'

'Cup of tea and two rounds of toast do you?' Jess pushed open the door and walked in carrying a tray. 'We need to get over things, don't we, and today is the day.'

'Really?'

'Yes, we have Grandpops to organise, and we both know he wouldn't want all this ignoring it, as we're doing at the moment. So once you've eaten, I want you to seriously consider getting up, having a shower, and I'll dry your hair for you.'

'Really?'

'Yes, today is the day we have to be the strong women we are. It's time we showed the world how the Wheeler women react in a crisis.'

'Really?'

'Nan, you've just said really three times. You not fully awake yet?'

'Well, I am now after this conversation, even if I wasn't before. Where's Mabel?'

'Having her breakfast. She's fine, don't worry about her. It's the rest of our lives we have to be concerned with. Now, eat that toast, no arguments. I don't want you ill because you're wasting away. So, I suggest we go see the funeral place that Chantelle has used for Andrew, because they've been amazing with her. They've taken away all the stress about organising everything, and she's been able to get her head around the rest of her life with the children. That's her priority now. Your priority is to be able to sleep at night instead of all this being on your mind, so we're going to do something about it. Yes?'

'If you say so, my darling.' Nora bit into her toast. 'This is nice. I can't actually remember eating yesterday. I'll finish this, then jump in the shower.'

Jess stood from where she'd been perched on the end of the bed. 'Good. Give me a shout when you're dressed, and I'll come back up and do your hair. Okay?'

Nora smiled and nodded, then watched as her granddaughter left the room. She pulled a few tissues out of her tissue box and wrapped the toast in them. She really wasn't hungry, but that young Jess would only fret if she thought she hadn't eaten the toast. And Mabel was the perfect receptacle for uneaten food...

* * *

The hairdryer was soothing for Nora, and she closed her eyes and enjoyed the precious time with Jess. She had talents, this wonderful girl, and yet that blasted husband of hers squashed everything out of her.

'Nan, if I tell you something, will you keep quiet about it?'

'Do you need to ask?'

'No, of course not. It's just that it's about one of us, and we never talk about each other. But Chantelle is so unhappy.'

'Chantelle? She'll be unhappy for a long time, Jess. She's coping with the girls?'

Jess switched off the hairdryer for a moment. 'She is. It's Andrew who's causing her grief, and it's not all stemming from his death. He had another woman. Somebody he worked with.'

'My God. And Chantelle knew?'

'She found out about it accidentally, just a few days before his accident. She hadn't confronted him, she was leading up to that when he was killed. I'd rather tell you than you pick up on it, because we seem to all be together here a lot. Nobody wants you to be on your own at the moment, but if one of us lets it slip about this other woman, you'd be shocked. So I'd rather you knew, and I know you won't spill the beans to anyone.'

'Of course I won't. Is there anything we can do for the poor girl?'

'Only what we've been doing, which is to support her as much as we can. Her mum and dad don't know about it, and they've been absolute stars staying with her, but I'm starting to get the feeling she needs some alone time with just her and the girls now. She's admitted there were problems between her and Andrew before she saw him with this woman from work, so she's maybe not as upset about that as she would have been if she'd thought it was all hunky-dory. But it's more about the death of the man she has loved for a long time.'

'I can relate to that,' Nora said quietly. 'I promise I won't say anything to anyone else, but I really do feel for her, bless her.'

Jess finished doing Nora's hair, and the older woman swung backwards and forwards in front of the mirror. 'This looks lovely. Thank you, Jess. I feel a bit more human now.' Her mobile phone began to vibrate and play the tune she didn't hear all that often. She stared at it. 'There's only you ever rings me, and you're here.'

Jess laughed. 'Best answer it then. It could be the funeral directors we chatted to yesterday, or it could be St Luke's. Just answer it and find out!'

She did, laughing at her granddaughter's words. The laughter faded as she listened to the voice on the incoming call. 'Yes, of course you'll be very welcome. I'll text you our address. See you soon.'

She disconnected and turned to Jess.

'That was Anna's wife. She's just finishing her breakfast and then she wants to drive over to see us.'

'Do I have to be here?'

'You do. Are we tidy downstairs?'

'Of course. When is it not tidy?'

'I'd best text her the address then.' Nora tapped away on her phone, and pinged it to the number she hadn't recognised on her phone. 'That's done. Let's go and meet the woman who I suspect knew absolutely nothing about us.'

* * *

Siân pulled up outside the well-presented detached house, and climbed out of her car. She looked around her, reflecting quietly that the last time Anna had been here was the day she had walked away from Sheffield. And her parents. What had gone so wrong with that relationship that would make Anna not approach them for a further thirty-five years? She felt there was so much she didn't know about the woman she had married, and yet she also felt it had never been obvious there was stuff to know.

They had decided early on in their relationship not to have children, to concentrate on their business, their creativity, and their love for each other. They'd never regretted remaining as a couple, and their wedding had been a small affair, attended only by friends from the village. Things could have been different, but Anna had been happy to leave it as a friends-only celebration. Siân felt a shiver course through her as she remembered that day, the greyness of the skies in November, followed by the sunshine in Florida as they had closed everything down in the shop and set off for their honeymoon. All memories she could cling on to, as she spent the rest of her life without Anna.

The front door opened and a grey-haired woman was standing on the doorstep, waiting to welcome her. Siân locked the car and walked towards the woman she guessed was Anna's mother. It felt strange, almost frightening. She had never been the most confident woman on the planet, and this was way out of her comfort zone. But it had to be done. She had to meet the woman she had always assumed had turned her daughter out of the family home, had driven her away to lead her own adult life without the back-up of a family.

'Mrs Wheeler?'

'I am,' Nora confirmed. 'But please call me Nora. We don't stand on ceremony in Yorkshire,' she added with a smile. She could see Siân was nervous.

'Hi, I'm Siân.' Nora stepped back and Siân walked through and into the large hallway.

'First room on the left,' Nora said. 'Tea or coffee?'

'Thank you, I'd love a coffee. Milk, no sugar.'

'Then make yourself comfortable, the drink will only be a moment.'

Siân entered the lounge and was impressed. The walls were a

gentle shade of light green, and everything else had been bought to reflect the ambience of that colour. She sat on the sofa, and tried to subdue the tremble in her hands. She didn't need to make a good impression, she would be back in Criccieth before she knew it, able to cry when she wanted, and at any volume. She just needed to get through this difficult meeting, and she could submerge herself back in the life she had shared with Anna. It briefly occurred to her that Nora might not be forthcoming about the disagreement that had forced the split between parents and daughter, the fight that had driven Anna away, but did it truly matter? She would probably only see Nora one more time if she came to Wales for the funeral.

The door opened and Nora moved into the room, taking the rocking chair. 'I seem to be sitting in this chair all the time,' she explained. 'It was Arthur's favourite, he loved to rock while he was reading his books. I feel closer to him when I'm sitting here.'

'Can I help with the drinks? I should have asked...'

'No, it's fine. They'll be here in a couple of minutes. The police are looking after you?'

'They are. I was with DI Marshall and PC Ginny Keswick yesterday. They were with me when I identified my wife, and then Ginny stayed with me and tried to feed me, bless her, before taking me to a police compound to retrieve our car. It seems they had to check it, but it was never seen as being part of the crime. I'm glad I got it back, it makes life easier because I can drive back to Criccieth under my own steam and at my own pace, now.'

The lounge door opened and Jess nudged it with her bum, carefully balancing the tray holding three mugs and a plate of biscuits. She placed it on the coffee table, and Nora spoke.

'Siân, this is Anna's daughter, Jessica, although she's always called Jess. Jess, this is Anna's wife, Siân. And the little dog is Mabel.'

28

The two women stared at each other, both without speaking. Nora eventually clicked on what the problem was, and her hand went to her mouth automatically.

'You didn't know, did you, Siân? Anna never told you she'd had a baby.'

Still the two women didn't speak. Jess realised she couldn't think of a worse nightmare scenario than what was happening in her nan's lounge, and eventually she spoke. 'I think I'd better sit down.'

She deliberately chose to sit next to Siân on the sofa, although she wasn't sure why she did that. Maybe it was because the woman looked as though she might need physically propping up very shortly. She reached across to the tray and handed Siân a mug of tea. 'Drink this,' she said, 'then we'll talk. It seems you didn't know of my existence.'

And still the small, dark-haired pretty Welsh woman didn't speak. She sipped slowly at the hot tea, and tried to gather her thoughts. Initially they were thoughts of escape. How could she get out of the house without looking ridiculous? Then she began to query why she had to come. Anna had never wanted to visit, so why should she?

The reasons for Anna's reticence were now becoming very clear. Why had Anna walked away from her child? She looked at Nora, and spotted tell-tale tears in her eyes.

'I can't believe she never told you,' Nora said. 'I'm so sorry it was such a blunt introduction, but it never occurred to me for a minute that Anna wouldn't have told you. You're her wife!'

Finally Siân spoke. 'I'm so sorry. This has knocked me for six. What I don't understand is why the police haven't mentioned Anna's daughter.'

Nora picked up her own cup. 'They probably assumed, like us, that Anna would have told you. The police said you'd been together thirty years?'

Siân nodded. 'We have. And you're right, of course. Anybody would have thought I knew. But I promise you, I didn't.' She turned to Jess. 'I'm so sorry, Jessica. You must think I'm a horrible person, and I promise you I'm not. Maybe between you the full story can be handed on to me?'

* * *

And it was. It became obvious that the colour disappearing from Siân's cheeks was telling its own story, but Nora talked of thirty-five years without Anna in their lives, of having no idea where she was, what she was doing, or even if she was alive. She spoke of Arthur's devastation at what his daughter had done, but he always believed she would return one day. And she had, but Arthur had been too near death to know she was there.

Jess spoke very little. She listened to her nan tell of the years of heartbreak, the frequent talks of employing a private investigator to track her down, but it all came to nothing when common sense prevailed. The true fact was that Anna wanted to remain hidden, and as an adult, they had to respect that wish.

'And Jessica – sorry, Jess – was only a month old when Anna left Sheffield?' Siân's voice reflected the emotion she felt – and it was one of disbelief that the woman she had loved for so many years could have kept the biggest secret of all, that she had given birth to a daughter.

Nora went to her sideboard and took out an envelope with three copies of a newspaper in it. 'I think you should have one of these,' she said. 'One is my copy, one is a copy for Jess, and one was kept for Anna in case she ever returned. We took part in an interview for *The Star*, a Sheffield newspaper, when the girls had just been born. There were four born within a six-month period, all living on this tiny little close. It must have been a slow news day, because this feller turned up, interviewed us, took pictures and this came out a couple of days later.'

She handed one of the papers to Siân. 'The four girls are like sisters. There's Jess, Chantelle, Melissa and Erin. They grew up together, they stand together, and don't ever cross any one of them, it simply wouldn't be worth it because you couldn't win. If they told me milk was delivered by handcart from the moon, I would simply agree because if I didn't it would be the word of four women against me. Not good odds. My Arthur loved them all dearly. He was their football coach, their gymnastics coach, he never said no to anything they wanted. And now all four of them are looking after me. Obviously the other girls had parents much younger than Arthur and me, but that never mattered. Jess was our baby, our granddaughter, and we shared the four girls, baby-sitting when needed, birthday parties galore, it was a wonderful upbringing for all of them. But Anna missed it all. She didn't even take a photo of Jess with her when she left. To us it seemed as if she'd simply vanished. She made it quite clear in the letter she left us that she didn't want to be found, and we could either keep Jess or put her up for adoption.'

There was a sharp intake of breath from Siân. 'She actually wrote that? This doesn't seem like the Anna I've known for thirty years. She was lovely with the kids who came into the shop. We always kept a jar of lollipops for handing out to them, and Anna developed a particular skill for whittling. She used to make little doll figures about six inches or so tall, and she made them for handing out to what she called the nicer kids.'

'You have to understand, Siân, Anna wasn't in a place where she had worries or anything. She was fine once she'd got over the shock of being pregnant, or so we thought. She gathered everything together for the baby's arrival, did everything any normal mother would do. We talked through any fears and worries we felt she might have, and let her know we were with her every step of the way. Then she changed. About a week after the birth, she began to ask me to change nappies, prepare bottles, that sort of thing. I did it willingly, of course, never realising she'd probably already made plans to go. She changed. She became introspective, quiet, moody, and I began to fear that post-natal depression had hit her. Then she went. As I've already said, she took nothing of Jess's, so she meant to have no memorabilia of her daughter, and we headed straight to a solicitor to secure Jess remaining with us. We initially thought she just needed time out and she would be back, but there was nothing.'

Siân sighed. 'This is killing me to hear all of this. It's so new to me and yet I thought I knew her so well.'

'You knew the new Anna, not the old one. You met the one who gave birth and became somebody else. And hid her past from you.'

Siân finished her tea and placed the cup back on the tray. 'I need to go now and be on my own for a time. I'll keep in touch if that's okay?'

Nora stood. 'Of course it's okay. I know we haven't exactly cleared anything up, and what we've discussed doesn't lead us in any way to the killer of my daughter and your wife, but at least you must feel you know Anna better now. Take care, Siân, and ring anytime. All of this is going to make you feel very down. We're here if you need to talk. And of course we'd like to go to Criccieth for Anna's funeral service.'

'You've booked Mr Wheeler's service?'

'Not yet. Possibly tomorrow. So it will be sometime in the next two or three weeks. I hope you feel you can attend, but I'll understand if you can't. You may feel differently about the whole situation once you start to think things through, and may not want Anna's family in your life at all. Just know we're here if you need us.'

The FaceTime chat with the Coven was extra interesting that night as Jess detailed Siân's visit.

She spoke of all that had been discussed, although had to confess to keeping out of it as much as possible. As she tried to explain to them, mother isn't just a name, it's a person who devotes their life to a child, and her mother was Nan.

Erin also had news of a fall-out with the man who brought such a lot of money into her business.

'He turned up at the shop,' she explained, 'and I treated him exactly as always, with deference.' She gave a small laugh. 'Only this time Mel was in the shop with me, and she inadvertently called me "love". He picked up on it, I could see it in his face, and he asked if Mel was a new employee. I said no, she was my girl-friend, and he accused me of leading him on!'

'Oops,' Chantelle said. 'The end of a beautiful friendship, then. I guess he'll be going elsewhere for his books now.'

'Well, I can assure you he'll not get the antiquarian sort from Amazon,' Erin responded. 'Honestly, I've never given him any reason to think I might fancy him. When he asked me to go for a meal, I put him off. He'll be back, I reckon, when he sees what books I'm putting in the online trade papers. He'll not be able to resist.'

'His face was a picture when Erin said I was her girlfriend,' Mel said. 'I didn't quite know what to say other than hello. And it was so noisy because for about half an hour they were knocking something down next door. He just happened to turn up in that half hour. He didn't buy anything and left very quickly.'

'He'll be back,' Erin repeated. 'So let's move on and forget Alistair Jones. Chantelle, how're the babies?'

'In bed, fast asleep, thank goodness. I do have some news, though. Sandford's have given me Andrew's car. So I can finally get rid of the clapped-out thing I've been driving since before I had the twins. And I won't need to go to work, the insurance he had through Sandford's is considerable, it appears, so I feel as though a load has been lifted from me. I did have a bit of a moment today, I must admit. I suddenly missed him and it was like an ache in my heart. I suppose it's because we've been together for such a long time, it's like a part of me has gone, no matter how things evolved at the end.'

'Why didn't you ring one of us? We can all drop what we're doing at a moment's notice, as we've all proved over the years.' Mel's tone was quite pushy. 'It's what we're here for, our own little support system. I hate to think of you being upset about anything, not when we're only at the end of a phone.'

'I came round,' Chantelle said. 'Went and lay on the bed when Mum and Dad took the twins out for a walk, had half an hour's sleep until the postman knocked on the door, but felt much better after that. Mum and Dad are going home on Friday, then coming back the night before the funeral. I think they're missing their own bed and I'll find it a relief knowing it's just me and my girls in the house. I'm seriously thinking of getting a rescue dog, a little bit of extra security around our place, and the girls would love a dog. I don't want a big one, though.'

'That's good news,' Jess said. 'I love my Mabel, as you know, and let's face it, she was the reason I found Grandpops when I did. I went to the shed to collect her. I heard her bark as I went down the garden path, so I think she knew he needed help. She was standing by him when I opened the shed door, not waiting to get out to me because she'd heard my footsteps. A dog is a really good idea, Chantelle.'

They ended the chat with messages of support, and Wednesday drifted slowly through to Thursday.

29

It took almost the whole of Thursday for Jess and Nora to sort out arrangements for Arthur's funeral. The first part was easy because they placed everything in the hands of the funeral director, who reassured them they would have no concerns. Everything would be taken care of, from ordering the flowers to a death notification in *The Star*, and he would keep them fully informed every step of the way in case they wanted to add or take something away.

It was a relief to both of them to have taken that first step in saying goodbye to the man they had loved forever, and they returned home to discuss what to do about the wake. Should they go to a pub? Come home and cater themselves? In the end, they decided to contact a pub near the local golf course and spent an hour in the afternoon going there to discuss what they would require. It seemed everybody was being completely helpful, and they returned home feeling a strong sense of accomplishment.

Jess messaged the other three on the Coven group chat giving them the details, and all three responded with tearful emojis in acknowledgement that they had read and understood.

It was Nora who messaged Siân to give her the relevant information. Siân rang her within seconds of reading it.

'You're okay?' Siân asked. 'I sensed yesterday this was something you really didn't want to do. Believe me, I recognise that feeling.'

'I actually feel better for having done it. It was the black cloud over me, putting things in motion to say goodbye, but now that it's done, I feel so much better. I think Jess is the same. But what about you?'

'The police have been here to see me. They're really trying to track down who it was gave Anna the information that her dad was seriously poorly. They want to search the shop and our home just in case she didn't bring this second mobile phone with her. I told them that I'd never seen one in all the years we've lived there, but if they go to the shop next door, they have keys to our shop and our home and they can go in and look. I did stress I expected the shop to be exactly the same as I left it, upon my return, so hopefully they won't cause too much upset to our home. My home, now, I suppose. Luckily our neighbour is also a friend, so she'll go in with them.'

'You know, it could be something as simple as the killer took the phone away with them,' said Nora.

'So you think whoever contacted my Anna to tell her Arthur was seriously ill then went to meet her in that room for the sole purpose of killing her? Why? Why would they do that? Anna would never have hurt a fly. And she would also never have suspected that whoever visited her was there to kill her.'

'She was always a gentle girl when she was growing up, and I have no reason to think that changed. Likewise, I can't imagine why anyone would want to kill her. Maybe someone has waited a long time for her to surface, I simply don't know, and it's probably just my imagination working overtime here.' Nora sighed. 'Suddenly my life is in tatters with no explanation for it. It's early days in the investigation, I know, but I need to know why this happened to my girl.'

* * *

Closer to the city centre on that Thursday, work was pushing forward in Fully Booked. Jess walked into the shop and Erin thought she had aged in a matter of days.

Mel looked at Erin, and nodded to indicate they should go upstairs to the flat.

Erin smiled at Jess. 'Lovely to see you out and about. Tea?'

'Not bothered about the tea, it was more the company I needed. Are you busy?'

'Mum and Tia can manage. I've been doing a stock check and getting an order together so everything can wait. Nothing's that urgent that I'd put it before you.'

'Your mum's in?'

'Somewhere around the back of Crime. We're having a general tidy up, making sure the books are all in alphabetical order after a busy couple of days. I spotted some romance in the crime section when I opened up, so Mum volunteered to check everything, and leave Tia to see to the serving. But I can leave them to manage. Let's go upstairs.'

She disappeared towards the crime section, told Suzanne what they were doing, and Suzanne popped her head around the shelves. She went towards Jess and hugged her. 'So very sorry, lovely girl. Grandpops went very quickly, but sometimes it can be for the best when it's cancer. Tell you what, though, he'll bring a smile to the face of anyone who ever thinks about him, he was such a lovely man. We'll all be there to give him the send-off he deserves.'

'Thank you, Suzanne. It's hard. I've left Nan on her own, and all the time I'm worrying about her. She's taken to sitting in his rocking chair, and she kind of disappears inside herself when she does. I know it's only natural she'll be like that, but it's changing her. She said last night she'd lost her reason for living because Grandpops was her reason for living. And I feel some of that as well. I know it will pass with time, but it's bloody awful at the moment.'

'Oh, Jess, I wish I could do something about it. You know I'd do anything for all four of you, and it hurts so much whenever any of you are hurting. And now I'll make it five girls, because I'll include Nan in that.'

Mel slipped her arm through Jess's. 'Come on, it's cup of tea time for us, so we might as well make one for you. Let's get off the shop floor and leave it to the customers.'

Suzanne watched as the three of them headed upstairs, before returning to the crime books. It was a period of change. It now seemed that not only had Mel moved into the upstairs flat, but so had her cat. She was struggling to imagine a Mel and Erin combination beyond the sisterhood relationship, but as had always been the case, she had to accept all the decisions made by Erin. And that clearly involved having a cat. She felt the now familiar pain in her stomach threaten to overwhelm her, and she leaned her head against the shelf she had previously dusted. She stood immobile until she felt it begin to subside, then headed towards the kitchen for a glass of water. Two of her tablets would help, but she was all too aware she was an hour early taking them.

Tia was serving when the door opened and Alistair Jones entered. Tia really didn't like this man, and took her time with the sale, chatting for some time with the customer. He then stepped forward, and she said, 'Mr Jones.'

'Hello, Tia. Is Erin around?'

'Not at the moment. I mean, she is around, but she's with a customer upstairs. She may be some time.'

'An antiquarian customer?'

'I don't talk about Erin's business, I'm sorry.'

'No, of course not, and I'm sorry I asked. We had a bit of a fall-out, and I thought I'd call in to apologise. Can you tell her I was here, and I'll be in touch?'

'Of course.' She wrote his name on a Post-it note, and stuck it on the till. 'Thank you for calling in.'

He disappeared through the door, and her eyes followed him as he returned to his car. She screwed up the Post-it note and threw it in the bin. Erin had been quite vocal about future communications from the man, and what the boss said was what the boss wanted. No more Alistair Jones.

She watched as Suzanne finished on crime and turned to the next section. Suzanne leaned against the large bookshelf, and simply stood there, unmoving, and unaware Tia's eyes were on her.

The older woman seemed to be deep in thought, and didn't stir until the bell above the door pinged to announce the entry of another customer. She shook her head as if to wake herself up, and then moved onto the thrillers section, where she began to change a few of the books, replacing them alphabetically, standing them upright where they had been left flat on the shelf, and dusting the shelves once they were tidy again. Then she crossed towards the tiny kitchen, leaving Tia on her own.

Ten minutes later, Suzanne walked across to speak to Tia, once the thriller section was back to its normal appearance. 'I'm going home,' she announced, sounding quite belligerent, almost as if daring Tia to argue with her.

'Okay.' Tia smiled. 'Do you want me to tell Erin when she comes down, or have you messaged her?'

'I'll message her from the car. I started to think about the awful stuff that's happening, and I need time out, I think. I'm feeling a bit overwhelmed by it all, I thought a lot about Jess's grandpops, and there's Andrew, who never came home from his bike ride, along with Jess's mother's death – it just feels too much to take in at the moment. Are you okay on your own?'

'Of course. Erin leaves me on my own quite a lot, especially since she has to keep nipping next door if the builder needs to discuss something. I'm absolutely fine, and Erin is only upstairs anyway.'

'I'll see you next week then, unless Erin asks me to come in for anything. You're a good girl, Tia. I know Erin is very impressed, and believe me, this shop is her life. She wouldn't leave you in here on your own if she didn't fully believe you could handle it. Can you pass me my bag from under the counter, please?'

Tia reached down into the cupboard and brought out a leather handbag. 'This one?'

'It is. I didn't sleep much last night, so I'm going to have a couple of hours in bed, and hope I feel livelier when I wake up.'

The door closed behind her and she walked to her car, dropping into the driving seat with a sigh of relief. It was all too much at the moment, grieving, working, supporting, dealing with intensifying pain – she definitely needed time on her own, an afternoon nap followed by a long rose-scented bath and a gin and tonic.

* * *

Erin wasn't surprised to find Tia on her own. Her mother had been very quiet all morning, and she had actually volunteered to do a job that meant she would be working on her own and not particularly having to deal with customers. This was so unlike the normally garrulous Suzanne, and Erin wondered if it was their present situation, or was she not feeling good?

'She wasn't ill?' Erin asked, concern flashing across her face.

'No, she said she was tired because she hadn't slept much last night. She looked tired, so it wasn't just an excuse.'

'She doesn't actually need a reason to go home. Let's not forget I don't pay her a penny for working here, she just loves being among the books and says that's enough for her, so it's a very ad hoc sort of employment. I'm just a bit concerned. I'll ring her later, have a mother and daughter chat.'

Jess smiled. 'Seems like it's your day for sorting everybody out.' She leaned across and kissed both Erin and Mel on their cheeks. 'I know I don't always show how I feel, but I love the bones of you two, and you're always my first port of call when I need cheering up. And you've done it again. I feel so much better than when I arrived here, and we've done it on tea and coffee, no wine! I'm going to call round to Chantelle's now and pass a little of this sunshine on to her.'

30
<hr>

Laura and Samuel were outside Chantelle's house, with the twins clinging on to their mother. Jess parked her car and walked across the road to them.

'Problem?' she asked and Laura shook her head.

'Not at all. Samuel has a hospital appointment this afternoon, so we're going to head home after that. Chantelle says she's feeling so much better, and let's face it, we're not a million miles away if she does need us to come back. Are you and your nan okay?'

Jess shrugged. 'We're feeling a bit lighter for having booked the funeral, but we miss him so much. Chantelle said she felt better after doing the same thing for Andrew. I'll take care of her and the twins, so don't be sat at home worrying about them. I'd ring you if there was a problem, but there won't be. Chantelle is our grown-up, she's the sensible one, she'll be absolutely fine.'

'Thank you, Jess.' Laura and Samuel got into the car, and Samuel started the engine. They all waved as the car disappeared down the road, and Chantelle gave a huge sigh of relief.

'I'm so grateful to them, I really am, because they've been

amazing with Daisy and Lily, and have allowed me to sort out my life without having to take the girls everywhere, but...'

Jess laughed. 'There's always a "but".'

'It feels like being back at school and living with my parents again. I'm thirty-five, for heaven's sake. And they're so worried about me, but I haven't said anything about what Andrew did to me, so they don't need to be worried. And that is actually the biggest thing in my life, but I'm handling it. Come on, let's get the little monsters inside, it's quite cool out here.'

* * *

The little monsters cooked sausages for Aunty Jess, sausages made out of rolled-up pieces of paper.

'Dad made them,' Chantelle explained. 'You know, the house feels so much lighter. Isn't that awful of me? They've been so good, but it's as if they daren't smile, not in this house of sorrows. And I can't tell them it's not really a house of sorrows; there's a definite sense of relief that I won't have to go through all the rigmarole of divorce, custody, sharing my girls with him and the new girlfriend...'

'Have you heard from her?'

'Not a word. Seems to me she's scuttled under some stone somewhere, and she's hoping it will all fade away once Andrew's funeral is out of the way. She could be quite embarrassed that she's the only employee from Sandford's who isn't at the funeral, and if that does turn out to be the case, she'll have to come up with some brilliant excuse for her absence, won't she? Isn't it strange how you can hate someone without knowing them at all?'

'I've never known you actually dislike somebody, and definitely not hate anybody. Don't let this fester inside you, Chan. You can get counselling, you know.'

'It's more counselling for Andrew's death I think I need.' She looked forlorn. 'It just seems so strange. And the police have never once said they were looking at it as anything but an accident, but the back wheel was bent, according to them. I just want to see what they're seeing, and put my mind at rest. All of this goes through my mind every night, and of course there are no answers.'

Jess hugged her. 'Oh, Chan, I don't know what to say. People keep saying to me that losing Grandpops will ease with time, and I want to say that to you, but nobody ever specifies how much time. Surely you don't believe, deep down, that somebody tried to kill Andrew?'

'I don't suppose I do believe it to that extent, I suppose I'm just raging against the injustice of a man of thirty-six being dead, and it not being due to natural causes. I can't say all of this to Mum and Dad, though, they'd have me sectioned. You're not going to have me sectioned, are you, Jess?'

Jess frowned. 'No, you daft bat. There's nothing stupid about anything you've said, but I do think maybe we need to put your mind at rest. Are we too late to get this bike back? Will they have already scrapped it, do you think?'

It seemed as if Chantelle's back suddenly became straight. 'I can find out. What shall I say? I suppose I should have a reason for wanting it back.'

'Why? It's your property. Just say you've changed your mind, and you'd like to dispose of it yourself, along with the broken helmet.'

'God, Jess, you're such a cool customer. I think of all sorts of convoluted and twisted reasons, and you say just tell them you want it. Put the kettle on, I'll ring DS Royce, and tell him. Of course, it may already have been scrapped, in which case I'll have to stop thinking about it and start my life over again.'

* * *

It hadn't been scrapped. Royce gave her directions to go to the compound and collect it, adding that he would tell the staff there that she wanted the bike returning to her.

'Why?' he asked.

'I don't know, to be honest. Maybe if his helmet was no longer hung up in the garage it wouldn't trouble me so much, but it is, and it was always hung next to the bike on the wall. It'll be like a memento to my husband, I suppose. And I hate the thought of it being crushed, it was such a large part of his life. Am I being silly?'

'No, of course you're not. It's just that once it's been returned to you, you'll have to dispose of it yourself if you change your mind. And I think you've enough on your plate at the moment.'

'I'll cope,' she said. 'And in a couple of years, when life is more on an even keel, maybe I'll consider having a clear-out of all his stuff in the garage and the shed, but not yet. For now, I want him here with me.'

They said goodbye and disconnected. Chantelle turned to Jess, who gave her a clap, and her cup of tea.

'Oscar for that,' Jess said. 'Even I believed you. But I'll go with you to collect it. We'll take my car for the bike, and the twins can travel as usual in yours.' She sipped at her own drink, then sat on the sofa.

'Mike's coming home tomorrow.'

'About bloody time,' Chantelle responded. 'The man's a moron just as much as Andrew was over the last six months or so.'

Jess laughed. 'Say it like it is, oh wise woman. He has contacted me fairly frequently, and don't forget he's been moving around the Far East, so I don't suppose it's been easy for him to keep in touch.'

'Jess, you're making excuses for him. He's always put his career before you, and made sure you were at home instead of at work so he'd always got clean clothes in the wardrobe.'

'Well, he's due for a surprise then, if that's all he thinks of me. I've not even been at home for longer than a couple of hours; Mabel and I are quite comfortable at Nan's place. And I need to be there. So he might be coming home but I won't be there with him. I actually think he's coming home earlier than he said when he disappeared. But you know what, Chan, I really don't care any more.'

'Wow! Go you. You going to tell him?'

'I'm going to tell him I want a baby. Then I'll give him a choice. What do you think he'll decide? Stay with me and father a child he doesn't want, or leave and find somebody else who doesn't want a baby and who will wash his shirts – and iron them!'

Chantelle sipped at her drink, hardly aware she was holding it, thoughtfully mulling the problem over. 'I think he'll stick to his guns.'

Jess laughed. 'I'm counting on it. I've been so unhappy for such a long time, and, truth is, I want out, but it will work so much better if it's a mutual agreement to split up, instead of me storming out to find somebody to sleep with who looks like David Beckham. Preferably.'

* * *

With the bike collected and balanced against the garage wall, Chantelle felt a huge waft of grief wash over her. Jess was aware as they stared at the battered appearance of it of just how sickening it was; the man who had ridden it for so many years was now in a coffin.

It felt as if it was a momentous point in such a sad part of

Chantelle's story as they stood looking at it, Daisy in Chantelle's arms and Lily in Jess's arms.

Lily spoke first. 'Daddy's bike,' she said.

'It is Daddy's bike,' Chantelle said, and felt Daisy squeeze her neck as if to comfort her. The girls didn't really understand, but knew enough to realise this was something unusual going on in the garage.

'Thank you,' Chantelle said quietly to Jess. 'Thank you for not telling me I'm an idiot, for supporting me and helping me bring this back here. When the girls are in bed, I'll get it put back on its hanger and cover it with the waterproof he had for it. He really took care of this,' she said pensively. 'Really took care of it. It was an expensive model, and he was proud of it. He didn't cover it at night, just if we went on holiday, or he was going away for a longish trip. I don't want to feel shocked every time I come into the garage, but after I've given it a good going over, I'll cover it until the time comes when I feel I can get rid of it. Come on, let's go in the house, it's quite cool in here. And I need to get the little monsters bathed ready for bed.'

'I not a monster,' Lily giggled.

'And I not a monster,' added Daisy.

Jess agreed with them. What she wouldn't give to have her own little monster...

'So can Aunty Jess sort bath time out, or does it have to be Mummy?'

They both squealed and wriggled out of their captors' arms. 'Aunty Jess!' shouted Lily, and they ran up the step out of the garage and through to the kitchen.

The two women looked at each other, and followed them.

'I hope you know what you've just let yourself in for.' Chantelle smiled. 'You'll be a soppy wet mess when you next exit that bathroom. Don't say I haven't warned you.'

She watched the three of them scamper upstairs, then briefly returned to the garage. Bending down, she stared at the rear of the bike. How the hell had that much damage happened to the back wheel? It must have been a hell of a rock it hit on its short journey across the field, after leaving the tarmacked road...

31

Mike Armstrong waited impatiently at the baggage return carousel, not looking forward to the long drive over the Pennines. The Woodhead Pass was a beautiful route but so damn long. Maybe he could talk to Jess about moving a little nearer to Manchester airport if the two aborted attempts to get a viable airport at Sheffield meant they wouldn't get a third chance – would she go for it? He had been told the Far East was going to be his speciality from now on, which meant many more flights and ergo many more trips across the massive range of hills running up the spine of the country. Definitely not a good thought. He spotted his suitcase come through the hatch and waited for it to reach his outstretched hand, then moved quickly to head across to the car park to collect his car.

He was soon heading along the motorways that linked him to the Woodhead, but it was only as he was dropping down the long road that culminated in Tintwistle that he realised he was closing his eyes every time the traffic drew to a halt. He was tired. Over-tired.

Once through the traffic lights at the bottom of the hill, he waited until he spotted a café, then pulled off the main road and parked up. Coffee time. He couldn't take chances on such an eminently dangerous road, he had to be fully awake.

Buns and Sarnies proved to be just what he needed, and he even approved of the bell that rang as he opened the door.

He walked along the counter, ordered a strong black coffee and a croissant, and headed towards a table for two in the corner. His sigh was deep. He really was tired, and now beginning to regret working most of the way home, instead of sleeping on the plane as most of his fellow passengers had done.

He was looking forward to being home. Jess was a remarkable homemaker, and he knew the house would be warm and welcoming for him. He glanced up at the waitress as she brought his order and thanked her before returning to his newspaper.

He ordered a second coffee once he'd drunk his first one, finished that and folded his paper before replacing it in his briefcase. He felt a little surprised that Jess hadn't responded to his text message to say he was back and on his way home but then guessed she was possibly out walking Mabel.

Setting off once more, he was pleased to realise the coffee had worked and he was now awake and able to properly concentrate on the winding mountain pass. By the time he reached the M1 for the last stretch back to his home, the effects of the coffee were beginning to wear off, his heart was no longer a little erratic, and he knew he was almost home when his bad language increased as he took on the overwhelming traffic of the M1. Fortunately he wasn't on it very long, and exited at the Catcliffe junction, knowing he was only ten minutes from home.

* * *

Mike was a little surprised to see no car on the drive, but inserted his key into the door and walked into his home. His cold home.

'Jess? Jessica? You upstairs?'

There was no answer and no bark. His brain might have been tired, but it only took seconds to figure out he was alone in the house.

She answered on the third ring.

'I'm here,' he said.

'Where?'

'Home.'

'Oh. Welcome home, Mike.'

'Where are you? It's cold in this house.'

'If it's that cold, put the heating on. I'll maybe pop round later to see you.'

There was a silence while he worked out what to say. I'll maybe pop round later to see you? She lived here, didn't she?

'Jess, where are you?'

'Where on God's earth do you think I am? Grandpops died last week and I'm at Nan's house with Mabel.'

'But I'm home now.'

'That should have happened a week ago.' Her tone was icy as she realised just how selfish he was being.

'You know I couldn't just up and leave Japan. My job doesn't work like that.'

'Maybe it should have. Anyway, that's where I am, but I'm sure Nan will be pleased to see you if you want to come over. And try to remember she's lost her daughter as well as her husband, and only about twelve hours apart.'

'But aren't you coming here? I need to...' He realised he was speaking to nobody. She had disconnected without even saying goodbye, and it slowly dawned on him he'd done something wrong. It wasn't very often Jess took umbrage about anything, but

she seemed to be a bit pissed off with him at the moment. Whatever he had done, he decided, it was mistake number one.

Mistake number two was in going upstairs and just lying on the bed for a minute. He woke five hours later desperate for a wee, to find the house still empty apart from himself.

Life seemed to have taken a turn for the worse, and he hurriedly showered and jumped in the car to go to the Wheeler house.

* * *

Mike gave a brief knock on the back door and walked into the kitchen; he sensed the atmosphere immediately. There was a sorrow in the air. A deep sorrow. And suddenly he knew his marriage wasn't going to recover from this. He should have left Japan the second he'd received Jess's phone call, his company would have understood. But he put his job first, his wife second. Again.

He stood for a moment, listening for any sounds that would indicate where anyone was. He could hear a faint murmur of voices, so decided they must be downstairs, and probably in the lounge.

He walked quietly through and heard his wife speaking.

'I no longer care,' she was saying. 'I've had it with him. This past week has been the worst time of my life, and where was he? In bloody Japan.'

He waited, expecting somebody to answer her, but they didn't. She continued to speak and he realised she was on her phone. And from her tone of voice, it was probably another Coven member. This left the question: where was Nora? Jess wouldn't have been talking like that to one of her gang of four, as he thought of them, if her nan had been in the room.

He headed back to the kitchen, and the door opened; Nora walked in carrying a bunch of chrysanthemums.

She looked at him for a moment. 'You're back then. Took your time, didn't you?'

'I fell asleep,' he admitted. 'I worked on the flight coming back, so didn't get any sleep. When I got in, I absolutely zonked out.'

'Well, that's a real pity, Mike.' She brushed past him towards the sink. 'I just need to put these in some water.' She busied herself finding the right size vase for the highly perfumed blooms, and then turned to him. 'I know I should keep out of this, but I love my granddaughter more than life, as you know. So I am going to say it, and what you do with it is up to you. Okay?'

He couldn't speak. Nora had never said a word out of place to him, so this woman standing before him, like a lioness defending her cub, was a stranger in his life.

'Currently, in Jess's mind, she wants two things. The first is a job and the second is a baby. If you say no to either of those two things, she'll say yes. If you don't want a divorce, you have to learn to go with what she wants for a change. I know so much more, but it's up to Jess to tell you. However, if you don't listen to me today, you'll be able to continue to act like the single man you obviously think you are, with a housemaid to attend to all your needs. Only the housemaid will have flown the coop, understand?'

He sat on the kitchen chair with a thud. He'd only heard a tiny part of the phone conversation from a couple of minutes earlier, but it was enough to confirm Nora's words.

'Brandy?' she asked when she saw the colour of his cheeks.

He shook his head. 'Is Grandpops's shed open?'

'It is. When you come back up, lock it after you, will you, please? It'll save me going down later.'

He stood and walked to the end of the back garden path, opened the door and slipped inside. The chair was an old wooden armchair, and he sank down onto the cushion. This had always been the thinking place for Grandpops, and he had spent some hours in the little eight-foot-long wooden building. This was his first time in it without the older man.

He stayed there for an hour or so, just thinking through everything. It appeared, from the harsh words Nora had used, that he was the world's worst husband. But he'd never cheated, he'd loved Jess ever since they'd met, and he'd always considered them the perfect match. Apparently that wasn't so.

He mulled over the various options available to him for the rest of his life; even the sword of Damocles now hanging over him wouldn't push him into making rash decisions, but he knew Nora wouldn't have been so vociferous if she hadn't cared. Although he did wonder if it was just her granddaughter she cared about and not her grandson-in-law.

Had she been implying he was a bully? That's how it felt, but having certain expectations in life didn't mean it was bullying. Did it? His mind was moving out of control, and he laid back his head and closed his eyes. He still hadn't seen his wife, and she hadn't ventured down the garden to him, even though he knew Nora would have told her where he was. She would have said he was doing an Arthur, taking time out to sort out his head.

'Where is he then?'

'I've told you, he's in the shed. Leave him be, he obviously needs thinking time. Give him ten more minutes then take him a hot drink down if you're so keen to speak with him, but he looked quite shaken to the core when he first went down the garden. I might have been a bit abrupt with him.'

Jess grinned at her nan. 'A bit abrupt? What the hell did you say that's made him go off to commune with the fairies in the shed at the bottom of the garden? Grandpops always said that was what he was doing, didn't he?' She felt tears prickle her eyes, and wondered if this would continue to happen every time she thought of Arthur. She guessed it would.

She made tea, automatically making it in the teapot because that was the way Mike liked it, and carried the mug down the garden. She stopped to sniff the late season roses, thinking how much love Grandpops had put into his rose garden, and how he would frequently bring one into the house to present it with a flourish to the love of his life, his Nora. And Nora would smile and accept it graciously.

She reached the shed, and pulled open the door. Mike immediately stood, but didn't move.

'I've brought you a tea. I've made it in the teapot, as you like it.'

And that was the moment all of Mike's jumbled thoughts reached fruition. He took the cup from her and placed it on the workbench so lovingly crafted and installed by Arthur.

'Thank you. And I've been thinking, Jess. I've sat here for the last hour with Grandpops's fairies, and I've reached a decision. You can have what you want.'

Jess stared at him. 'A baby?'

'No. Not quite. A divorce.'

32

Jess watched him walk back up the garden and round the side of the house, listening for the sound of his car starting before heading back up to the kitchen. On the way up, she broke off a yellow rose and carried it up with her.

Nan was in the lounge, attempting to read a book, but all the time listening for sounds from the kitchen. She'd had the feeling all day that it was a make-or-break day for her granddaughter and the husband she had grown away from, and recognising that she had gone through a similar situation over thirty years earlier, she wanted to make sure she was there for Jess, no matter what solution was reached. It was so hard to make life decisions like giving up completely, or struggling on and learning to love again with the original person. And she had done that for sure. Her illicit love would always be in her heart, but she had loved Arthur very deeply.

Which was why she completely fell apart when Jess walked in with the rose, and performed the Arthur flourish as she presented it to her nan.

'Oh, Jess,' she sobbed. 'If there was anything designed to bring me to my knees, this is it.'

Jess pulled her nan into her arms and simply held her. 'Thank goodness you're crying. You've needed to do this, it's all part of the healing. We'll have many more tears, so don't hold back.'

'You've sorted things with Mike?' Nora scrubbed her eyes with a tissue.

'Kind of. I feel as if it should be me that's crying and blubbering all over the place, and I'm sure I will when the decree absolute comes through, but today I feel a sense of relief. It's over, Nan.'

Nora tried to hide the shock she was feeling. Of all the things she could have envisaged, this was the most unexpected outcome. She had thought Mike would see how unhappy Jess was, but once again the selfish Mike had surfaced.

'You'll stay here?'

'If that's okay. Once we've settled everything, I can start to look for a place of my own, but at the moment I think we need each other.'

'You seem very calm about it.'

'I am. I actually think I made the decision it was over when Erin offered me the job in the tea shop. I knew it would cause an argument at home, and I knew I was worth more than that.'

'So much more, Jess. So much more.'

* * *

Siân checked out of the Hilton, stowed her luggage in the car boot and left Sheffield with a feeling of sadness. So much had changed. She felt as if she had lived a lie for the past thirty years, and wondered just how, and with who, there had managed to be communication with Sheffield over the years. Anna had obviously set up some sort of system to cover an emergency situation, and it had been triggered for the first time recently, causing Anna to scurry off to Sheffield. And that had cost her.

It seemed even the police were baffled. They had called her to thank her for allowing full access to the shop and her home, and had confirmed no additional mobile phone had been found. She had been tempted to say *I told you so* but resisted. However, somewhere there was another phone, one that wasn't helping them at all, one that Anna had used before she was murdered.

How she hated that word. Murder. It was brutal, and her Anna wasn't a brutal person. If Anna had died of natural causes, she could have taken that, and she could have been with her in her last moments, but this was another brutal side to it, this knowing Anna had died alone, scared and defenceless against a knife.

She switched on Radio 2, wanting music that wasn't irritating. Middle-of-the-road stuff was about all she could handle at the moment. She settled back for the long journey over the Pennines and into her heritage, Wales.

* * *

The FaceTime Coven call that night was later than usual. The twins didn't want to go to bed, they wanted to go to the sand. They hadn't believed their mother when she tried to tell them that Sheffield didn't possess any sand, not like Whitby did anyway.

As a result, World War III had erupted, the bathroom had turned into an ocean and buckets and spades had been used in the bath, in the absence of sand.

By the time Chantelle called everyone back, she looked and felt like a drowned rat. 'They're in bed,' she said. 'They're actually in bed. An hour late but peace is back in my house. I've read *Three Little Pigs* five times! Is this normal?'

'No idea, but well done on not strangling them.'

'How do you know I haven't?' Chantelle said, lowering her voice to its spooky best.

''Cos ya loves them babies with everything you've got,' Jess joined in, smiling at her friend.

'Okay, maybe I gave them a bunch of kisses, but they're asleep now, thank goodness. So, is everybody okay?'

Jess held up her hand as if she was in school. 'Can I speak first so nobody makes me cry?'

'Course you can. What's wrong?' There was concern in Mel's voice.

'Mike and I have split up.'

There was a moment of stunned silence, and then all three spoke together. Jess held up a hand, but this time it was to calm everyone down.

'Let me tell you what happened, or as much of it as I know. It seems my nan had a go at him about me being unhappy. He went down into Grandpops's shed and sat for an hour or so thinking things through. Anyway, it seems he can't accept his wife going out to work, and he definitely can't accept her wanting a baby, so he's going down the divorce route. So, do any of you know David Beckham?'

'I don't, but my builder's quite nice,' Erin said with a laugh. 'He's currently footloose and fancy free, so he says.'

'Didn't he have a wife when he did your upstairs room? I thought she came with him on a couple of days.'

'He did, but she liked somebody from work better than she liked him.' Erin laughed. 'I can always put in a word...'

'Don't you bloody dare,' Jess exploded. 'I'm not interested in anybody till I've got rid of the current one, thank you very much. Anyway, obviously it's upset me, but I'm not exactly devastated. It's very liberating to have a useless husband start talking about divorce.'

'Then good for you,' Erin said. 'We're here for you when it gets a bit rough, as I'm sure it will. He'll want everything his own way. Perhaps Mel can get you an appointment with her friend, Caroline?'

'Definitely. I'll give her a call for you on Monday. That okay with you, Jess?'

'It is. I was going to ask anyway. I really don't know what I'd do without you three supporting me. Nan had a good cry today, which was good, and it was all because I brought her a rose in from the garden. Grandpops used to do that for her.'

Erin laughed. 'He used to do that cavalier thing for her, and bend at the waist before presenting it to her.'

'Exactly. I did the same, and she burst out crying. I actually think it did her good to cry because she's not been heartbroken. Know what I mean? It's like she was holding it all back.'

Chantelle began to speak. 'Are we done? Anything else to report?'

'Only that Siân has returned to Wales until Grandpops's funeral, then she'll come back. We've not heard anything else from the police today, but when Siân rang Nan to say she was going home she said the police hadn't found any second phone. They've searched their home and their shop. It's such a mess.'

'We all feel so sorry for you, Jess. You've had a shitty few days, and there's nothing the rest of us can do to help except be here. We love you and Nan, never forget that.'

'I won't. Speak to you all tomorrow probably.'

* * *

Saturday drifted to an end. Jess made hot chocolates for the two of them, and Nan felt warmed by the thought as much as by the drink. They played two games of Scrabble, winning one game each but feeling too tired and a little too affected by memories to play the decider. Playing Scrabble had been something they had both done with Arthur, and knowing that could never happen again was daunting.

As they put the tiles into the little bag, Nora spoke softly. 'Did he say when he was going away again?'

'Mike? I think it's Monday. Why?'

'We should go to your house on Monday and get as much of your stuff as we can bring. You have little bits and bobs that are important to you, plus all your clothes, and I think we need to get them out of harm's way, don't you?'

'You think he'd be so vindictive as to destroy stuff?'

'I do. Because although you've told me it was him that specifically said he wanted a divorce, I think his mind will twist that round to it being you that wanted it. He's been thwarted by you wanting a baby, that's what the true issue is, but because that's not normal he'll look for something to blame you with, and that will be seen in his mind as you walking away from him.'

'Thwarted. What a wonderful word. But you're probably right. I obviously can't ask him when he's going and where he's going to, but I can ask Rosa, his secretary. She books all his airline and train tickets so I'll invent a fictitious holiday I want to book but I need to know when he's free and when he's going next because I want to book a weekend away in a couple of weeks.'

Nora laughed. 'Make sure you get your thoughts properly in place before you ring her, because even I could tell you were winging it on that bit of invention. You can ring her tomorrow?'

'I can. He made sure I had her mobile number just in case. Says she knows his itinerary down to the last minute. Let's hope he is going Monday, because it doesn't give him any time to do anything. Am I being paranoid now?'

'No, but I don't trust him. He's all about himself, isn't he? Let's not leave anything to chance. Make a list of all your stuff you need to remember to collect, and we'll go together.'

Jess packed the entire game away into the box that was starting to require sticky tape to hold it together, and replaced it in Nan's sideboard. She spotted some packets of medication, and some that were in bottles. She picked one up and looked at it. It bore her grandfather's name.

'Did you know, Nan?' she asked, and waved the box.

'Not how close to the end he was. I've known for some time what it was that would eventually kill him, and we had discussed when would be the right time to tell you. He knew it would change you once you found out, and he didn't want that to happen. But we thought he still had around six months left.'

'But I could have supported you more.'

'Jess, my darling, you have always supported us. You couldn't have done any more for us, and Grandpops knew that, so don't fret. He knew how much you loved him, just as I'll know that when it's time for me to go.'

33

Monday morning saw Sergeant Owen Donald staring at his screen and thinking, 'Sod it.' It might be autumnally cold outside but it was better than being in the heat inside caused by a newly refurbished heating system that wanted to prove how well it was working.

'Cerys!' he called. 'You're with me today.'

Cerys held up a thumb to signify she'd heard his summons, and stood. He was putting on his jacket, which meant he wanted out of the office right now, so she grabbed her own padded coat. It had been a smart move to go back inside and grab it once she'd stepped outside her home that morning and felt the unusual chill in the air.

She caught up with him as he was trying to persuade his car to unlock, something they had to contend with every time they got in it. 'Time you got that lock fixed, boss,' she said, knowing it was the same words she used every time they took his car.

'Oh, shut up,' he said. Familiar words to her in retaliation for the words she always used.

'So where are we going?'

'Costa.'

'Right. Burglary? Murder? Kidnap? You want to fill me in?'

'Coffee. And not drive through. We're going inside.'

'You definitely know how to treat a girl, sarge.'

'I know. It's your turn to pay.'

He pulled into the car park and they walked across to the coffee shop, where Owen found them a table. Even at this early hour it was busy, and Owen cast a casual glance around. He recognised one or two faces – living in such a close community meant he knew many people that hadn't come under the police radar for any reason, and he raised his hand in acknowledgement of a lady who one day had lost her kitten and called the police for help. He had found it for her, and she always seemed to want to kiss him now. He hoped it wouldn't happen again in front of Cerys, who never failed to take the mickey out of him for being irresistible to the elderly of their area.

Cerys sat down, carefully placing the tray with its over-full drinks on the table. 'I got us a packet of biscuits as well,' she announced.

'Living the high life today, then.'

'We are. We got anything to do after this?'

'We have. We're actually out killing a bit of time. I need to take the keys for Anna Wheeler's home and shop back to the lady who owns the shop next door. They're the spare keys she keeps for them in case they ever lose their keys. She doesn't open till ten, so we'll give her time to warm the shop up before we intrude. And I'd tell you her name if I could remember it.'

'Dilys Braine. I typed it into my report.'

'Thanks. I knew there was a reason I'd rescued you from the heat of that office this morning.'

'Strange we didn't find a spare phone, isn't it?'

He shrugged. 'In one way it is, because if anybody were ever to search my house for one, they'd probably find about four because I never get rid of them when I get an upgrade, but not everybody's like that. And it was only a theory that she was contacted via burner phones set up specifically for emergency calls from Sheffield to her. Still, it's not our case, we're just the dogsbodies for South Yorkshire Police on this one, so we don't have to do much thinking, just complete the task and get out of it. I've got one of her pieces, you know.'

'Anna Wheeler?'

'Yes. She always signs Anna W. She was so talented. I walked past the shop one day and bang in the centre was a display of her pottery. The focal point was a bear. I wanted to go in and buy it right there and then. It was like a real one, you felt you could touch the fur. It didn't have a price on it that was visible, but I told my wife about it. I went past a couple of days later and it had gone. I felt gutted I wouldn't see it again, but it was in my Christmas stocking that year.'

'Well, it will increase in value now,' ever-pragmatic Cerys said, and sipped at her coffee.

'I regret never meeting her. I could have called into that shop at any point and told her I'd got the bear, but I didn't. I'll always regret that.'

'You're turning soft, sarge.'

He grinned. 'I'll toughen up. I picked the bear up and had a good look at it last night, and it really is a perfect piece of work.'

'Wonder what will happen to the shop now. If she built up a stock, it won't last for ever, and nobody could replicate her. Maybe Siân Jefferies will sell up. She was devastated, wasn't she?'

'They'd been together for many years. And survived all the shitty times when two women living together wasn't acceptable, to now, when nobody thinks twice about it.' Owen reached across and helped himself to a ginger biscuit. 'Delicious,' he added as he crunched on it. 'Don't tell the wife, she's put me on a diet.'

'We had fish and chips for lunch on Friday.'

'I told her I'd had a seafood salad.'

'I won't lie for you,' she warned him, with a little wag of her finger. 'You're on your own, buster, if she asks me the direct question.'

'Spoilsport,' he grumbled, and reached for a second biscuit. 'And I thought you were a friend.'

It was just after ten when they reached Dilys Crystals. The shop had been there seemingly forever, but in reality had only opened six months before Anna and Siân opened their Artisans of Criccieth shop.

The two shops had always complemented each other, and customers who wandered around inspecting the wares made by artists from the community tended to head straight for Dilys Crystals as their next port of call. With the growth of Criccieth as a spectacular place to visit and stay, the two shops had grown, along with the friendship between the owners. They each held keys for the other's shop and helped out when deliveries were expected during the long winter months when they tended to take their sunshine holidays, and it had always worked out to the benefit of everyone.

Dilys saw the two police officers as they paused outside the shop window to look at the huge amethyst crystal on display all on its own. It needed nothing else to set it off other than a scrunched-up piece of deep purple silk at its base.

She watched as their eyes never left the centrepiece. It was a magnificent piece, and she prayed her security was enough to protect it. She greeted them with a smile as they came through the door.

'Have you come to return the keys?'

'We have, and thank you for being so understanding. We needed to check there wasn't a mobile phone hidden somewhere on the premises that would give us a clue as to who contacted Siân to get her to travel to Sheffield.'

Dilys stared at him. 'Is that what it was all about? If you hadn't been so secretive about needing the keys, maybe I could have helped you out.'

'You have Anna's second phone?' Just for a second, Owen's heart rate jumped.

But she shook her head. 'No, nothing so technical. What I do have is a twenty-odd-year arrangement in place that could possibly help you. I'll start at the beginning, shall I?'

She sat down on the high stool behind her counter then stood up again. 'I'll close up for ten minutes, because if this is police information, we don't want anybody walking in, do we? God, they'll spread rumours about me being a police informant, and I'd never get to know any gossip ever again.'

Cerys grinned at Owen, and they waited until Dilys returned to her stool, the door securely locked, with the 'CLOSED' sign in place.

'Okay, now bear with me because this all happened many years ago. The three of us got a bit tipsy, me, Anna and Siân. Siân fell asleep because she's a lightweight when it comes to alcohol, and Anna and I carried on drinking and talking about our younger years. It's how I discovered Anna came from Sheffield. Her Yorkshire accent gave away her county, but she told me that night that she had a mum and dad in Sheffield, and that she'd walked away to make her own way in life, ending up in Cardiff. It's where she met Siân,' she added as an afterthought.

'We chatted far into the night, getting drunker and drunker, and she confessed to me that her only worry was the health of her parents as they got older and could I be a go-between. I hadn't a clue what she wanted, but it turned out she didn't want Siân bringing into her family issues. The Welsh part of her life was a separate entity, but whether Siân knew it or not, she did still have parents who weren't getting any younger. She asked me if it was okay if she gave my phone number to an old friend in Sheffield, and if ever either her mum or her dad needed her help the friend would contact me to tell her to ring Sheffield. It effectively kept Siân away from asking questions, or pushing her to visit Sheffield. Or taking phone calls from people she didn't know even existed.'

She paused for a moment and looked at the two officers. 'You still with me? It was a very drunken night, and of course I agreed. Until last week, I never thought about it again but one night I got a call. Sunday, I think. It was a woman and she asked me to pass on a message. The message was simply "Ask Anna to ring Sheffield", and it brought that night back to me. I went round to their place straight away, using a tiny crystal as a pretext. It had been carved into a tiny giraffe, and I had saved it for Siân anyway, as she collects giraffes. Not real ones,' she added.

'You passed on the message?'

'I did, and all Anna did was nod. Then she went out to make the phone call, but not on her mobile. She wanted no information anywhere until it was unavoidable. You see, that night she told me something else. She always rings Sheffield on 23 April, every year. She didn't say why, but I assumed it was possibly to speak to a married woman who she'd not been able to be with. It was pure guesswork, believe me, but she uses the public phone box up at the top of that road opposite the Spar shop down the village.'

'And she used that phone box that Sunday night?'

'She did. I'd seen her use it before on that special date, so I watched for where she went. She was there for about a minute then walked back down. What a disaster Sheffield proved to be for her.'

Cerys rang forensics, explained they needed the call log for one specific phone box, and within five minutes the call box was sealed with crime scene tape. BT were contacted for an immediate print-out of all calls both in and out of the call box for that Sunday evening and Owen was left to put Dilys's twisted and convoluted tale into a statement that would actually make some sense once this case came to court.

Much to everyone's surprise, it only took BT an hour to produce the information they needed. It hadn't been an arduous task; hardly anybody uses call boxes, the BT operative had explained. And there was one call to a Sheffield landline listed. The landline was registered to a Suzanne Chatterton of Larkspur Close in Sheffield.

34

The ruse of ringing Rosa, Mike's secretary, with her story of wanting to book a surprise holiday left Jess with the knowledge that on that Monday morning Mike was already on his way to a series of conferences in the south of England, the last one being Thursday evening. She could expect him home sometime Friday.

'Then let's take both cars and we'll go and remove everything you want to bring away from this bloody awful marriage. Do we need any of the girls to help? Fully Booked is closed on Mondays, so maybe Mel and Erin are free.'

'We'll ask if we need them, but I don't think we will. There's not that much I want, it's mainly my journals, my books, stuff like that. Things that have made me who I am. I'd hate him to take his annoyance out on my journals, he knows how much I cherish them. My life from being eighteen is in them. There's a couple of suitcases I can use to pack my clothes, but to be honest, when I do get my own place, I won't want anything I had with him, so it's stuff that's personal to only me that we'll be bringing back with us. All Mabel's things are already here apart from a couple of bags of food, so we'll bring that as well. He'll not want dog food unless he suddenly realises nobody is there to do any food shopping, and he's a bit hungry.'

Jess giggled, and Nora felt heartened by it. There had hardly been a smile all weekend. Then she broke out into giggles at the thought of Mike only having dog food in the house. Would he know how to make some gravy to mush it up a bit?

'Right, let's put Mabel in the kitchen with some food, water and her bed, then we can get off and get it over with. We have a lot of other stuff on our minds that's a bit more important than Mike Armstrong and his selfishness.'

* * *

The cars were groaning with extra weight despite protestations from Jess that she had hardly anything to bring. It was only as she was walking around the house for what she hoped was the last time that she spotted things like her laptop, the sewing machine and everything that went with that major item, the Christmas tree that he didn't want her to buy because he said it was too showy; everything and more was loaded into both cars, and by just after one o'clock they were ready for their journey back to Nora's house.

'Does Mike have a key for my house?' Nora asked.

Jess shook her head. 'No, he never needed one. Why?'

'I didn't want him turning up one day and taking stuff back. If he has a key, we can't call it burglary as such, but if he doesn't, it's breaking and entering.'

'You think he will turn up?'

'Not really. It's called forward planning, Jess. I'm just preparing for the what ifs in this life.'

They took their time driving home, recognising instantly that the cars weren't responding in quite the same way as when they had no weight in them. Nora pulled her car onto the drive first, as she rarely drove. Jess would be in and out frequently.

'Use the third bedroom, Jess. You don't want all of this in your room, so until you do get your own place you can store everything in the spare room.'

'Thanks, Nan. I hadn't given much thought to what I wanted to do with it once I'd got it here. I'm just glad that's over, I kept expecting Mike to walk in while we were packing things up. That could have been a bit awkward.'

'You think?' Nora laughed at her granddaughter. 'My money's still on you to come out the winner. And he'd have had to get past me to get to you. That wouldn't have been the easiest thing to do.'

Jess pretended to be hungry. The truth was that she felt sick, as the fact that her marriage was over rolled around her in waves. Nora volunteered to make them a sandwich and a hot drink, while Jess took some of the things upstairs, so Jess then cracked on with it, knowing her nan was busy in the kitchen. Having a nan who refused to accept she was getting older and thought she could still do things that thirty-year-olds did was ludicrous. But Nan was Nan, so Jess had to take everything upstairs at a hundred miles an hour.

They sat down to eat their lunch, and Nan said she would give her a hand with the rest of the things after they'd eaten.

'It's done, thanks, Nan,' Jess said. 'I've got it all up there, and tomorrow I'll go through it all and get it stashed away as tidily as I can. It looks a bit of a mess at the moment, so I closed the door.'

'What? All of it is up there?'

'All of it except the sewing machine, and I've purposely left that down here to repair those curtains for you.'

'You're a good girl,' Nan said, then frowned. 'I think. Have I just been conned into doing some lunch so that you could run up and down stairs, stopping me doing it?'

Jess grinned. 'As if I'd do something like that. Now shut up, old woman, and eat your yoghurt.'

* * *

Suzanne couldn't eat anything. She took an extra morphine tablet, despite the doctor telling her not to until the time came when it was really painful, but this afternoon the time had arrived. She was finding it increasingly difficult helping out at Fully Booked, and knew confessions of what was wrong with her were looming if she didn't take matters into her own hands pretty soon.

She felt a sense of relief that Mel and Erin had finally found each other, because Erin was going to need massive levels of support for all sorts of reasons over the next few weeks, and Suzanne knew she wouldn't be here to support her. It seemed that she and Arthur had reached the same decision: to hide the diagnosis until it was too late. Protect the girls. That was what it was all about, protecting the girls from the more horrible parts of life that couldn't be changed. She had spent her entire life protecting the girls – and Jake Chatterton, the ex-husband, had been the first to go.

She couldn't trust him. He had touched Erin when she was little, and Erin had told her mother, without actually realising what she was talking about. At three years of age, the little girl knew it wasn't a nice feeling, but she didn't know why. Jake was out within the hour, and out of Suzanne's life for good a few months later. Jake Chatterton got away light. She now knew she could have done so much more.

Living on her own meant she wasn't answerable to anyone, and nobody had seen the stock of high-dosage morphine that she had accumulated. Soon it would diminish considerably, and then everyone would know. Except her. She wouldn't know anything, and she was at that point.

She thought Tia had noticed she wasn't functioning properly when she had tidied and dusted the shelves, and the pain had been almost unbearable, hence the early finish. But Tia hadn't realised, because if she had, Erin would have been round to see what was going on.

Protect the girls, tell them nothing. It was all everybody had done since the day they were born. Four girls in six months, a joyous time, with only one fly in the ointment. Anna.

If Anna had told them what was on her mind, they would have been there for her. But one day she was there, the next she wasn't, and only Suzanne had known her secret. Anna had to give up her daughter, her beautiful Jessica, to keep her mother with her father, the man who would have had nothing to live for if Nora left him. Anna had seen Graham Barker and Nora in his car, and they weren't having driving lessons.

Suzanne was afraid of forgetting something. She had to make sure Laura and Samuel, Tracy Marsden and all four girls knew why she had done what she'd known she had to do. And Nora Wheeler. With Arthur gone, the whole world could know about her now, the sanctimonious cow. She had been the start of it all, the one to drive Anna away and cause pain to Jess, who would never know a mother's love. She intended that Nora would, one day very soon, realise she was the cheating wife who had started all of this.

Some of her girls had been hurting; but Chantelle and her babies had now had the hurt taken away, Jess likewise it seemed, if Erin had got the story correct, and Erin and Mel were no longer hurting, so Suzanne knew it was time. Her job was done; two deaths and her girls were all back on the right tracks.

She sat at the kitchen table, holding tightly to a stomach that was so full of pain. She prayed the tablets would work quickly and she prayed she could get them all down.

The piece of paper had been on the table since the day she had had to leave Fully Booked early, her story waiting to be written. She would take the paper into the lounge along with the dish full of tablets, and begin to take them as she finished off the already partially completed letter. By the time her brain started to close down, the letter would be finished and she prayed all her girls would know how much she had loved them, and why she had used her own special way of protecting them.

She pulled the boxes and tubs of tablets towards her and began to pop them out of the blister packs into a bowl that she would, in her previous pain-free life, have used to eat cornflakes for breakfast. Now she couldn't face the thought of breakfast, or lunch, or dinner. Slowly she filled the dish, and even she was surprised by the number of tablets. She would die quickly, of that she was sure. She already had a very weakened system, and it wouldn't cope with the amount of medication she was about to introduce into her body.

She put everything onto a tray and carried it through to the lounge, pausing in the doorway as waves of intense pain washed through her. She stumbled as she reached the sofa, but manged to stop the wine from falling over. She pulled the coffee table closer to her, poured out a glass full of wine and took two tablets out of the dish. She took ten minutes to finish off the letter and then stroked it, folding it carefully into three. She liked to be neat.

And now she had to leave the letter for everyone to see. Including the police. Her resignation letter.

I resign from this life. Signed Suzanne Chatterton. PS Don't let Jake Chatterton come to my funeral.

* * *

DI Marshall received the phone call from Owen Donald in Criccieth before he received the email from him confirming the details. He'd been feeling so frustrated by everything coming through as negative, and suddenly the answer was in front of him.

'Ginny,' he called, 'sort out a second car with two uniforms in, and you come with me in my car. We're going to pick up our suspect.'

The two cars left the car park at the same time, and headed out to Larkspur Close, with Paul Marshall filling Ginny in on the information he had just been given.

'Who is she?'

'No idea, but I reckon we're about to find out. It seems she was the go-between for keeping Anna Wheeler informed of all that was going on with her parents, but Anna was also ringing Suzanne Chatterton every 23 April because that is Anna's daughter's birthday. So she kept tabs on Jess, albeit from some distance. Strange world, isn't it?'

35

Both police cars pulled up outside the house on Larkspur Close that had been Suzanne's home for over thirty-five years. Since Erin had inherited Fully Booked, she had lived there alone.

And died there alone.

The two uniformed officers remained in their car, patiently waiting until they got the call from Ginny to say they were needed inside. Paul Marshall and Ginny Keswick walked up the garden path, and Ginny knocked on the front door.

'She should be in, there's a car parked on her front.'

'No guarantee, Sherlock,' Ginny said with a smile. 'She could be out jogging, or taken the dog for a walk. I know it feels like this is the end of the case, but have a little patience.' She knocked again. 'This is the road where all those baby girls were born back in the day. It's kind of gone full circle, hasn't it? Hope that germ's gone away now.'

They waited a further minute then Owen banged hard with his fist, bent down and called through the letterbox, 'Ms Chatterton? It's the police. Please come to your door.'

He moved along the front of the house and lifted his hand to his forehead to peer in through the bay window. Then he banged on the window. Ginny reached him quickly. 'She's on the sofa,' he said, 'but not moving. Not responding to all this banging – that doesn't sound good. We've got to get in here. See if you can find an unlocked back door, Ginny, and I'll get the other two out of their car and we'll try to get in the front door. I've a bad feeling about this.'

Ginny ran, and forced open a locked gate that kept intruders out of the back garden. It didn't keep her out, but the rear door was locked anyway, so she made her way around to the front, where the main door lock suddenly gave, and they were in.

Paul went straight to the woman on the sofa, and held his fingers to her neck. He looked up at Ginny and shook his head. 'Get a paramedic here urgently, stress overdose, but we're much too late. She's already starting to go cold.'

He slipped on some gloves and picked up the letter. He quickly scanned it, and turned to Ginny with a nod. 'It's all explained, and more, in this. She meant it.'

Ginny used her own gloved hand to pick up one of the empty tablet boxes. 'Powerful stuff,' she said. 'And it's in her name. These are the tablets my dad had when he was nearing the end with pancreatic cancer. Really strong pain control. He used to ask me for an extra half dozen when the pain was really bad, and I was tempted...'

'You didn't?'

She shook her head. 'He said I didn't love him enough to help him, but the truth was I loved him too much to let him go before his time was up. Obviously Suzanne guessed we would be coming round at some point, and made her own decision. I'm not sure I could be this brave, no matter how bad the pain is.'

'Don't read the letter yet, you need to read it slowly, but take a photo of it as this letter will be whisked away and handed to the coroner. We have stuff to follow up as a result of Suzanne Chatterton's death.'

He held the letter open for Ginny to take the photograph, and then she forwarded it to his phone. He folded it back up and left it where he had found it, on the coffee table amidst the detritus of the empty tablet boxes, and still half-full bowl of tablets. He then photographed the entire coffee table.

With the arrival of the paramedic who confirmed life extinct, and the arrival a few minutes later of the vehicle that would be used to transport Suzanne to the morgue for post-mortem, it suddenly became a very busy scene. Paul walked outside, leaving Ginny to deal with the medics. He recognised the two women standing at the garden fence; Jess was on her phone and speaking quickly.

'Hi, Mrs Wheeler,' he said to the older woman. 'You know this lady?'

'Very well,' Nora said. 'We've lived here as long as Suzanne has. What's happened? Is this connected to Anna being killed?'

'I'm sorry, we have to speak with next of kin before I can say anything.'

Nora pointed to Jess. 'Jess is on the phone to her daughter right now, and they're just getting in the car to shoot over here. Her name is Erin Chatterton, and she's the owner of the Fully Booked bookshop. Her partner will be with her, and she's called Melissa Marsden.'

As she spoke, Mel's dark blue Toyota came round the corner at considerable speed and pulled up outside Suzanne's home. Paul Marshall moved to stop her going inside, and then said a few words to her.

Jess and Nora walked over towards Mel, who was clinging on to Erin, trying to stop her crumpling towards the ground. Jess helped her hold Erin, and Paul led them gently to the squad car, which was empty. Erin and Mel sat in the back seat, and Jess waited by the side of it, knowing that if Erin looked bad now, she was going to look a lot worse in a couple of minutes. She locked eyes with Mel, and they both shook their heads.

Nora had lost all her colour. These girls were clearly suffering and for the moment she couldn't do anything to help them. She spoke softly to Jess, telling her she was going home and she would put the kettle on. 'Bring Mel and Erin over when they take Suzanne away, because it seems to me that Suzanne is dead, even though the policeman wouldn't confirm it. And don't forget to ring Chantelle. She may need to make arrangements to get the twins to Laura and Samuel.'

Jess gave a quick nod, and watched Nora as she walked back across the tiny cul-de-sac to get to their home.

Erin was crying, and although Jess couldn't tell what the DI was saying, it was obvious it was the worst news. Mel was holding her, so Jess took out her phone and spoke with Chantelle.

'I'll be there in two minutes. The girls have gone super-market shopping with Mum and Dad. I'll ring Mum and ask her to stay here when they bring the girls home, so I can be wher-ever I'm needed. Shit, Jess, what the hell is going on? And why Suzanne? Was she poorly and we didn't know? This was how I felt about Grandpops, he was poorly and we didn't know. Okay, I've kind of got a coat on, I'm leaving the house now. Be there in no time.'

And so it was that all four women were at the house when Suzanne was taken away. Erin was the only one not mopping up her tears, because she couldn't find any more tears to cry. She felt dead. This was her mother, who, it seemed, had this massive pile of painkillers to handle the cancer that, once again, nobody had known about.

Jess shepherded them all across to Nora's, where teas and

coffees began to make them feel a little more normal, but the unexpectedness of what had happened would never leave them.

* * *

Paul Marshall and Ginny Keswick felt a little numb themselves. Although they hadn't known Suzanne Chatterton, or even her name until that morning, it was clear she was a much-loved woman who had decided enough was enough as far as cancer pain went. But had that been her sole reason for such a final act on that particular day? Had she realised that a net was closing in on her? After reading her final letter, he knew she had completed every-thing she wanted to complete, that the protection and love she felt for the four women who she considered to all be her daughters was sorted.

The final sentence in the letter was particularly telling. She had spent most of the afternoon following Anna's exclusion from her father's bedside in Anna's hotel room with her talking over old times, reminiscing. They had shared sandwiches and a bottle of wine and Anna spoke of her gratitude for Suzanne's availability through the long years spent away from her daughter. She was still with Anna when Siân rang her, but the knife was waiting at the bottom of her bag. After she was sure Anna was dead and had paid for abandoning her daughter, she walked away by dropping her clothes out of the window, then wrapping a towel around her head and her body as if she had just showered. She walked down to reception, bought something from the vending machine, then slipped out of the front doors and round the side to collect her clothes. She simply looked like every other guest wandering the Premier Inn corridors after a shower and needing a snack.

Anna died for two reasons – the first was to punish her for walking away from Jess, who hadn't deserved to lose her mother, and the second and main reason was to punish Nora for starting the affair with Graham Barker which caused a very young Anna to leave home. Because Anna had known that her mother would have to look after baby Jess. And as a result she would have to stay with Arthur Wheeler.

Suzanne Chatterton blamed Nora Wheeler for causing such disruption in their lives, and all because she fell in love with someone else, while still married to Arthur. And it seemed only Suzanne and Anna knew.

Paul and Ginny held a long discussion about the entire situation. For everything to come out wouldn't benefit anybody, but the letter carried confessions to crimes, not least Suzanne following Andrew French when he went out on that last bike ride. She had deliberately caught his back wheel. The absence of a helmet was a bonus.

Ginny stared at the printed-out enlargement from the tiny photo on her phone and sighed. 'She really did want to sort them all out before the cancer took her, didn't she? These four women meant the world to her, and she protected them with everything she had. She removed Andrew, possibly even more thoroughly than she had envisaged, she removed Anna, when this comes out she'll have destroyed Nora Wheeler, and she's seen her daughter begin the relationship she wanted her to have. She knows Jessica Armstrong has separated from her husband, so that suits her. At least she didn't bump him off, although I should imagine it was a plan if he didn't voluntarily leave Jess. This woman was heading towards serial killer status, and yet that would never have occurred to her. She was just being mother hen to her girls, wasn't she? Thank God there's nothing to link her to the death of Arthur Wheeler.'

'Maybe there was something of the cancer partnership in that. She recognised some drug he was taking because she was taking it? We'll never fully know, but she didn't have to deal with him, nature was doing that for her. I'm going to have to talk to the DCI about where we go from here, but according to this letter, which is a little bit garbled in places, everything was down to her. And there's nothing we can do about that except release the facts. We could try saying the Anna Wheeler case is closed, but I don't think for one minute we'll get away with that.'

He stood. 'Go home, Ginny. I'll go and talk to the DCI, and tomorrow we'll have everybody in for a briefing where I'll confirm what we're going to do about it all.'

'Thanks, boss. It's been a shitty day. I know we've achieved a clear-up rate second to none with this letter, but I don't know how I feel about it all. See you tomorrow,' she called as he left the room with a wave of his hand.

EPILOGUE
FIVE WEEKS LATER

More people than Erin could have imagined turned up for her mother's funeral. There had been an initial reveal of why Suzanne had taken her own life, but the emphasis had been put on the cancer pain becoming unbearable, and she had decided not to put her daughter through the stress of caring for her and watching her die slowly and in massive pain.

Mel's apartment was bigger than Erin's flat above the shop, so they decided to have a wake at her place for the close friends they knew would attend; but Suzanne had been well-known and well-liked, and at one point they were considering sending out for pizzas to replace the rapidly disappearing sandwiches.

Jess, Erin, Mel and Chantelle took on the organisation and serving, and tried to hide the anguish they were all feeling. Since the day Suzanne's body had been found, they had hardly slept. The revelations in the letter she had left, which DI Marshall had revealed to Erin and which she had photocopied before handing it back to him, had knocked them all for six.

Suzanne had always been their go-to person if they wanted things that their own parents couldn't or wouldn't provide, and they had loved her. It seemed from her letter that she had loved them to such an extent that she had killed for them to give them the happiness that was missing in their lives.

Nora felt she would never recover from the past few weeks. It began with Andrew's funeral, progressed to saying goodbye to her Arthur, then that was to be followed by the trip to Wales to finally say goodbye to Anna. That, she hoped, was the last one until it was her turn to face her maker.

She looked around Mel's apartment. She hadn't been for a long time, but she had seen it on the day Mel moved in and it definitely had needed some work doing to it. The walls were now a delicate shade of lilac, and she imagined Mel may have to bring in a carpet cleaning company to deal with the cream carpet after the number of feet that had walked all over it. It did seem though that Mel and Erin had committed very firmly to living together in the tinier flat over Fully Booked.

Mel put some crisps on her plate and began to nibble at them. She was feeling a little woozy from lack of food, and although she didn't want a three-course meal, half a dozen cheese and onion crisps would help. Considering it was a wake, it was a bit noisy. She looked around the room, and realised nobody had left. Would it be impolite, she wondered, if she went round suggesting they might want to pick up their kids from school, or go to the pub or something? She needed time out, she needed some peace. Thinking time.

She had reached an agreement with a lawyer specialising in pro bono work to start in two months, so at the moment it didn't really matter that she wasn't living at home, this beautiful place she had spent lots of money on. However, she knew that accommodation requirements could possibly change when she started her new job. For one thing, she was hugely excited about doing the work she had always wanted to do, and secondly she was excited about the future with Erin. For now, they had room, but during talks about her new job it seemed that she would be doing a lot of working from home, which would be difficult without the space for an office.

There had to be an answer to accommodate them both and she had the glimmer of an idea, but she needed to be back at Fully Booked to see whether the idea was dead in the water or feasible. Could the prefabricated office Erin used for Fully Booked possibly have a central wall installed, so they could have an office each?

Erin looked across the room and smiled for the first time that day. It had been so hard for her, and Mel had been afraid to leave her, but the multitudes that had arrived at the apartment had prevented them getting anywhere close to each other.

Eventually, as funerals do, it all ended, and the apartment was left to its own devices until the following day. Time enough then to start the big clean up. And still nobody slept through the night. Their thoughts were with all the people they had laid to rest, but especially their imminent trip to Wales.

Siân had kept her promise to be in Sheffield for Arthur's service, and she had done so, knowing that one week later she would be saying goodbye to the love of her life, who she suspected was also the love of Arthur's life.

She had learned of what had happened in Anna's final few moments from the two police officers, Owen Donald and Cerys Kitchen, who had kept her fully informed from the very beginning. She had been stunned to hear it was the woman who had facilitated everything between Sheffield and Criccieth over the years, as little as it was, who had killed Anna. They had held nothing back, and she had cried all over again. Would this hurt never go away?

Alongside Nora, all four women attended Anna's funeral. Jess had felt some reluctance but accepted she needed to be there by Nora's side anyway, and Erin, Mel and Chantelle went because they needed to support Jess and Nora. It was a burial, and that actually broke Jess. It suddenly hit her that it was her mother who was being placed in that hole, and she couldn't stem the tears. They had intended driving straight home after the service, but chose instead to stay in a seafront hotel, and travel back the following day.

It calmed Jess, and the sea and the beach brought back all the lovely memories of Grandpops taking all four of them to the coast, teaching them how to build sandcastles.

Nan bought a small glass of brandy at the hotel bar, and took herself off to bed. She didn't think she would sleep, but she knew she wanted time alone to think about Anna, and the lovely Welsh people, mostly Criccieth natives, who had come up to her and said what a good woman Anna had been.

* * *

The four women sat on the large rocks on Criccieth beach, well wrapped up in winter coats as it was a windy, cold evening, and stared out across the water.

'We've done it,' Jess said. 'We've got through today, although I must say I don't want burying. You put me in a furnace, right?'

They all nodded and said right, their eyes still on the far horizon, and the water creeping ever closer to their perches on the rocks.

'We've all lost so much this year,' Erin said. 'I'll be so glad when it's over. It feels as if we've gone through the rest of our life with nothing much happening, just normal stuff, and then bam. We get the lot thrown at us. We've all seen and digested the contents of the letter that Mum left?' She looked round at the others. They nodded.

'Would you have thought she would have done all of that? Do you think the cancer was affecting her brain?' she asked them.

'It does affect the brain.' Jess spoke, still staring out across the water. 'Grandpops thought every person who came into the room was Anna, at the end. The nurses explained the tumours had spread to the brain.'

'And why would she refuse chemo? She could have had a few months longer with us.'

'Oh, Erin.' Jess took hold of her hand. 'Your mum was the master of her own destiny by refusing that chemo. It would have made her ill, she would have lost all her beautiful hair, and we would have guessed what was wrong. If I'm ever in that situation, I'd like to think I'm as brave as she was in tackling it head on, and under her own terms.'

'Am I being selfish then?' Erin's eyes were full of tears. 'And poor Chantelle. Mum took away her husband. It's all such a mess.'

'Hey, come on.' Chantelle leaned over and gave Erin a hug. 'I'll never blame her for that. If anything, it was my fault for printing off that picture. She wouldn't have known we were having problems if she hadn't seen that. So let's stop with the allocation of blame for anything. What's done is done, and now all our loved ones will be where we can visit them with bunches of flowers. We have to get on with our lives, or this will eventually overwhelm us.'

'You're always our sensible one, Chantelle. Thank you. But Mum did take away your children's father, and for you to forgive her is... well, it shows you are exactly as we've always thought of you, a lovely, lovely person.' Erin smiled at her. 'Should we all take a small brandy to bed with us and hope it will make us sleep?'

Jess laughed. 'Don't let Nan fool you. The brandy has no effect on her sleep patterns, she just likes brandy. Come on, let's head back, it's turning even colder, and the water's getting closer.'

Chantelle stood and took a fairly dangerous step back. 'Before we leave the beach, I need to tell you something. On the night that Andrew died, Suzanne saw me returning home. The kids were at Whitby, remember? I was crying, because... truth be told, I'd just sent my husband off the road and over a field full of rocks, where, although I didn't see this part, he came off the bike and smashed his head on a rock. Earlier, he'd left our house and I followed him. Hitting his back wheel was a sudden impulse, a need to show him I couldn't be sidelined. It was dark; I switched off my lights and nudged his back wheel with the passenger side of the car. Then I spun the car round and drove home at breakneck speed. That's when your mum found me, took me inside, and I told her what I'd done. She talked to me for hours, really calmed me down, told me to act super dumb when the police arrived, because I had two children who needed me. It was pretty much a certainty he was injured and the police would be telling me he was in hospital. When they did turn up, obviously it was to tell me he was dead. I phoned Suzanne immediately, once they had gone. In her letter she took the blame, she protected me. Erin, this was your mum, not the person the police have portrayed to us. Now you can do what you want with that knowledge but I'm just glad I've told you. Nan doesn't know, before you ask. It's just the four of us. And Suzanne.'

The wind howled, and the other three stood and helped a shaking Chantelle back up the slope to the beach road.

They linked arms and Jess giggled. 'Sisters always. And tomorrow at breakfast I want the three of you to do me a favour. I want us all to talk about milk being delivered from the moon on a handcart. Then watch Nan's face.'

ACKNOWLEDGEMENTS

As always, my gratitude by the bucketful goes to the amazing team at Boldwood Books. All of them have helped me through this time of editing, and believe me it is much more difficult than writing the book! A massive thank you goes to all of them.

I also have thanks to give to people who have volunteered their names for use in this book. Nora and Arthur Wheeler, thank you so much. Nora, is milk delivered on a handcart from the moon?

The name of the bookshop came from a competition I ran on Crime Fiction Addict, and Susan Middler came up with Fully Booked, which I loved. Thank you so much, Susan.

And speaking of Crime Fiction Addict, my fellow admins, Susan Hunter, Tara Lyons and Sean Campbell have been such strong supporters of my work, and I am so grateful for that. And what on earth can I say about our almost 13,000 strong membership? Awesome, the lot of you.

My beta readers deserve a massive thank you as well, Tina Jackson, Nicki Murphy, Alyson Read and Denise Cutler, as does my entire ARC reading team of forty members.

Judith Baker (J A Baker) and Valerie Dickenson (Valerie Keogh), you keep me sane, focused and informed. You are my rocks in this strange fictional world we inhabit, and I love you both for it.

I have a large family of people who love and support me, buy my books, look after my website (thank you, Dom), and stop me when I really am too tired to carry on. Thank you to all of you, but especially to Dave who waits until book delivery day, accepts the book I hand him and sits down to read it. His normal reading preferences are Roman era novels, historical novels in general, Jack Reacher... anything but psychological thrillers. Oh dear.

Anita Waller, Sheffield 2024

ABOUT THE AUTHOR

Anita Waller is the author of many bestselling psychological thrillers and the Kat and Mouse crime series. She lives in Sheffield, which continues to be the setting of many of her thrillers, and was first published by Bloodhound at the age of sixty-nine.

Sign up to Anita Waller's mailing list for news, competitions and updates on future books.

Visit Anita's website: https://anitawaller.co.uk/

Follow Anita on social media here:

facebook.com/anita.m.waller
x.com/anitamayw
instagram.com/anitawallerauthor

ALSO BY ANITA WALLER

One Hot Summer

The Family at No. 12

The Couple Across The Street

The Girls Next Door

The Forrester Detective Agency Mysteries

Fatal Secrets

Fatal Lies

THE
Murder
LIST

**THE MURDER LIST IS A NEWSLETTER
DEDICATED TO SPINE-CHILLING FICTION
AND GRIPPING PAGE-TURNERS!**

**SIGN UP TO MAKE SURE YOU'RE ON OUR
HIT LIST FOR EXCLUSIVE DEALS, AUTHOR
CONTENT, AND COMPETITIONS.**

SIGN UP TO OUR
NEWSLETTER

BIT.LY/THEMURDERLISTNEWS

Boldwood

Boldwood Books is an award-winning fiction publishing company seeking out the best stories from around the world.

Find out more at www.boldwoodbooks.com

Join our reader community for brilliant books, competitions and offers!

Follow us
@BoldwoodBooks
@TheBoldBookClub

Sign up to our weekly deals newsletter

https://bit.ly/BoldwoodBNewsletter